Bruce Hennigan's *The Twelfth Demon* is the redemptive answer to books like the Twilight Saga.

—MIKE YORKEY
COAUTHOR OF *CHASING MONA LISA*
AND THE EVERY MAN'S BATTLE SERIES

Jonathan Steel fans rejoice! Bruce Hennigan is back with a quick-paced thriller, chock-full of action, plot twists, and some great slam-bang monster action. *The Twelfth Demon* is a fun read that puts a fascinating new spin on the vampire genre—combining spirituality and real-world vampire subculture with the fictional mythology of Dracula.

—GREG MITCHELL
AUTHOR OF *THE STRANGE MAN* AND *ENEMIES OF THE CROSS*

Bruce Hennigan has done it again. *The Twelth Demon* is everything a good suspense novel should be and will have you realizing you've been holding your breath for way too long. Interesting characters, a plot that speeds along, and a message you can ponder for a very long time convince me of two things...*The Twelth Demon* is a hit, and Bruce Hennigan is the real deal.

—MIKE DELLOSSO
AUTHOR OF *FRANTIC*, *DARKNESS FOLLOWS*, AND *SCREAM*

The 12th DEMON

Mark of the Wolf Dragon

BRUCE HENNIGAN

REALMS

Most CHARISMA HOUSE BOOK GROUP products are available at special quantity discounts for bulk purchase for sales promotions, premiums, fund-raising, and educational needs. For details, write Charisma House Book Group, 600 Rinehart Road, Lake Mary, Florida 32746, or telephone (407) 333-0600.

THE TWELFTH DEMON, MARK OF THE WOLF DRAGON
  by Bruce Hennigan
Published by Realms
Charisma Media/Charisma House Book Group
600 Rinehart Road
Lake Mary, Florida 32746
www.charismahouse.com

All Scripture quotations are from the New King James Version of the Bible. Copyright © 1979, 1980, 1982 by Thomas Nelson, Inc., publishers. Used by permission..

This is a work of fiction. The characters portrayed in this book are fictitious unless they are historical figures explicitly named. Otherwise, any resemblance to actual people, whether living or dead, is coincidental.

Cover design by Justin Evans
Design Director: Bill Johnson

Visit the author's website at www.brucehennigan.com.

Library of Congress Cataloging-in-Publication Data:

Hennigan, Bruce, 1955-
  The twelfth demon, mark of the wolf dragon / Bruce Hennigan.
    p. cm. -- (The chronicles of Jonathan Steel ; bk. 2)
  ISBN 978-1-61638-839-3 (trade paper) -- ISBN 978-1-61638-840-9 (e-book)
  1. Demonology--Fiction. 2. Vampires--Fiction. 3. Psychological fiction.
I. Title.
  PS3608.E56453T94 2012
  813'.6--dc23
                                    2012026305

12 13 14 15 16 — 9 8 7 6 5 4 3 2
Printed in Canada

To Mark Sutton for years of encouragement

Special thanks to Andy, the world's greatest editor

Assemble yourselves and come; gather together from all sides
to My sacrificial meal
which I am sacrificing for you,
a great sacrificial meal
on the mountains of Israel,
that you may eat flesh and drink blood. You shall eat
the flesh of the mighty, drink the blood of the princes
of the earth…and drink blood till you are drunk.

EZEKIEL 39:17–19

[Chapter 1]

THE ASSASSIN'S GARROTE was woven from three sturdy strings: a black string for death, a red string for the bloody necklace it would leave around the jogger's neck, and a bright green string for surprise. She had plucked all three strings from the body of her first kill, and they had served her well over the years, but only in a pinch. The garrote was not her preferred method of execution. Unfortunately for the approaching jogger, she would put the garrote to good use once again. He had interrupted her carefully planned approach to the maintenance door on the shopping mall roof. Only a fool would jog in a thunderstorm. She pressed her back against the air conditioning unit and waited.

She drew in a deep breath to calm her nerves and gripped the handles on her garrote tightly. She listened to the approaching footfalls, sensed the emergence of the labored breathing, smelled the odor of sweat. She opened her eyes, muscles coiled just as the jogger passed the threshold of the doorway. But the jogger never turned her way, oblivious to her presence. At the last second she held back. He had not seen her as he exited the rooftop. He would live to be a fool another day.

She gathered her oiled gunnysack and hoisted it over her coveralls. Walking calmly, she stepped across the track and made her way toward the maintenance entrance. Through the glass roof she watched children skating on the ice rink six floors below her. They were so unaware of the cruel world that awaited them. With gloved hands she slid a metal pick into the lock of the maintenance door. Rain trickled down her back. Even though it was the middle of July, the water was cold, and it sent a chill down her spine. The lock clicked, and she opened the door and stepped into a small, metal enclosure. Ahead catwalks branched out across the underside of the roof to allow maintenance workers access to every nook and cranny. Delighted shrieks from the children ice-skating echoed hauntingly. For a moment she saw a young girl in a pink dress with her hair pulled back in a ponytail. The girl blew out the candles on a cake and smiled as her stepfather cut into the cake. She heard the girl scream. The assassin closed her eyes and wrapped the memory in a bundle of gray twine until it stopped moving, stopped twitching, and then she shoved it into a dark corner of her memory cabinet where it would not interfere with her job.

Reaching the end of the catwalk, she stepped out onto an overhang enclosed with wire mesh and knelt to the corrugated metal floor. She slid a rifle from the gunnysack and attached the wooden stock to the barrel in quick, fluid movements. Tied around the narrow portion of the stock were twenty-seven colored strings, one for each kill. She took the string for her next victim from her pocket. It was dark red, and she had woven it into the shape of heart. She hung it on the wire before her then lay down on the floor of the cage. She braced her elbows and slid the thin barrel through the crisscrossing wire.

The Chinese restaurant had an exterior dining area with twelve tables nestled onto an overhanging balcony. The table closest to the edge carried a reserved sign each day at noon. She didn't have to look to know her victim waited for his bullet. He was too much of a creature of habit to make the change that would save his life.

She felt tranquility flow over her, filling her with tightly coiled power ready to be unleashed. She rested her cheek against the gun and felt the coarse touch of the strings. The strings reached and connected the disjointed chaos around her. In her mind she traced a dark red thread across the space to the man's heart. From there the string turned and moved across space to a dilapidated doublewide in Tyler, Texas. It wound its way around the waist of a young woman who looked far older than her twenty-one years, and then the string moved on to the hands of a snotty-nosed toddler who would never know his father was the man sitting at the table, a man who had taken advantage of an eighteen-year-old girl and then paid her off with a pitiful sum and a nondisclosure agreement. The young thing had lost all her money at the casinos in Shreveport, and the future of this unwanted child was filled with endless misery.

Suddenly the string turned blood red, and her mind disappeared into the past—to another man whose cruelty had known no bounds, until she had stopped him just as she now stopped them all.

The assassin pushed these thoughts away and looked through the gun's scope. The man was sipping his hot, green tea. She cast the string again, down the line of vision, through the teacup, and right through the man's chest. She would blow out his heart. She noticed the movement of a shadow and lifted the gun's barrel ever so slightly. A teenage boy sat at the far end of the table. He had short reddish-blond hair and wore a beige T-shirt. His eyes were directed at her. But she did not worry. He could not see her through the crisscross wires.

Another shadow fell over the table. Someone sat behind the support beam, out of sight. She saw strong, lean arms laid out on the table. And then the man sat forward, bringing his face fully into view. He turned his head and looked up in her direction, revealing bright, turquoise eyes.

For the first time in years the assassin's heart rate accelerated, and her strings frayed and broke. Every muscle in her body contracted at the sight of that man. Without realizing, she pulled the trigger. The explosion echoed through the shopping mall. The ice-skaters screamed beneath her. She bolted up, and the rifle barrel snared in the wires. She jerked at it, and it flew backward out of her grasp, skittering across the catwalk. It slid beneath the wire mesh and fell toward the ice below. As she watched it fall, she noticed the man with the turquoise eyes standing over the target, and his fierce gaze was directed toward her. He bolted for the stairs to the roof. He was coming for her! She brushed the red heart from the wall and stepped on it as she hurried toward the roof.

"I still don't know how I let Grace talk me into this." Charles Atchison adjusted his napkin and studied his silverware. He sighed and motioned to a waitress. "This fork has food on it. I want a clean set. Now!"

Jonathan Steel drew a deep breath and tried not to be irritated. "I'm sorry about your schedule, Mr. Atchison. But Josh has to go back to his house today for the first time since his mother died."

Atchison poured green tea from a teapot into a tiny cup. "Yes, so I've been told." He pushed his frameless glasses back up on his thin nose and nodded toward the boy sitting next to him. Josh Knight was nervous and twitchy, and he kept touching the hole in his lower lip. He was looking up toward the ceiling of the shopping mall.

"I've tried to get in touch with Cephas…" Steel said.

"Dr. Lawrence, yes I know. The boy's uncle. Look, Mr. Steed…"

"Steel."

"I'm in corporate law. I'm already missing an important board of directors meeting the idiots scheduled during my lunch. *My* lunch! So you're lucky I worked you in. But I don't handle child custody or estate matters." He poured two yellow packs of sweetener into the cup.

"I asked for Ruth Branson." Steel said. "We've worked together."

"She's in Europe." Atchison stirred the tea and then pointed the tiny spoon at Steel. "Look, I'll get things started so Dr. Lawrence can come and claim the boy, and then Ruth can finish it."

"Dude, you are unbelievable." Josh said, his gaze still on the ceiling. "Jonathan, I think somebody's up there with a gun."

Atchison lifted the cup toward his lips as Steel leaned forward to look around the support beam. The man's teacup shattered, and hot tea splattered over the tabletop. Wood splintered from the edge of the table just inches from Josh's hand, and the teenager fell over in his chair. The bullet came to lodge in the concrete floor of the walkway in a puff of pulverized tile and dust.

Steel dove across the table and pushed Atchison behind the balcony wall. He glanced up toward the source of the gunfire and saw a small puff of smoke near the ceiling by a maintenance walkway. A slight figure in maintenance coveralls stood up and moved quickly inside the walkway as a rifle somersaulted through the air into a huge hanging fixture of tiny white lights.

Steel glanced once at Josh to make sure he wasn't hit and then rushed toward the nearby stairs. In his haste he shoved aside shoppers and stumbled over people prone on the floor. Reaching the doorway to the stairs, he bolted up them two steps at a time. He paused at the doorway leading onto the roof. Standing to the side, he shoved it open and waited for gunfire. Only rain cascaded through the opening, and he rushed through the door out into the storm.

The assassin crashed through the maintenance door. Rain swirled around her as she hopped onto the metal support between the glass panels of the roof. Of all the people to surface out of nowhere, why him? He had nothing to do with Atchison! Or did he? She cursed her employer for not warning her.

She heard the stairwell door bang open and knew it would be him. She pulled the brim of her cap down to hide her face and slid her hand into the coverall pocket for her knife. Irony of all ironies, it was the same knife she had used on the man years before. She spun and watched the man awkwardly run toward her. She slowed her breathing, concentrated, and visualized a yellow string connecting her hand with the man's chest. She released the knife even as she completed her turn.

The man stopped, and his hand lashed out with inhuman speed. He caught the knife, and his gaze fixed on hers. For a moment that seemed to stretch into eternity the rain slowed, the air grew thick, and they looked at each other over the intervening years. She saw his hideously beautiful eyes, his square jaw, smelled his masculine fragrance, felt the stubble of his cheek on her hand, tasted the saltiness of his lips—and then she was back in the present. Their stare broke, and he stumbled sideways and fell onto a glass panel. With a sudden explosion of cold air it collapsed. The man's free hand lashed out, and he snared the edge of the support beam. He hung over the vast expanse of the shopping mall.

She walked gingerly along the beam and squatted down. He looked up at her, and rain pooled in his haunting eyes. She grabbed his hand just as it was about to slip and pulled him up onto the beam. The man turned over onto his back and gasped for breath. She took the knife out of his hand.

"You're supposed to be dead."

"Raven?" he mumbled.

There was a shout from the distance, and she glanced up. Three security men were coming out onto the rooftop. She slid the knife back into her pocket as she hurried along the beam and down onto the roof. A short hop over the retaining wall led to where the rope waited, and she rappelled down to her waiting car. She sped off toward the now uncertain future. Her gun was gone. Her target was still alive. She glanced once into the rearview mirror and saw the man standing at the edge of the shopping mall roof. She would have to kill him. Again.

[Chapter 2]

ERGEANT RAFFLE, I have appointments to see to. And I haven't had lunch." Atchison ran his bandaged hand through his unruly hair.

"You're welcome to grab a bite at our café." Sergeant Raffle, an African-American man in a Dallas Police Department uniform nodded down the hall. "It's very energy efficient."

"I don't do institutional food."

Raffle shrugged and tapped the notepad on his desk. "You aren't going anywhere until I finish with your statement. You are a material witness to this assassination attempt on Mr. Steam."

"Steel." Steel sat stiffly next to Atchison. Josh Knight sat next to him.

Raffle glanced at him. "Steel. Got it. Lieutenant Kane will be here in a moment to ask a few questions."

"Haven't you asked enough?" Atchison sat forward and pointed to the notepad in front of Raffle. "You've got my statement. I was meeting them about succession issues, and someone took a shot at him."

"And, how do we know you weren't the target?" A short, trim woman in a three-piece suit appeared behind Raffle. She had shoulder-length dark hair and the kind of face that didn't need makeup. She seemed tense and rigid as she picked up the notepad and studied it. "I'm Lieutenant Sue Kane, homicide division. Mr. Atchison, you wouldn't know a young woman by the name of Gloria Sanchez would you?"

Atchison shook his head. "No. What does that have to do with anything?"

Kane glanced up from the notepad. "She's seventeen."

Atchison paled and pushed his glasses back onto his nose. "Be careful, officer. Slander and libel are grounds for a good lawsuit."

"And I know you're good at all three." Kane dropped the notepad on Raffle's desk. "I need a list of your current clients."

"No!"

"That bullet could have been meant for you, Atchison." Kane said.

"Get a warrant, Kane. I have appointments." He stood up. "Besides, if you take a gander at Steel's past, you'd see he was the target. I'm out of here."

"What about Josh?" Steel said.

"I'll have some paperwork for you to sign this afternoon." Atchison opened his hands and glared at Kane. "Anything else?"

"I'll be in touch," Kane said. "Oh, and the reason I'm asking about Gloria Sanchez? I just came from her house. Murder/suicide. But she wasn't pregnant, so don't worry."

Atchison walked away, and Kane pulled his chair around and sat it in, facing Steel. "Now, who are you?"

"Jonathan Steel."

"Josh Knight," Josh added.

"What's your role in all of this?" Kane asked.

"Josh's mother died three weeks ago. I'm waiting for his uncle to come down from New York. Atchison represents the law firm handling..." Steel cleared his throat. "Claire's affairs."

Josh nodded and touched the hole in his lower lip. "We were meeting the dude for lunch."

Kane frowned. "I'm sorry, I didn't know. My condolences. So, your presence here was a fluke?"

"Yes." Steel nodded. "I called Ruth Branson's office this morning."

"I know Ruth. Good lawyer." Raffle said. "Pennington, Crandle, and Frost, right?"

"Yeah. Turns out Grace Pennington put Atchison on the case. He asked us to meet him for lunch. He's the only person who knew we were here."

Kane picked up the notepad and studied Raffle's notes. "So, how did this assassin know?"

"She didn't."

Kane jerked her gaze up from the notepad. "She?"

"Yes. A woman dressed in a maintenance uniform. I recognized her face."

"Let me get this straight. No one knew you would be meeting with Mr. Atchison? And yet someone you know shows up to shoot at you?"

Steel flinched. How did he get into these things? "I have amnesia, Lieutenant. Every now and then something triggers a memory. When I saw the woman on the roof, I remembered her. I was close to her."

"Close?" Kane raised an eyebrow. "How close, Mr. Steel?"

Steel drew a deep breath. In his memory he could smell her perfume and feel her breath on his face. "Very. And her name is Raven."

Kane sat back and sighed. "Raven, you say?"

"Yes."

Kane looked over her shoulder toward the door to a conference room. "I have a visitor in that conference room looking for an assassin with the code name Raven. Coincidence? I hardly think so. He'll want to talk to you."

"What about Josh?"

"Dude, I can wait in the truck."

"There's an assassin after me." Steel said. Josh had already been through enough with the thirteenth demon.

"Wrong, bro." Josh shook his head. "Look, you weren't the target."

"Oh, and how do you know that?" Kane asked.

Josh pointed to the computer screen in front of Raffle. "You got the pictures right there. Look at the bullet trajectory. Jonathan was sitting behind a support beam. No way he could be seen. The bullet went right through Atchison's teacup. He was the target, not Jonathan."

Kane leaned over Raffle's shoulder, and they studied the screen. "Not bad. You might ought to apply for the police academy."

"I think he's right, Lieutenant. Mr. Atchison is the one in danger, not Mr. Steel."

Kane straightened up and rubbed her eyes. "Well, get a hold of him and offer him protection. And Raffle, when you get to his office, don't leave without those names."

"Why would anyone want to kill Atchison?" Steel asked.

"The man has a history, Steel. Likes young women. He's gotten a couple pregnant and paid them off. He confessed to his wife, and she's so gullible, she forgives him and takes him back. He's very open about it. Says he has an 'addiction.' Truth is, he's a creep."

Raffle stood up. "I'll get over to Atchison's. Hope your interview with Ross goes well."

Steel stiffened. "Ross? Not Franklin Ross?"

Kane blinked. "Don't tell me you know him too?"

"I've broken his nose a time or two."

Kane pointed to the conference room door. "Well, you go in. I've got a suspect in the Sanchez murders to interrogate, and then we'll all have a little sit-down to talk about Raven."

Josh stood up. "I'll be in the truck charging up my new iPhone."

Steel was still recovering from the shock. Ross was here? The man had been in Lakeside when the thirteenth demon had tried to kill Emily Parker. And Ross had thought Steel was in on the scheme. "Fine. I won't be long, and then we'll head to your house."

Josh froze and touched the healing hole in his lip where he had once worn a lip bead. "Yeah, I guess so."

Steel reached toward Josh and paused. His hand fell back to his side. He wasn't good at this. He would be glad when Cephas got here. "The sooner we're done with Atchison, the better."

Josh just shook his head and headed out the door. Kane picked up a phone. "I'll inform Special FBI Agent Ross he has another witness."

Raven sat in her rental car with her cap pulled down over her face. She had followed the boy and the man to the police station. How had he survived? She had shoved the knife between his ribs. He should be dead, and yet here he was with Atchison, of all people. Her hand drifted up to her neck and to the silver amulet she always wore to remind her of *him*.

She had tied it around her neck with a dark blue twine. Over the years the twine had frayed very little, and it held the amulet close to her heart. She squinted her eyes and saw the dark blue thread stretching back into the past to a restaurant, to the man with the turquoise eyes, to the amulet he held in his hand, to the gift given out of affection. Affection! She had taken it, but it hadn't kept her from killing him the next day. Now it was a daily reminder of the weakness of *affection*.

A policeman brushed against her car, and she dropped the amulet into her shirt. He ignored her as he slid into a patrol car and left the parking lot. What should she do? Atchison was still alive. And the man with the turquoise eyes had recognized her. She would have to kill them both.

The teenager exited the building and climbed into the beaten-up old truck they had arrived in. Raven had placed a tiny GPS device on the truck to track them down later. But first, she had to take care of a certain client. She had never said anything about the man with the turquoise eyes. It was an unexpected string stretching out of nowhere and intersecting Raven's careful plans. She would follow that string back to Vivian Darbonne Ketrick.

[Chapter 3]

FORTY-FIVE FLOORS ABOVE Dallas Vivian stood at the conference room window and watched lightning splinter across a gray sky. She wore a tight, short black dress with a high neck that buttoned at her throat. A discreet slit in the skirt revealed passing flashes of her right thigh. She had pulled her dark hair into a severe bun beneath a black pillbox hat. A fine, dark net hung over her face. She let a tear trickle down her right cheek and turned to face the conference table.

"I'm so sorry, but losing my poor Robert is almost more than I can handle." She tucked a pale handkerchief beneath the net and dabbed at her eye carefully, as to not mess up her mascara.

"Ms. Darbonne…" A portly man sitting at the opposite end of the table motioned to the other ten members of the board of directors. "You actually expect us to believe you and Mr. Ketrick…?"

"Please, Mr. Shaw, it's Mrs. Ketrick." Her voice trembled. "Now, I know you don't think I know one little ole thing about business, but I was his executive administrative assistant in Lakeside and, now, his wife." She stepped slowly toward the table and stumbled. A man sitting close by stood up and caught her. She nodded toward him as he helped her to the chair at the end of the table. "Thank you, Mr. Forbin."

"I think that's enough, Bryce." He glanced at Mr. Shaw.

Shaw stood up, and his chins shook as he spoke. "There is no way Robert Ketrick would agree to make this woman the next CEO of Ketrick Enterprises."

"We've all seen the will." Forbin sat back down.

Vivian reached over and patted Mr. Forbin's hand. "There,

there, Mr. Forbin. We can't blame Mr. Shaw for being suspicious. After all, he is next in line for that position. However, I understand there is to be a vote?"

Shaw motioned to an empty chair. "We can't vote. Atchison is missing."

Vivian frowned. "Well, I have it on good authority Mr. Atchison is no longer able to fulfill his duties. And"—Vivian stood up and pressed a button on a tiny control panel in front of her—"Robert did tell me that if you had any questions about the transition, he wanted you to see this."

A computer panel slid up in front of each of the directors. Vivian suppressed her smile as Shaw paled and slumped into his seat. Vivian walked slowly around the table, pausing to regain her steadiness by occasionally touching the back of each director as she peeked over their shoulders at their deepest secrets playing across the screens. She stopped behind Shaw. "Oh my, Mr. Shaw. How young is that man you're with? Why, he's young enough to be your son. I would just hate for your wife to see this video."

Shaw slammed the screen back into the tabletop. "You couldn't get anything on Atchison?"

"Me?" Vivian sniffed. "I don't know what you're talking about. Mr. Atchison *was* an upstanding member of this board, and while he does have some shadowy activities in his past, I understand his wife had forgiven him."

"In other words, you couldn't blackmail him."

"Poor Mr. Atchison," Vivian continued. "We will miss him."

"Miss him?" Forbin said from the other end of the table. His face was as white as a sheet.

Vivian frowned and touched the handkerchief to her lips. "I'm afraid he has met with a most unfortunate accident. Now, if all of you would be so good as to sign the form in the folder before you, you can honor Robert's memory and see that his wishes are fulfilled. And we can keep these little ole secrets tucked safely away in my vault."

Raven ignored the secretary at Ketrick Enterprises and burst through the double doors into the penthouse conference room. Vivian Ketrick whirled around from a conference table. Her eyes widened and she threw back the black net from over her face.

"What are you doing here?"

"We need to talk. Now!" Raven kept her voice low because Vivian thought she was a man.

Vivian's eyes filled with fiery anger, and she turned back to the conference room. "Thank you for signing, gentlemen. I look forward to continuing Robert's legacy."

The people around the table filtered past Raven, and she kept her face averted. An older man at the head of the table threw down his pen as he stood up. "You still have to get Atchison to sign these papers. We'll fight you until the end, Ms. Darbonne."

"Mrs. Ketrick." Vivian smiled at him. He stormed out and slammed the doors behind him. Vivian glared at Raven and tossed a handkerchief on the table. "I told you never to come to my office!"

"You couldn't blackmail Atchison, so you paid me to kill him?" Raven glared from under the brim of her hat.

"The man tells his wife everything. And the idiot believes him." Vivian said tersely. "So, is he dead?"

"You didn't tell me he had a bodyguard."

Vivian raised an eyebrow in surprise. "That's impossible. There's no way he could have known there would be an attempt on his life."

"I know the bodyguard, and he is dangerous."

"So, kill him too. I'll pay for both." Vivian shrugged as she unbuttoned the tight collar around her neck. "I need this to move quickly so I can move onto the Council."

"The Council?"

"You don't have to talk like that anymore." Vivian frowned. "I know you're a woman."

No one knew her true identity. Except for the man with the turquoise eyes. She pulled the knife from her pocket, but Vivian skittered to the other side of the large table and Raven's knife passed through empty air.

"I have good reflexes, dear." Vivian slowly paced farther away from Raven. "Now, it's simple. Take care of both of them, and do it soon."

"It will cost you more." Raven tried to regain control.

"I have plenty of money. I..." A buzz sounded on an intercom in the center of the table.

"Mrs. Ketrick, there's a gentleman here who insists on seeing you. He says his name is Rudolph Wulf."

"Tell him to make an appointment."

The secretary's voice was replaced by that of a man with a heavy Eastern European accent. "Madame Vivian, the twelfth demon will speak to you. Now."

Steel opened the conference room door, and cigarette smoke drifted into the hallway. He stepped into the darkened interior. The opposite wall contained a one-way glass covered by closed blinds. But his attention was drawn to the man standing in the far corner. The man inhaled his cigarette, and red light illuminated his face.

"The sign on the door says 'No Smoking.'"

FBI Special Agent Franklin Ross dropped the cigarette and

stepped on it. He smiled and motioned to another man seated at the conference room table.

The man stood up. "Juan Destillo. Ross's partner."

"Not partner. I work alone."

"Jonathan Steel." He shook Destillo's hand. "I wouldn't want to be his partner."

Destillo picked up a plastic wrapped bundle on the table. "I'll just go check the rifle into evidence." But Ross held out an open hand, halting him.

Ross hadn't changed. His dark hair was perfectly combed. His black overcoat hung open to reveal a white shirt and red tie. In the middle of July he wore an overcoat. Ross had been following Steel for the past two years, convinced he had something to do with the murders committed by Rocky Braxton. Braxton had died on the beach the same night Steel had lost someone he loved.

But Ross continued dogging Steel's footsteps in hopes of catching him in criminal activity. Instead Ross had been able to close the case on Braxton and his mentor, Robert Ketrick. "Steel, every time I turn around, you pop up."

"Seems true for you too."

"I live here. Regional headquarters." He took the rifle from Destillo and pointed to the stock. "Notice the strings tied around the stock. One for each assassination." He handed the rifle back. "She likes strings." He pulled a tiny plastic bag out of his pocket and held it up. "Dallas PD wants the evidence. I'm fighting Kane tooth and nail. We found this in the catwalk. Red string woven into the shape of a heart." He tossed it on the table, and it slid in front of Steel. "Looks like you broke Raven's heart, so she was going to break yours. Were you a loose thread?"

Steel felt the fury build, felt his face grow warm. "I thought you had changed your mind about me."

Ross motioned to the heart, and Destillo picked it up. "Leave us alone." Destillo took the rifle and left. "I find evidence Raven is in town for her next target, and she takes a shot at you. Coincidence?"

"I didn't ask to get involved, Ross." Steel said. "I just happened to be at the wrong place at the wrong time."

Ross sat on the corner of the conference table. "Yeah, that's always your excuse. Only a few people in the agency know her code name." Ross crossed his arms. "Was she your partner?"

"I don't know, Ross. When I saw her, I remembered her name." Steel looked away. If he had been Raven's partner, did that mean he was as assassin? "But Atchison was the target, not me."

"Yeah, right. You show up in Dallas, and your old partner decides to tie up loose ends." He walked around the table toward Steel. "Or same assassin decides to shoot a lawyer from one of the most prestigious law firms in Dallas. Why?"

"I don't know."

"But there is a motive for shooting you." Ross poked him in the chest, and Steel stepped back.

"Don't do that."

"What are you going to do about it? You're in a police station. My turf. I could break *your* nose this time."

Steel clenched his fists and drew a deep breath. "Forget it, Ross. I'm not giving you the pleasure."

Ross shrugged and turned back to the interrogation window. He reached down and turned a volume knob on the speaker beneath the window and opened the blinds. "Well, as soon as Kane finishes with this riffraff, we'll get down to asking you a few questions that might jog your memory."

Kane sat at a table with her back to the window. Across from her sat a young man with shoulder-length black hair and a gold bead in his lower lip. He was dressed in a long, black coat, and his skin was pale. His eyes were alive with a burgundy glow. Probably tinted contacts. He slouched in the chair.

"I asked you how you knew Gloria Sanchez," Kane said.

The man glanced down at the tabletop. "We used to go to school together."

Kane stood up and circled the table and paused behind the young man. "She was in your clan."

"What's a clan?"

"Your vampire clan, Winston."

"My name is Armando now."

Kane's glare bore down on the man's scalp. If her eyes had been laser beams, Armando's brain would be cooked squash. "Three witnesses place you at Gloria's house last night. Two hours later she goes into her mother's bedroom and rips out her throat with a set of false fangs. Then she goes into the bathroom and cuts her own wrists."

"What can I tell you, Ms. Kane…" Armando shrugged.

"Lieutenant Kane."

"Maybe her mom wouldn't give her an allowance." A ghost of a smile played across his lips.

Kane came back around to her side of the table. "I know your *secret* name, Armando."

Armando's gaze popped up from the table, and Steel saw fear in them for a brief second. "Secret name?"

"I know your *name*. Gloria was your thrall, and I found a photograph of you. You missed it when you were cleaning up. What did you tell her to do? Did you tell her to kill her own mother, drink her blood, and then you would accept her back into your clan? I know who made the fangs, Armando. And soon I'll have enough evidence to hold you. You killed Gloria and her mother, and I will prove it. Now get out of here!" Kane hissed. A uniformed policeman came in and motioned Armando toward the door.

The young man stood up. "Be careful in the dark, Ms. Kane." He was still laughing when the officer closed the other door.

[Chapter 4]

RAVEN WATCHED FEAR etch its way across the face of Vivian Ketrick at the mention of the twelfth demon. The woman was usually as cool as a penguin at the South Pole. Vivian pointed toward a huge mirror. "Get in there and be quiet." Vivian keyed a hidden switch, and a door swung inward. Raven stepped into a darkened office, and the door eased closed behind her. The wall held one-way glass, the other side of the mirror.

Raven watched Vivian cast a worried look at the mirror and pull the black net back down over her face. The doors to the conference room opened, and a tall man stepped in. He flicked his hand, and the doors closed behind him. His posture was regal and imperious, and he wore a dark gray overcoat draped over his shoulders. His dark blue shirt and bright yellow tie were perfect. He carried about him the sense of age, and yet his face was smooth and seamless. His silver gray hair was thick, and every hair was in place. His eyes were almost the same shade of gray as his hair. He carried a shiny black cane, which he placed carefully on the table before he shrugged off the huge overcoat. He folded it carefully and placed it beside the cane. "Vivian Darbonne Ketrick. I have come to claim the territory of the thirteenth demon."

Raven drew a deep breath. Vivian leaned wearily against the table and picked up her handkerchief. She dabbed at her eyes. "Wulf, you'll have to be patient with me. I just lost my husband and…"

"Spare me your theatrics. You are not that good, Vivian."

Vivian straightened and tossed the handkerchief back on the table. She lifted the net away from her face. "Fine. But I took out Robert Ketrick and the thirteenth demon. *I will have his territory."*

Raven stepped away from the window. Demons. Where there were demons, there were angels. And where there were angels, there was God. She had pushed away her belief in God. She suddenly saw silver threads emerging from the very fabric of space, reaching toward heaven, glowing with love and forgiveness. She swept away the strings with a swipe of her deep-seated anger. She had cut those strings long ago, on her twelfth birthday. Her life now was to sever those strings in others. One minute her victims were alive and moving to the machinations of their own misery. The next they were dead. Simple. Clean.

But now she felt uneasy again, as if from the depths of her unconsciousness the reality of good and evil was suddenly very real. New strings appeared that threatened to bind her, restrict her, remove her freedom, pull her back into her past. She couldn't allow it. To believe again would destroy her. She had become the predator, and she had killed those who deserved judgment. Her justice had been complete and irreversible. The idea that God had been watching her all along was intolerable.

Wulf's laughter was deep and filled the room with an eerie echo. Then Wulf's mouth opened wide, exposing fangs, and an unearthly howl filled the air. Raven fell back away from the window onto a huge mahogany desk, and she watched as Wulf floated up into the air as his face elongated into a wolflike snout and his fingers became claws. Leathery wings sprouted from his shoulders and beat the air with ferocious fervor. Papers scattered in the sudden wind. A long, serpentine tail appeared from his back and wrapped itself around Vivian's waist. He was an unholy blend of wolf and dragon.

He launched himself across the table into Vivian, and they disappeared from view. Raven's heart raced as she leaned forward toward the mirror. Two dark figures heaved up into the glass, and it shattered as they hurled into her hidden room. Raven rolled across the desk and into its leg space as the two bodies thudded onto the mahogany desk. Tentacles fell from the desk and writhed just inches from her face.

Raven realized she was about to scream, and she shoved her hand into her mouth. What were these people?

"Your bottom-feeding demons are no match for me! I can crush your skull like a ripe plum. Do you yield the territory of the thirteenth demon?" Wulf's voice was harsh and deformed by the wolflike shape of his mouth. The tentacles retreated, and Raven heard Vivian scrape across the desk. Dung beetles materialized out of the very air and rained down upon her. Roots sprang up from the carpet and encased the desk.

"Never!" Vivian screamed.

The desk lurched backward against the wall, trapping Raven in a beetle-infested nightmare. They ran across her face and into her hair. The roots from the floor began to intertwine around her legs. She tried to scream, but sound would not come from her open mouth.

Against the back wall she saw the shadow of Wulf in his transformed state holding Vivian. "I can do this for hours, Vivian. Yield now, or die!"

"I yield!" Vivian screamed. Their bodies thudded against the desk, and the roots and dung beetles disappeared into thin air. Raven raked her hands through her hair. Nothing! She pressed her back against the wall as the desk trembled with the weight of the two creatures. Then silence descended. Were they gone? She dared not move. Then she heard glass crunch and discerned movement. She eased forward in the cramped space under the desk and peered through two elliptical openings for computer cables.

Vivian moved into view, and for a second her head and face were deformed, as if she too had assumed the shape of some kind of bizarre creature. She shook her head, and her dark hair cascaded back around her shoulders. She pulled the pillbox hat from her head and tossed it aside. Wulf was human again. The two faced each other in the destroyed conference room as if nothing had happened. Vivian uncoiled what was left of the tight bun of her hair.

"You win, Wulf. But I claim your second."

Wulf nodded and clasped his hands behind his back. "That is much better, my servant. Remember this little scuffle in the future. I have spent centuries planning what is about to happen, and nothing will stop me."

"Not even the Council?"

Wulf smiled, and Raven could not believe that just seconds before he had been a wolf thing. "Let me just say that the Council is grateful for your neutralization of the thirteenth demon. He was never a member of the Council and was more of a nuisance. As you have become. They do not need you, Vivian. However, I need you. Tell me about your vampires." Wulf swept the scattered papers off the table. Had he said vampires?

Vivian turned away from him. "Vampires? Vampires are boring."

Wulf examined his fingernails. "Don't toy with me, Vivian. I know you were involved with a clan here in Dallas as fodder for Ketrick's games."

"I did play around with them for a while. But not anymore."

"I visited a member of one of the clans last night. She said her allegiance was pledged to a vampire named Armando." Wulf smiled and touched his fingertips to his nose. "Her blood was so fragrant, so fresh, so rich. She betrayed her clan leader when she told me his name, Vivian. I value loyalty. I punish betrayal." He licked his lips and walked calmly around the table toward Vivian. "Don't make the same mistake. I believe you are hiding your fangs."

"What are you talking about?"

Wulf's cane had fallen off the table during the fight. Papers rattled in the far corner, and the cane flew through the air and into his grasp. The top was a gold wolf's head. Etched around the black shaft of the cane was the golden trace of a dragon's tail. Wulf pressed a button and revealed a long, gold blade. He raised its tip in front of her face. "One touch, Vivian, and the poison will kill you within seconds. Your trinity of demons will flee you and find another host. Now, show me your fangs."

Vivian hissed at Wulf, and Raven watched in horror as her bicuspids lengthened into fangs. Wulf smiled and sheathed the sword.

"There, that wasn't so bad. If you aren't associating with vampires, then why do you have fangs?"

"Okay! I tried to use one of the clans to recover a boy who slipped through my hands."

"Tried? And failed, I take it. Well, my dear, I have something that will make you more than a rank amateur." Wulf reached back into his jacket and took out a leather pouch. Raven could make out a red and gold emblem on the front of the pouch. It looked like a dragon with a wolf head. The beast was circled upon itself, and the jaws of the wolf had snared the tip of the dragon's tail. Wulf unfolded the pouch and revealed five glass vials about six inches long secured by elastic. Also tucked into a clear plastic sleeve next to the vials was a memory card the size of a postage stamp. He slid a vial out of its bindings and held it up in his perfectly manicured hands. Red liquid glowed in the vial.

"My latest development. Years of work have gone into this, Vivian. And you shall be the first conduit of this vampire magick."

Vivian took the vial. "Blood?"

"Of course. Special blood. Go ahead, drink it."

"Why?"

"So you can join in the new world order, Vivian. You are my second, remember?"

Raven found herself pressed against the hole in the desk, and her eyes were riveted on the glass vial. What would make blood glow like that?

"What will it do to me?" Vivian uncapped the glowing vial and inhaled.

"Nothing." Wulf smiled. "It is not intended for you. It is intended for your clan."

Vivian's downed the contents in one quick swallow. Vivian closed her eyes in ecstasy. "Exquisite!"

"It should be. It's from my blood." Wulf capped the vial and slid it back into its bindings.

Vivian reached out and touched Wulf's tie, straightening it. "So what is your blood supposed to do?"

Wulf smiled and brushed her hands away. "If it works as I intend, then you will still be alive when we finish this conversation. If it fails, you will die, and I will go back to my laboratory and start over."

Vivian's body tensed, and Wulf ignored her. He pried the tiny memory card from its plastic sleeve and held it up. "On this card you will find a wealth of information that details my plan. You need to review it in depth. Also on this card are documents detailing my life's story gleaned from the Grimvox, a grand and glorious tale that has unfolded over the millennia. You are familiar with the Grimvox? The repository for our stories? Mine is the story of the mark of the wolf dragon." His gaze came to rest on her neck. "Ah, I see the blood is working." He reached down and picked up a shard of broken mirror. "Take a look."

Vivian grabbed the piece of mirror and studied her reflection.

Raven could see a dark tattoo of the wolf dragon symbol appear just below Vivian's right collarbone.

"It is my symbol, Vivian. It means you belong to me."

Vivian frowned and dropped the mirror shard. She held up the memory card. "This is why I should learn about your past?"

Wulf glanced past Vivian and stared at Raven's desk. She gasped and shoved her fist into her mouth. He seemed to be staring right into her eyes.

"Yes, my dear Vivian. One day I shall be in charge of the Council, and all who bow before me will know of my grand story. I shall be exalted above all of the Master's servants. And everyone will bear the mark." He smiled, and his gaze turned back to Vivian. "On the memory card you will find your instructions in detail. Follow them to the letter. An astronomical event that has not occurred in over two thousand years is about to happen. I have waited patiently for it. Do you understand?"

Vivian nodded. "Yes."

"Good. After you have committed the plans to memory, erase them. My story you can leave so you can digest it slowly. But as for the plan, time is crucial. You need to start with your young friend, Armando. He was there with the girl, but I tampered with his memory. He will be in trouble with your constabulary, and this vampire magick will help, shall we say, forestall any complications." Wulf glared down at her with his gray eyes. "It seems my blood has not killed you. Tick, tock, my dear Vivian. You have work to do."

"What will you be doing?"

Wulf smiled and threw the cloak over his shoulders. "I want to sample some American pleasure. We get so little in Romania. You are making a wise decision, Vivian." He strode across the piles of paper, pushing aside the shards of shattered mirror with his cane, and left the room.

[Chapter 5]

IEUTENANT KANE OPENED the door into the observation room and waved Ross and Steel in. "That scum has ruined dozens of kids. I'm going to nail him if it's the last thing I do."

Ross closed the door behind them. "Vampire cult?"

"Yeah. They actually drink each other's blood, if you believe it." Kane slumped into her chair and rubbed her tired eyes.

"Tell me about these clans," Steel said.

Kane tilted her head. "I'm the one asking questions, Steel."

"Josh had a lip bead like Armando's," Steel explained. "Maybe he was in one of these clans."

"Kids want to belong to something, Steel. They get together and pretend to be vampires. Shiny ones. Victorian ones. Alien vamps. You name it. But some of these kids take the lifestyle seriously. They swear on pain of death to keep their 'clan' a secret. They drink each other's blood. They sleep during the day and go out at night. It's Goth. It's emo. It's fantasy come to life. And sometimes the kids go too far. Like Armando. They blur the lines between fantasy and reality, and someone gets hurt. Or killed."

Steel stared at the closed door. What were the chances Armando and Josh were connected in some way? If so, it had to be more than a coincidence he was here, now, confronted with the growing acknowledgment that perhaps God wanted him to intervene. He gritted his teeth. He wasn't ready for another confrontation like this. He had to take care of Josh. He glanced down at the open folder on the table and the picture of Armando. Reluctantly he reached out and picked up the folder.

"Hey, Steel, that's police property." Kane reached for the folder. "I'm interrogating you now."

"You can't stop him, Kane. He's constantly sticking his nose where it doesn't belong. Orders from the top," Ross said, pointing to the ceiling.

"What, the chief?"

"No. He's God's private investigator."

Kane's eyes widened. "This is ridiculous. I ought to throw you in a retaining cell."

Steel flipped through the pages in the file and drew in a sudden breath at the sight of Gloria's mother. The images were blanched by the cold, sterile flash of the cameras, but the sinews and motionless arteries visible through the torn flesh of her neck were laid out in vivid detail. He shuffled the photographs and studied the ones of Gloria. The girl's eyes were partially open, and her mouth gaped, revealing fangs on both of her incisors. Dried blood was crusted on her cheeks. "Look at the close-ups of Gloria's wrists."

Kane sighed. "What about it?"

"Hesitation marks on the left wrist. Several. But your profile here says she was right-handed. She would have gone after her left wrist first. But on her right wrist the cut is neat and deep. No hesitation."

"I'm not a doofus, Steel. That is why I brought Winston Poole in for questioning."

"You may be on to something. Look at this reference. Her last job was with Ketrick Enterprises." Ross pointed to the profile.

"I thought Ketrick's office was located in Lakeside," Steel said.

"His corporate headquarters is here in Dallas. According to this, Gloria Sanchez worked for Ketrick for three months as a student office worker."

Kane placed a hand on Ross's arm and turned him toward her. "What's a Ketrick?"

"An egomaniacal killer."

"He tried to kill me and my friends. Claire Knight, Josh's mother, died saving us from Ketrick." Steel stared off into space. For a fleeting second the odor of burning wood engulfed him, and the flames of the incinerator flickered over the face of Claire as she bolted over the stone altar and carried Ketrick with her into the fire. "I promised her I would make sure Josh and his uncle Cephas got together."

Ross took out a cigarette and played with it. He ran it lovingly across his upper lip as he thought. "Ketrick was into the occult—he lured young, disturbed men into his clutches and turned them into killers."

Kane seemed to relax. "Young, disturbed men like Armando?"

"If there is a connection, it would explain Gloria's death. Ketrick used his 'nephews,' as he called them, to do his dirty work. When was this picture taken of Armando?" Steel asked.

"Looks like it was two weeks ago." Ross pointed to a time and date stamp in the corner.

"No spiral tattoo around the right eye. If he had been under the influence of the thirteenth demon, there would have been a spiral."

"Thirteenth demon?" Kane's mouth fell open. "Spiral tattoo?"

Ross nodded toward Steel. "God's PI, remember? Casts out demons. Defeats evil spirits. Leaps tall sepulchers in a single bound."

"You've got to be kidding!"

Steel heard the disbelief in her voice and ignored it. "This man could still be carrying on with Ketrick's plans. He doesn't have to be demon possessed."

Kane took the folder from Steel's hands and shut it. She pointed to the seat on the opposite side of the table. "I've heard enough of this hocus pocus, Mr. Demonbuster. Sit."

Steel felt the anger roll off of him at her remark. His mind was still on Armando. Deep inside the voice of God nudged him. Something was about to happen, and Steel would be involved.

"Before my interrogation, Ross told me about your past. A little over two years ago you woke up on a beach with amnesia. Spent the fall as a caretaker for a condominium after your therapy. Serial killer Rocky Braxton killed the owner and his daughter. But you were cleared of any connection. Ross filled me in on some of your other 'cases,' the last one three weeks ago in Lakeside. I guess that's the one in which you were involved with this Robert Ketrick?"

"Who turned out to be the mastermind behind Braxton's murder spree as well as dozens of others," Steel said. "Did Ross mention Ketrick's videos? He liked to watch."

Kane glared at Ross. "No."

"Lieutenant Kane, I'm not interested in your murder/suicide. I am after Raven. You and Steel can bond later. Right now I want answers from Steel." Ross pushed the folder aside. "So spill it."

"All I can give you is what I remember. It was just a glimpse of my past. You know more than I do."

Ross tapped the tabletop and looked away. "She is very careful. We won't find any DNA evidence on that rifle. She seeds every crime site with a dozen different types of DNA from her former victims. Once I found a partial fingerprint. I got a hit, but when we went to download the name and match, the computer network died. Just dropped out for only a second. And when it came back, the matching information was gone. I don't know how she does it. My theory is she has backing from some powerful person who has his or her fingers in every governmental security agency in the world."

"Wow. Paranoid," Kane said.

Ross leaned back in his chair and popped the cigarette in his mouth. "You realize she'll be back. Whoever her target was supposed to be, she missed. And I know Raven. She never leaves a job unfinished. She ties up all the loose strings. She'll be back for that rifle, Kane. I hope your evidence room is secure." He pulled a lighter out of his pocket.

"This is still my investigation, Ross." She jerked the cigarette out of his mouth. She looked at it and tucked in between her lips. "I haven't smoked in three years. But today the two of you are driving me to smoke."

Ross raised an eyebrow and lit the cigarette. She took one long pull and sighed.

"Get out of here, both of you. I've got work to do."

Steel stood up. "If you need help on the Sanchez case, I'm available."

Kane blew smoke in his face. "I'll save you a tankard of holy water."

[Chapter 6]

As SOON AS Rudolph Wulf disappeared from the conference room, Raven climbed out from under the desk and shook shards of glass out of her hair. "What are you?"

"I think you know what I am," Vivian said.

"I used to believe in God. But now...I guess that means I don't believe in Satan and demons and..."

"I don't care what you believe. And it's Lucifer, honey. That's his name." Vivian paced around the room. "This changes everything. I need you to get rid of Wulf."

"What?"

"I'm not going to stand around and let him take my place on the Council!"

"Wait a minute! I'm not about to help you fight that wolf-dragon thing. You're not even human yourself."

Vivian stopped her pacing and glared at Raven. "How many people have you killed?"

Raven had lost her cap during the scuffle, so there was no way to hide anymore. Vivian had seen her face. "Twenty-seven."

"Then you and I are more alike than you think, sweetie." Vivian walked across the room and leaned into her face. "I need it to be twenty-eight so I can get rid of number twelve."

"No way. I saw what he became."

"If I go near him, he will sense my demons. But you're demon free." Vivian paused and her eyes widened. "Wait! You said you used to believe in God? What happened to change your mind?"

"None of your business!"

"What turned *you* into a killer?"

33

Raven stumbled back from Vivian and slumped into a chair at the table. She turned away and felt the strings emerge from the dark cabinet of her memories. She shoved her hands over her eyes and fought the memories, but the strings vibrated with life and she was there again.

"Where's your daddy?" Katie asked.

Victoria looked around the yard. It was a perfect spring day. Flowers bloomed around the picnic table in the front yard of the dilapidated house.

"He made me a special birthday cake! Wait until you see it."

"When can we play with your lamb?" Judy asked.

"He's in the backyard. Father said he might run away. We can play with him after we have cake."

Suzie, the fourth girl, sighed. "Vickie, don't you think your dress is too fancy?"

Victoria smoothed down the front of her satin dress and touched the bow in her hair. "My mother picked this out for me for Easter."

Katie glanced at Judy. "But your mother is in heaven."

"She picked this out for me before she died." Victoria fought back tears. She missed her mother so much. Ever since Mother had died, her stepfather had become meaner and meaner. He wouldn't let her go to church. But she had fooled him. While he was sleeping on Sunday mornings, she had gone to church with Katie and Judy. And then, just last week, she had realized that she really wanted one day to see Mother again in heaven. And she didn't want to become like

her stepfather, mean and nasty and... well, the other things too. So she had asked God to take her in his arms and keep her safe.

"It's okay, Katie. When I prayed to God last week, I gave him my heart for safekeeping. One day I'll see Mother again."

Suzie rolled her eyes. "Can we have cake?"

Victoria heard him shuffling through the unmowed grass before she smelled the drink on his breath. She turned and saw her stepfather stumbling across the yard with the cake in his hands. She hurried to him and took the cake.

"Thanks, Father. Thank you for letting me have a party."

Her stepfather rubbed at his stubbled cheek and belched. "Yeah, whatever."

Victoria studied the cake as she placed it on the picnic table. It was shaped like a lamb, her favorite animal. But her stepfather had done a terrible job of icing it. She wanted to cry but realized he had done something nice for a change.

"Now, girls," her stepfather sat at the table. "I have something for each of you."

"No, Father, I made them some treats..." Victoria tried to stop him. He frowned at her and pulled strings out of his pocket.

"Nonsense. Now, what's your name?"

"Katie."

Her stepfather held out his hand, and in it was a coil of bright blue twine tied in a circle. "Now watch." He threaded the circle over his fingers and crisscrossed them until he had a cat's cradle formed with five points. "Now put your hand in the middle."

Katie stuck her hand through the center as Suzie shook her head. "I've seen this before, Katie. It's a trick."

Father released all of his fingers but two, and the string snapped into a tight circle around Katie's wrist. Victoria swallowed as she saw the look on her stepfather's face. He grinned as he tightened the string around Katie's wrist. Katie pulled back.

"Ow! You're hurting me."

"Just a minute," Father said as he rewove the cat's cradle. "Now put your hand back through the center. Go on. Hurry."

Katie's face was red now, and she pushed her hand through the center. Father opened his mouth and revealed his stained teeth. "Now, let's see if you can get free." He released his fingers and the string snapped away from Katie's wrist. She backed away and rubbed her skin. "That hurt. You're mean."

Victoria grabbed the string from Father. "It's okay. We'll have cake now."

Father glared at her and pulled out a huge knife. "Girls, let me introduce you to the KA-BAR fighting utility knife. This baby has gotten me out of trouble many times."

Judy sat back, eyes wide. "My uncle has one of those. He's a Marine. Were you a Marine?"

Father's smile faded, and he placed the knife on the table. "Not for long. We'll cut the cake after you make a wish and blow out the candle." He took a short, stubby candle from his shirt pocket and stuck it in some icing on the edge of the cake. He lit it with a lighter and dangled the string over the candle. The twine caught fire, and he laughed as he threw it across the table at Katie. Katie jumped back.

"Sorry, sweetums. Stamp it out before you catch the yard on fire."

Suzie got up and pushed Katie aside. She stepped on the string.

Victoria fought the nausea and the fear and closed her eyes. What should she wish for? God, You are protecting me, right? You still hear my prayers, right? I don't want a wish. I want a prayer. She drew in a deep breath, whispered under her breath, and blew out the candles. The girls clapped.

"What did you wish for?" her stepfather asked. She looked up into his intense, brown eyes.

"I can't tell you. It wouldn't come true." She felt hope grow in her heart. Could God change Father?

"Oh, this cake is so cute. I've never seen one shaped like a lamb," Judy said.

Father smiled, showing his stained, chipped teeth. "A lamb for my lambkins."

"Where's your pet lamb?" Suzie asked.

Father grinned and held the knife over the cake. He slammed it down and cut into it. Bright red blood pooled out onto the table. "Right here in the birthday cake."

The world tilted and skewed. Judy, Katie, and Suzie screamed in unison as the icing slid away from the fur and the cake shifted and moved in a final rigor and the dull, white eyes of the lamb showed through the icing. The other girls ran, and Victoria froze in horror.

Her stepfather grabbed Victoria and pulled her close. She could smell his sour breath. "I sacrificed your little lamb. Isn't that what your God did for you? Sacrificed His little lamb? You think about that next time you sneak off to church. You think about your little lamb." He plunged the knife into the heart of the lamb-shaped cake,

*and his handful of strings settled onto the icing. Her lamb twitched
one last time as Father stalked off across the yard.*

Raven managed to gather the loose threads of that horrible
memory and roll them up and tuck them back into the cabinet.
She opened her eyes, and Vivian sat across from her.

"You didn't answer my question. What turned you into an
assassin?" Vivian crossed her arms and shrugged. "Was it your
father or your mother? Huh? It was my mother. The witch!
After she killed my father, the things she did to me. Until I met
my first demon, and then we took care of her. So, which was it?"

"None of your business."

"Fine. Where does God fit into your life now?"

"Why?"

"I need to know whose side you're on."

Raven stood up. "I have no god. I'm on *my* side."

Vivian laughed. "Dream on, sweetie. We all serve someone."

Raven already felt the wheels turning in her head. Rudolph
Wulf represented everything she had rejected. He represented
a world in which good battled against evil. She knew that good
had long ago lost that battle for her heart. She hated being
reminded that it might win. If she could kill this man for
Vivian, she would be protecting a world in which she could continue to survive. She saw new strings emerge from her mind, red
with clotted blood, dark with coming death, strings that would
ensnare this new reality and strangle it.

"Can Wulf be killed?"

"Of course. After all, his host is only human."

"What about the other man?"

"What man?"

"The one at the mall. Atchison's bodyguard. Now that he knows I'm here in Dallas, he'll come and find me."

"Kill him first." Vivian waved a hand in her direction. "I'll pay you for all three of them."

Raven considered what she was being asked to do. Kill a man she had already killed once. And then kill a demon-possessed megalomaniac with delusions of godhood. She would be crazy to do such a thing. She should leave now and run away. But Vivian Darbonne Ketrick was more than human, and she had seen Raven's face. She would see that Raven did her job or track her down and kill her. Raven imagined this Council of monsters pursuing her around the globe. She already lived that lifestyle, and those who hunted her now were mere humans.

"I don't have much choice, do I?" It all boiled down to survival. It always had. "So I'll help you become the twelfth demon."

Interlude
Arcanus Premum Secundus Chapter 42, Section 2, Grimvox

"Sir, this is your doctor. Can you hear me?"

"Yes?"

"Please keep your eyes closed."

"Yes."

"The voice you hear is the only voice you will obey. Do you understand?"

"Yes."

"You asked me to help you with some of your distant memories. Do you remember asking me for that help?"

"Yes."

"Good. Now, I want you to think back to your earliest memories. When you have done so, tell me what you are seeing."

"A rocking horse."

"I want you to go further back in your memory. You told me you have memories of another place and time. You told me you have memories that are hidden and repressed, but you want to remember them and experience them. Isn't that correct?"

"Yes."

"Fine. Now think very hard about someplace far, far away from the rocking horse. What do you see?"

"I see stone. I see candlelight. I smell wet earth."

"Good, where are you?"

"I am . . ."

Kogain Sanctuary for King Zamolxis
Near the Danube River
Circa 500–400 B.C.

"Surely Master is not afraid." I bowed before Zamolxis. The king, resplendent in his dark robes, turned from his spy hole.

"Saitnoxis, I am the master of the Kogain. You are my chief priest, my ktistai. You have no right to question my wisdom."

From the shadows in the corner the other advisor appeared. His long, dark hair hung down upon his shoulders, and his greenish brown eyes gleamed with malice toward me. He was my greatest enemy, and I could not allow him to influence the king. Rofel placed a hand on the king's shoulder. "You are correct, my king."

I groveled on the floor in the most humble posture. "This plan of yours is bold, Master. Rofel and I may disagree on your techniques, but I know your followers have seen your magick. They have tasted your healing potions. They know of your wisdom. But they do not believe your teachings. This plan would convince them."

Zamolxis thudded his staff on the ground, and his handsome, chiseled face reddened. Beside him the insufferably insipid Rofel smiled in triumph. "I am aware of my own shortcomings, Saitnoxis. I came here from Pythagorus, my old master, with riches and wisdom your people had never seen. I have brought peace and contentment and wealth to the land of the Getae. In time my followers will believe me."

"Yes, Saitnoxis," Rofel spoke smoothly. "Do not question our king's authority."

In my heart hatred for Rofel deepened. He was so self-righteous and smug. I had to win over the heart of the king. For as I hugged the harsh rock of the cave, I sensed the measured beat of hammers and chisels far below where the other ktistai worked on Zamolxis's secret chamber. Above us the planets moved into their alignment, and it would be only three years until the Event. On that day great power would arise from the planet itself, and with the achievement of my plan, that power would be mine. But first I had to get Zamolxis to see the wisdom of my deceptions.

"Master, your plan would convince them." I put the most pleading expression on my face. "If they thought you were dead and yet your soul, as you teach, was immortal, then how great would be your second coming! How marvelous it would be when they see your power and glory."

Zamolxis's face softened as he thought on the merits of my plan. He sought the power that I spoke of. He craved it as all men did. It was their downfall: the power of choosing, the power of the knowledge of good and evil. Oh, to be a god! He pulled away from Rofel's grasp. Rofel knew he was losing. For, in the end, it was the choice of the man that mattered. No amount of persuasion or coercion could be forced upon the human heart. The choosing came from within, and in that choice was the power of the cosmos, for God Himself had given it to man. *That freedom could be turned to my advantage, and Rofel knew it. Ultimately it would be the choice that would shape the future.* Slowly Zamolxis sat on his bench before his table and looked around the cramped room. "I would be deceiving them, Saitnoxis. I have built my rule on wisdom…"

"Great wisdom. And truth," Rofel whispered as he drew nearer to Zamolxis.

"But also misdirection," I whispered. I crawled across the floor to the feet of the king and dared to sit up and look him in the face. I had to overcome his doubts. He was a great man far ahead of his time, but he was plagued with mercy. "We sit in a spy chamber so you can see and hear what transpires in the banquet room below where the great heads of all households are assembled."

He glared at me. He realized his own dark nature. He sensed his need for power. Quick, before he could look at Rofel for reassurance.

"Please, do not get angry, Master." I stood to my feet and moved to eclipse Rofel. "Your potions are pure and filled with science, but your magick is only illusion. Yet it gives the people hope. Can you not see that? And you have told them there is hope. You have taught them their soul is immortal and will one day journey to a place of everlasting wonder. This plan is no meaner, no more deceitful than your rule has been. I would be remiss if I did not point out that your goals have justified the means. Our country is powerful and rich."

I waited for his outburst. But Zamolxis only stared at me. His eyes slowly filled with moisture. "You are correct, Saitnoxis. I have combined truth with lies. I have built a kingdom of wisdom and deceit. Perhaps I can salvage my future. Tomorrow at the great feast when all of the heads of the major households are present, I will disappear."

"Yes, Master." My human heart raced with joy. He had followed my words down the path to his own destruction. I glanced at Rofel. He was already backing away in defeat. I placed a hand on my king's shoulder. "My king, you must retreat to your underground chamber. Your followers will think you have disappeared, but the priesthood will reassure them that one day you will return as a god! Your ktsitai will tend to you in your secret chamber for the next three years, and one day you will emerge to fill your kingdom with awe and glory and power."

Zamolxis's eyes turned up to mine. "Who will rule while I am gone?"

"Your wisdom will rule. By your example we will follow your teachings and look forward to your second coming." I smiled.

Zamolxis nodded, and his eyes grew dim. "Who will oversee the government while I am gone?"

I squeezed his shoulder. "I will, Master."

Chapter 7

JOSH BABBLED ON about his new iPad and iPhone and barely noticed they had pulled up in front of his house. Steel switched off the GPS. "Is this home?"

Josh looked out the passenger window. "We're here." He pulled the box with his new hardware to his chest as if it were a life preserver. "Bro, I'm not ready for this." He started breathing heavily.

"You have to go home sometime." Steel reached toward him awkwardly and then put his hand back on the steering wheel.

"Home is with Uncle Cephas now." Josh looked straight ahead. "New York City. I hear he has this weird, haunted building. Dude, what if you hadn't called him?" Josh whispered.

Steel averted his gaze. "Your mother would still be alive."

"Yeah, she would." Josh said quietly. "And Ketrick would still be alive. And I wouldn't be any different. Tell me how you met, dude." He looked right at Steel. "You and Uncle Cephas. How did you meet?"

The cab screeched to a halt in front of the old building, and Jonathan Steel slid out of the backseat. The driver snatched the money from Steel's hand, threw the car into gear, and roared off down the street. Steel drew in a deep breath of the smoky air. Definitely pot and probably crack cocaine. Across the street dirty, graffiti-covered high rises sat in somber dejection. There were people present, huddled on stoops, stairways, and fire escapes, all listless and insulated in their own world of pain and despair. No wonder the cabby wanted to get out of here.

Steel turned around to study the building behind him. It stretched upward all of twenty stories, its old stone and brick façade displaying a 1930s' deco motif. A stairway led up into an open foyer, and the doors were ripped from their frames.

"Yo, dude, where you think you're going?"

Steel turned slowly. Three men stood in the street with their heads covered in do rags and backward baseball caps. The largest strutted forward and pointed a pistol sideways at Steel.

"Now, you just give us whatever's in your pocket, man, and we might let you live." He laughed. Steel studied the young man's goatee, his dark brown eyes, pupils constricted in a narcotic glaze. The other two guys stood to the bigger one's side.

"No."

"Too bad, dude." The tall one cocked the pistol.

Steel whipped into action. He slapped the pistol out of the big guy's hand, gripping the barrel just as the bullet exploded from its end. The bullet ripped through the end of Steel's jacket sleeve and buried itself in the brick wall behind him. Steel caught the big guy in the temple with a left hook and then brought the pistol around, smacking the handle across the shorter companion's face. Steel dropped the pistol behind him and snared the tall skinny one by the shoulders even as the other two dropped to the pavement unconscious. Steel threw him across the pavement and stooped to retrieve the pistol. He slid the clip from the gun and pocketed the bullets. "Get out of here, and don't come back." He glared at the skinny one, who bolted to his feet and disappeared down the street.

Steel looked at the two unconscious men at his feet and checked to see if they were breathing. Nearby a car stripped of its interior sat on cinder blocks with its trunk open and empty. Steel picked up the men and threw them into the trunk of the car. He pulled a piece of wire from the open engine compartment and wired the trunk shut.

Steel looked at the gun in his hand and felt the familiarity, the comfort of its weight. In his former life he had used guns. He had shot people. He may have even killed them.

"Well, are you going to use the gun, or not?"

Steel whirled. A short, bushy-haired man stood in the open stairway of the building. Small glasses sat on the end of his nose, and he wore a flannel shirt, khaki pants, and a housecoat. "You could have shot them all, and no one would have cared."

Steel looked down at the gun and hurled it into an open sewer drain on the street. It clattered away into darkness. "I don't shoot people. Are you Cephas Lawrence?"

The graying man sighed and pulled his housecoat around him. "If I'm not, are you going to lock me in a car trunk?"

"They tried to kill me."

"Of course they did. It is what they do."

"I was only defending myself."

"I do not fault your actions." The man stepped down the stairs. "Just your motives. I assume you are Jonathan Steel."

"Yes."

"And why should I allow you into my home?" Lawrence raised a bushy eyebrow.

"I have an appointment with you."

"Yes, to talk about evil. And yet you bring evil with you." He gestured toward the car trunk.

"What would you have done?" Steel countered.

Lawrence chuckled. "I would have dropped dead of a heart attack. But I have a truce with the people in this neighborhood. They leave me alone. Of course, now if I invite you into my home, they will probably ignore the truce. I must at least give you a hard time, you understand."

Steel glanced around at the buildings surrounding them. "Why do you live in this neighborhood if it's so dangerous?"

"This building is my home. I own it. I leave the bottom floors to the homeless. Fall is here, and soon it will be very cold. They need a place to escape the elements. I give that to them. It is part of the compassion of our Lord that I show."

"I suppose I should have turned the other cheek?"

"No, of course not. You should have shot them. But you did not. You showed restraint. You chose a different solution." He turned and started up the stairs. He paused and motioned into the foyer. "And that is what I call turning the other cheek. Shall we?"

Lawrence opened an elevator door with a key. They ascended, and the door opened into a small foyer. Steel looked around in amazement at the interior. The entire floor was an open unfinished space interrupted in places by partial walls. Lawrence locked the foyer door behind him and keyed in a security code on a keypad by the door.

"I keep myself locked away up here. I am not fool enough to think that those people you ran up against wouldn't break their truce. After all, the enemy is quite devious, and we must never let down our guard. At the same time we must extend to those children around us the love and compassion of our Savior."

Steel shook his head as Lawrence led them past a room with a sofa and chairs and around a partition. A kitchen occupied the next space, and Lawrence motioned to the antique table and chairs. "Why don't you sit down? I shall make us some tea."

Steel sat at the table. Two monitors on the kitchen counter showed a video feed of the exterior of the building. "You own the entire building and you live on this one floor?"

"Yes. I bought it in an auction years ago. The top floor was unfinished and used as storage, so I am filling it up with my treasures." Lawrence filled a teakettle from a bottled water dispenser and placed it on the stove. "Come; while the water is heating, I will show you my world."

He led Steel around the partition to a huge open space filled with tables and shelves. Books covered the tables, some open, some stacked, and more books cluttered the shelves all around him. "I have here one of the most exclusive antique book collections in the world. Behind that partition is a vault with temperature and humidity control to store the rarest of the books." He led them past the tables and shelves into another room. This area was twice the size of the library and held suspended paintings, standing statues, tables covered with artifacts.

"Artifacts from around the world. Now, you would not recognize the names of many of these artists. I do not collect them for their fame. I collect art and books that open a window into the hearts and minds of the people of the past."

In the distance the teakettle whistled, and Lawrence led them back to the kitchen. He poured the steaming water into two mugs and lowered tea bags into each.

"These treasures give me a window into the past." Lawrence turned to his kitchen counter and retrieved a bowl of sugar cubes and a small container of cream. "The enemy cannot see the future. He has no power to predict the events that are to come. But he reveals himself in the events of the past."

Steel removed the tea bag and sipped the hot tea. It was pungent and spicy. "I read your book. You try to stop Satan's interventions into people's lives."

Lawrence studied him for a moment. "I know all about you, Jonathan Steel. You awoke on a beach with no memory. I am familiar with the events since, and now you come to me for advice concerning demons." Lawrence leaned back in his chair and sipped at his tea. "What do you really want, Mr. Steel?"

"To understand how they work."

"Why?"

Steel averted his eyes. "I made a promise."

"You want to find the demon that prompted this madman to kill someone you loved?"

Steel closed his eyes and sighed. "Yes."

"What will you do when you find it?"

Steel felt his anger boil, felt the fury grow. "Send it to hell."

"Come with me." Lawrence led them into the library. He crossed to one of the tables and sifted through the open books. "Ah, here we are. You know your Bible?"

Steel nodded. "Yes."

Lawrence adjusted his glasses and lifted an old Bible and opened it. "Then you remember this account. A man possessed by demons went by the name of Legion. Jesus cast out his demons into pigs because the demons did not want to be sent to a 'distant place.' That place is

Tartarus, a compartment of hell reserved for the worst demons of the worst. Some theologians think that Tartarus was designed for the demons who had sexual relations with humans that resulted in the Nephilim, the giants of old. The Philistines. Goliath. It is not easy to send a demon to Tartarus."

"Unless you know how to kill it."

Lawrence shut the book and placed it on the table before him. "You cannot kill a demon. Mr. Steel, I have participated in over a dozen exorcisms in the past thirty years. Casting out the devil is not some cavalier action like dispatching the thugs you encountered this afternoon." Lawrence slumped into a chair and suddenly seemed old and feeble. "It takes something out of you. Each exorcism was long and tedious and a great work. And never have I been able to send a single demon to Tartarus." Lawrence looked up at him, his eyes haunted with the memories. "I have wanted to. I have wanted to hurt these heinous things that destroy human lives. I have wanted to torture them. To destroy them."

Steel released his breath, suddenly aware he had held it. He looked at the books before him. "I can't let the demon go free, Dr. Lawrence. I promised April I would find it. I would fight it."

"Cephas, call me Cephas." Lawrence said.

"The rest you know." Steel finished. "I called him the night I saw the spiral of the thirteenth demon on the ceiling of the church in Lakeside. I needed a physicist. I had no idea he would call his niece."

Josh nodded. "Dude, it seems all of this is beyond our control, you know? Like God has something planned. I just can't wrap my brain around why my mother had to…"

Josh shoved open the truck door and left his stuff on the seat. He ran to the front door, fumbling in his pocket for his keys. Steel barely had time to get out of the driver's seat before Josh had the door open. He ran down the walkway, and Josh was standing just inside the foyer, his eyes wide and his face pale.

"She's not here, Jonathan. She's not here!"

A sound behind him had him whirling around.

"Am I interrupting something?" Steel looked through the open front door of Josh's house as Charles Atchison came up the walkway. Josh was collapsed on the floor, sobbing. Steel felt helpless.

Atchison pushed in past them. "It stinks in here." He walked over to the thermostat. With a whoosh, stale air began moving around the interior. Steel reached down, took Josh by the arm, and pulled him to his feet.

"You wouldn't believe the afternoon I had," Atchison said as Steel led Josh to the couch. He moved like a zombie. Atchison turned off the den, into the dining room. Steel followed and watched the lawyer spread out papers on the dining room table as he babbled. When the man finally decided to take a breath, Steel interrupted him.

"Atchison, someone tried to kill you today. After that, the afternoon should have been a piece of cake."

Atchison sighed. "Not me, Steel. You! I'm not the man with a checkered past."

"That's not what I heard."

"Don't believe everything Kane told you. I admit I have a problem. I'm in counseling. Now, sit."

Steel glanced over at the couch. Josh was sitting already, rigid and still. His eyes were rimmed in red. "We need to go sit down with Mr. Atchison, Josh."

Josh nodded emptily and came to the table. Atchison placed

a sheaf of papers in front of Josh. "Josh, if you'll just sign these papers so the state can assign you a guardian—"

Josh looked up and life returned to his vacant eyes. "I have a guardian."

Atchison paused with his mouth open in mid sentence. "Ah, well that could be a problem. I don't see your uncle Cephas. Where is he?"

Steel pulled his cell phone out of his pocket. "Let's find out."

Cephas Lawrence ran a hand through his gray hair and glared at the man in the three-piece suit. "Mr. Roberts, I will be out of this building by morning, I assure you. I have to catch a flight to Texas to take care of my great-nephew." He paused for a second as the old sorrow cascaded over him. He still could not believe Claire was dead.

Mr. Roberts glanced around the cavernous room that had once been Lawrence's home. The walls that separated the floor of the building into rooms had come down. A dozen men moved around the interior taping up boxes and moving them toward the freight elevator in the corner. "You must vacate the building by seven a.m. The demolition crew will be here to start right away." Mr. Roberts adjusted his coat. "I'd hate for you to get in the way, Dr. Lawrence."

"I assure you I will not. I wouldn't want to stand in the way of your precious 'urban renewal' project."

Roberts frowned. "My corporation is doing the best it can to reclaim portions of this great city…"

"Save it for your election speech, Mr. Roberts. And now you can give me my check and leave. Until the morning this is still my home, and you are no longer welcome."

Roberts sighed and reached into his pocket and took out an envelope. "Cashier's check for the agreed-upon amount."

"Agreed upon by the courts, Mr. Roberts. This building is worth far more than you're paying me. But it is only a building." Cephas tucked the envelope in his pocket.

Roberts opened his mouth to say something and then shook his head. He joined the others on the elevator. Cephas watched it disappear from sight. He walked across the huge, open expanse to a window, where his gaze traveled up to the skyline of New York City. The boxes of his treasures would be placed in safe storage until he could find another home large enough to hold them. As for himself, he had no idea where he would live. His cell phone rang, and he pulled it out of his pocket. He slid his tiny reading glasses down and studied the readout.

"Jonathan, good to hear from you." He said as he lifted the phone to his ear.

"Cephas, we're here with a lawyer who wants to turn Josh over to the state," Steel said.

"Let me speak to him." Cephas waited patiently.

"This is Mr. Atchison."

"Where is Ruth?"

"In Europe with most of the firm for a seminar. Josh is stuck with me."

"Grace is not in Europe. I spoke to her this morning."

"I don't like this anymore than you do, Dr. Lawrence. If you were here..."

"I am on my way. Mr. Steel is to be Josh's guardian until I arrive. Do I need to call Grace again?"

"No. I'll check with her this evening. Here's Steel."

"Jonathan," Cephas stood at the window and watched the sun setting behind the high-rises of the city he had grown to love over the past thirty years. The fading glory of the sunset filled his lonely room with subdued, reddish light. Three bright stars appeared on the horizon. "I'm afraid I am detained by powers beyond my control. Atchison will give you temporary custody."

"Fine. When will you be here?"

"When I get there." Cephas ended the call and sighed. He walked across the room to the one remaining box and picked up a framed picture that lay atop the other contents of the box. He studied the young woman's photograph. His gnarled hand drifted out to touch the glass, and he sighed. She had been so lovely, and he missed her so much. His gaze lingered briefly on the woman's face. How he missed the touch of those lips. He felt the warmth of the dying sun on his cheeks, and he closed his eyes. "Molly, what do you think? Is it time to go somewhere warmer?" He opened his eyes and placed the picture back in the box. "I think it is."

"Looks like Steel will be your temporary guardian." Atchison began gathering the papers and sliding them back into his briefcase.

Josh opened his mouth and glanced at Steel. "What?"

"Don't get all mushy on me." Steel said.

"Dude, we're not even related."

"I know. Cephas is late." Steel said.

"I guess I don't have a choice." Josh tried to hide his smile.

"You want me to be your guardian?" Steel asked.

"Dude, anything is better than some foster home."

"I'll have to file a brief with the juvenile court for you to gain temporary custody of Josh. And we'll have to move rapidly if you don't want him in a foster home this weekend." Atchison packed up the last of his paperwork. "I'm heading over to Grace Pennington's office now, and I'll let you know when the hearing will be."

"Hearing?" Steel asked.

Atchison stood up. "Yes, Mr. Steel, there will have to be a hearing no matter what Dr. Lawrence says. And you'll have to convince the judge that you're not the target of an assassin, if you want to keep the boy out of a home."

A couple of hours later they had emptied most of the trash, and the house was cool. Steel surveyed the contents of the refrigerator, and they decided not to risk an outbreak of E. *Coli* and go out to eat. The doorbell rang. Steel looked at Josh and pointed toward the foyer. "It's your house."

Josh sighed and opened the door. A short, dumpy woman stood on the threshold.

"Josh, you're home!" She threw herself on Josh and hugged him as her eyes filled with tears. "Is it true? About your mother?"

Josh's breath came faster, and his eyes were wild. Steel pulled him away from the woman. "I'm Jonathan Steel, a friend of Claire's. May I help you?"

"I'm sorry. I'm Mrs. Reeves from across the street. I saw lights in the house, and I wondered if Josh was home. We heard about Claire at church and…" She stopped and glanced around Steel to Josh, now slumped on the couch, his face hidden in his hands.

"I'm so sorry, Josh." Mrs. Reeves spoke over Steel's shoulder. "Forgive me. I just… Have you heard from Ila?"

Josh looked up. "What about Ila?"

Mrs. Reeves walked over and slumped onto the couch next to Josh. "She's gone. Two weeks now. I talked to the police, but they think she ran away from home."

"She never saw me. I promise. I don't know anything," Josh blurted. Steel watched the exchange and felt an uncomfortable tickle in his gut.

Mrs. Reeves found a tissue box on the coffee table and blew

her nose. "She went to the mall with some friends, and she never came home. Some of them are missing too."

"Who were the other kids?"

"She called them her clan." An odd look came over her face. "At first I thought it was a gang. But they didn't drink or smoke, and I didn't see a whole lot of harm in it. Until I met that older guy they were hanging out with. That's when I tried fixing her up with Josh." Mrs. Reeves put her hand to her mouth. "Oh, I'm sorry, Josh. I didn't want you to know that I wanted Ila to like you, not that Winny guy."

"Winny? You mean Winston Poole?" Josh asked.

Cold fury washed over Steel at the sound of the name. Pieces of a puzzle tumbled into place; rocks settled in the avalanche; the mist began to clear.

"Yes. I didn't think he was a good influence on her. But I had faith in you, Josh. I worried you'd get pulled into that stuff, but I knew your mother would help you get back to reality. And I hoped you'd bring Ila along with you. But I guess I was wrong." She dabbed at her eyes with the tissue.

"Mrs. Reeves, call police headquarters and ask to speak with Lieutenant Kane. She knows something about Winston Poole. She may be able to help you."

Josh looked up at him suddenly, his face was alive with interest. Mrs. Reeves nodded. "The house is so quiet without my Ila. And Claire was supposed to be back in a couple of days." She paused as realization dawned. "Oh, my, she's gone too."

Steel ushered her to the door before she could pull them all back down into the abyss of sorrow. Steel shut the door and turned to Josh. "You want to tell me something?"

Josh shook his head slightly. "Not right now, dude. I've got to think. Let's go to Eastwood Mall. I want TexMex."

"Why the mall?"

Josh met his stare with determined eyes. "They may be hanging out there. I want to ask them about Ila."

Steel let the statement rest while his own thoughts whirled around Armando, aka Winston Poole, and the chasm into which he was being pulled.

Chapter 8

RMANDO SLID THE dead bolt closed and turned to the darkened interior of his apartment. From the far corner Vivian Darbonne Ketrick watched him in silence. She saw his nostrils flair.

"Whoever you are, you are about to die. I am a vampire, and all bow down before me."

Vivian reached up and turned the overhead lights on. Armando squinted in the sudden brightness. "Save it for your clan, Armando."

He blinked, and his burgundy eyes gleamed with growing anger. "How did you get in here?"

"Magick." Vivian had tossed the black dress and chosen a dark red blouse with black jeans. She suddenly appeared behind Armando with her hands on his beautiful neck. He jerked in surprise, and she pressed her lips against his right ear. "Boo!"

Armando pulled away from her and collapsed in the chair in which she had been sitting. His eyes were wide with fear, and his hands shook. "Why are you here?"

"Robert Ketrick is dead. Haven't you heard?" She sat on a footrest in front of the chair. "Fried in his own crematorium."

"The tall zombie dude?"

"He was playing games, Armando." She squeezed his thighs and leaned toward him. "But I have something that is real magick."

"What?"

"The most perfect blood possible." She held up the vial. "Blood that will give you the power of vampire magick. Drink it."

"I only drink from my clan." Armando eyed the vial suspiciously.

Vivian leaned forward and touched the vial to his nose and ran it down to rest against his lips. Vivian pointed to the mark on her neck. "The mark of the wolf dragon can be the mark of your new clan. Power beyond anything you can imagine. Just try the blood. A little sip."

She popped the top off the vial and handed it to Armando. He inhaled the aroma of the blood then tipped his head back and swallowed the contents. He smacked his lips. "That was amazing."

"I said you could trust me. Now, we wait. When the fever hits, you'll receive the mark." Vivian backed away.

"Fever?" Armando looked around the room as if seeking an escape. "What have you done?"

"I have given you a wonderful gift that will make you a god."

Armando began to tremble, and sweat beaded on his forehead. "I have the shakes."

"Yes, I know." Vivian felt her heart race with anticipation.

Armando's eyes grew wider as his shakes worsened, and soon sweat poured down his face. "I feel strange."

"Of course you do. But soon you will feel better than you have ever felt in your life."

Armando's face began to relax, and his eyes closed as he slumped in the chair. His breathing became quieter, and his trembling subsided. After the debacle in the conference room, Vivian's plans seemed doomed. But she would snatch victory from the hands of Wulf just in case Raven failed to kill him. She leaned forward.

"Armando, open your eyes."

Armando's eyes opened in a vacant stare.

"Can you hear me?"

"Yes," Armando said in a monotone.

Vivian felt a thrill inside of her. "Then you must listen very carefully. You must pledge total allegiance to—"

"Rudolph Wulf."

She whirled. Wulf stood in the room. "How did you get here?"

"I flew." He smiled and pointed his cane at Armando. "It worked rapidly on him."

Vivian frowned and turned back to Armando. This was not going as she had planned. When she had read Wulf's instructions, she had hoped she could turn this new blood to her advantage. Now that Wulf was here, she had to come up with a new plan. For now she would play along. "Armando, you must pledge undying allegiance to Rudolph Wulf and to me as his second. Do you understand?"

"Yes."

"Recite the vampire creed," Vivian ordered.

"I am a vampire. I worship my ego, for I am the only god that is. I am proud that I am a predatory animal, and I honor my animal instincts." His voice grew stronger as he spoke. "I exalt my rational mind, and I recognize the difference between the worlds of truth and fantasy. I acknowledge the Powers of Darkness to be hidden natural laws, subject to no gods. I realize there is no heaven as there is no hell, and I view death as the destroyer of life. Therefore I will make the most of life here and now. I am a vampire. Bow down before me."

Vivian stood up and pulled him up with her. "My master has an important task for you, Armando. But first, the part in the creed regarding fantasy and reality?"

Armando's eyes were riveted on hers. "What about it?"

"What is fantasy is real. And what is real is fantasy."

For a fleeting second Armando's eyes filled with confusion. "I don't understand."

"Armando, do you wish to have the power to use your vampire magick?"

"Yes."

Wulf stepped between them. "Then you must invite the magick in. You must embrace the mark of the wolf dragon. Do you understand?"

Armando nodded. "Yes."

Vivian tried to reach around Wulf, but he pushed her away. "I will take care of this, Vivian." He gestured with his gloved hand, and the air above Armando glowed with a reddish light. Wulf swirled his hand, and a mist formed, coalescing, swirling, throbbing with dark energy. "Open your mouth."

Armando opened his mouth, and Wulf touched his fake fangs. They fell away, and his bicuspids lengthened, forming real fangs. "Now, take a deep breath."

Armando drew a deep, shuddering breath, and the cloud trickled into his mouth, swelling with power. Armando's face reddened, and he gasped for breath. Vivian grabbed him as he tried to pull away in sudden horror, then felt him grow limp as the evil spirit exercised control. Armando relaxed, and his eyes glowed a deep burgundy. The mark of the wolf dragon appeared on his lower neck.

"He's all mine." Wulf said.

Interlude

"Sir, it is your doctor speaking. Do you hear me?"

"Yes."

"How are you feeling today?"

"Much stronger."

"Good. The last session drained you of energy. I have to make sure you are stronger before we go any deeper into the trance. Do you understand?"

"Yes. I feel strong today."

"Excellent. Now, in your last session you told me all about Zamolxis. Go back to that life. Go back to that memory."

"I will."

"What do you see?"

"I see a banquet hall."

Kogain Sanctuary
Near the Danube River
From the annals of Zamolxis
Translated by Rudolph Wulf
Circa 500–400 B.C.

I studied the night sky. Somewhere behind the swirling rain clouds the planets were moving into alignment, and the moon would soon be eclipsed. Such an event only came every two thousand five hundred years. Timing was critical for the transition of the ktistai into my followers.

"Do you really think the people will believe your lies?" Rofel stepped out of the shadows of a nearby archway. His eyes gleamed in the bursts of lightning.

I laughed and pointed to the sky. "They have done so for the past three years, Rofel. You are defeated. You have tried to persuade the royalty to disobey the priesthood, but they are as chattel. Feed them, and they will follow. Please them, and they will grovel at your feet. Go back and tell your master that I have won."

Rofel leaned against the wall and frowned. "This is but a skirmish, Saitnoxis. The battle lost does not mean the war is lost. You and your kind are already defeated."

For a second I felt fear and doubt. But my imperious demeanor and all that I had accomplished in the last three years came flooding back to me. "Neither of us can know the future, Rofel. It can be changed."

"I must leave now. You are correct about the current situation. The choices have been made. They cannot be changed. But there is one task I will complete before I leave." His features settled into hardened determination.

I leaned into him. "You cannot stop me, Rofel. They"—I pointed through the archway toward the great banquet hall where all of the royalty were gathered—"have already chosen. And tonight I will bring forth their lost king in a flurry of magick and glory. Zamolxis will return, along with my army of ktistai to bring doom upon this world."

Rofel glared at me, turned, and strode off into the shadows. I smiled. It was time for victory!

I entered the banquet room and took my place at the head table. Thunder rumbled outside the great hall, and a cold wind circulated through the windows into the huge room. The gathered heads of households moved restlessly around the feasting tables. Their murmurs echoed the fading rumble of thunder. I sat quietly next to the empty throne of the king, watching their fear and frustration grow. Soon it would peak, and when it did, I would act. A tall, bearded man stood up from a table and strode across the great hall to the head table. He wore a simple tunic and sandals, and his handsome face was twisted in anger.

"Saitnoxis, I grow weary of waiting for this miracle you have promised. It has been three years since our king vanished from this hall. He is not going to return."

I smiled at him. "Of course he will return, as you will return to your table."

"I tire of your leadership, Saitnoxis. For three years you have ruled ruthlessly in our king's stead. Either he returns, or you abdicate the throne. Now!" The man pounded the table in front of me, and fruit rolled out of a wooden bowl. I picked up an apple and studied it.

"Bisudris, your wisdom is well known among the Getae. As a follower of Rofel's philosophy, your words are of great renown," I said calmly. I glanced beyond him where the other household leaders were eagerly awaiting the outcome of this confrontation. All I had to do was buy some time. And take care of this little rebellious ruffian. "When will you take a wife?"

Bisudris shook his head in confusion. "You ask me such a question while our kingdom flounders? You are truly mad. It is time for you to step aside. We must find a new king. Zamolxis is not returning."

I smiled and adjusted the white robes of my priesthood. Within me, my power, my master, stirred, and I knew it was time. Beneath my feet the doorways were opening, and this very night, Zamolxis would make his triumphant return. But before he did, I had one last deed to undertake.

"Perhaps, Bisudris, we need to send a message to the master. We could beseech our king to return to us." I laid the apple on the table before me.

Bisudris backed away, and his face clouded with confusion. "Send a message? To do so would assume he is still alive. That his soul, as he *taught, lives still.* How would we communicate with his soul in the beyond?"

I stood up and took a knife from beside my plate. I ran a finger along its sharp edge. Blood spurted out, and I sucked on my injured finger. Delicious! "I have ascertained the perfect method to communicate with Zamolxis. All we need is a willing messenger. He must be handsome, righteous, powerful, filled with wisdom, and having no guile. And unmarried. Only the perfect messenger can communicate with the master. Who do you suggest?"

I raised an eyebrow as I looked across the table at Bisudris. He glanced over his shoulder at the other tables. The heads of each household looked away. I counted on his pride to bring this charade to its conclusion. Bisudris turned back to me and seemed to be taller. "You are the high priest. You decide."

I waved a hand, and the knife blade flashed in the candlelight. "My choice would be inadequate. I suggest we let the people decide." Lightning flashed outside, and thunder rumbled across the room. Within me I sensed the power of the universe now at my disposal. The planets had aligned, and the moon was now obscured by the shadow of death. The doorway opened far beneath on the chamber of Zamolxis. Soon he would be here. "Good people of Geta, who would you choose as your messenger?"

The cries went almost in unison. Bisudris paled. "I do not deserve such an honor."

"You would turn down this honor, this chance to be the first messenger to Zamolxis?" I smiled, and a sudden pain lanced across my chest. I drew a deep breath and blinked. Beneath me something was amiss. Zamolxis had left his chamber, but the remainder of the ktistai, the hundreds of priests who had waited on him, were trapped, sealed behind the door! The transition had been complete. The ktistai were now my true servants of evil. But somehow they had been forbidden from exiting the chamber! How could such a thing happen? Rofel! I saw his eyes gleaming in the darkness of my mind. I drew a deep breath and recovered my composure. "Will you accept the position as messenger?"

Bisudris yielded to the inevitable. His handsome face returned to its normal color, and he nodded. "Of course."

I slammed the knife down into the apple and impaled it with sudden fury. "It is time."

Four men came forward and took Bisudris by the arms. At first he seemed confused, and then his eyes met mine. "What are you doing?"

I gestured to three other men carrying huge spears. "Sending a message to our master."

Bisudris's eyes widened as he saw the men coming forward. They lined up in front of the table with their spears held aloft.

"What are you doing?" Bisudris struggled. The four men pulled him back and swung his body upward into the air. Bisudris tried to fight the forward motion and failed. His body arched through the air and thudded onto the spears. Blood spurted over the table and the bowl of fruit. His eyes locked on mine, filled with pain and hatred. The emotion then faded as the life flowed out of him.

I wiped a droplet of blood from my cheek and turned to the people gathered in silence at their tables. Their faces were etched in horror and yet filled with a hunger for the violence they had just witnessed. It has always been so. In time they would yearn for more impalings. Now that Rofel had sealed my followers in the chamber, I would wreak havoc on these pitiful humans. They would pay for Rofel's insolence!

"The message has been sent," I proclaimed, gesturing to Bisudris's lifeless body impaled on the three spears. "Our master has heard, and behold, he returns."

I made a grand, sweeping gesture toward the throne. Zamolxis emerged from behind, using his secret entrance. His face was resplendent. His garment glowed with power and life. Outside the great hallway thunder greeted his appearance, and the people fell on their faces in awe.

Zamolxis stepped in front of his throne. His face was triumphant until his eyes fell on the body of Bisudris. He looked at me and leaned forward to whisper.

"Saitnoxis, what have you done?"

I smiled. "I have made you a god."

Chapter 9

RAVEN WATCHED FROM her car as Steel and the boy walked into the mall entrance. She had tracked the truck to a house in the suburbs and had arrived just in time to see them pull out. Now she had formulated a plan. She handled her pistol with gloved hands. She was dressed for an evening on the town and had pulled on the expensive cloth gloves to complement her ensemble. She opened the chamber and loaded three bullets in the correct order. The special bullet was the third one. She always carried such a bullet as a contingency. She was always prepared.

Raven had approached the homeless man she had spied huddling in the corner of the parking lot, and now he filled the passenger seat beside her.

"Did you see the man that just went into the mall?"

A shadow stirred beside her. "Yes, ma'am."

"I'll let you earn good money. When he comes out, act like you're robbing the man. Back him up against the wall, and then fire the gun into the air. Fire all three bullets. All of them, understand?" She held out the pistol. Tied around the trigger guard was a hangman's noose braided from black string. The shadow unfolded, and a huge, dark meaty hand took the gun. It seemed small and insubstantial in his grip. She took the braided string bracelet from the car console.

"Wear this for good luck." She tied the bracelet around the man's wrist. When they dug through the body parts, they would know who killed the man with the turquoise eyes.

"Yes, ma'am." His voice was flat and deep and filled with

68

phlegm. "I don't kill people, you know. I'm doing this for my woman back at the Purple Ape Café."

"Fine. After you fire the gun, run to the corner of the parking lot over there, and I'll be waiting for you with your cash. Understand?" Raven studied the face that appeared from the darkness. It was all dark planes and folds with eyes that were a deep yellow with a patina of drug induced hysteria.

"Yes, ma'am."

Raven knew this was risky, but she couldn't take the chance of facing Steel on his own ground. Her best bet was to take him out in the most unexpected way. The homeless man would never survive the attack. The third bullet was filled with explosive. It would take out the shooter and the man with the turquoise eyes. In a way it was sad the young man would have to be near the explosion. He might die also.

"Here's half the money." She tore a one-hundred-dollar bill in half. "You get the rest when you're done."

"You are my angel, aren't you?" the big man asked. "God told me He would send me someone to save me. Are you the angel?"

If he wanted to believe she was an angel, so be it. He would get to meet one soon enough, anyway. "Yes, an angel will visit you this night. Now get out there and hide in the bushes next to the exit."

The man shifted his bulk and unfolded from the car as a katydid would emerge from his old carapace. Raven watched him recede into the gathering darkness, and in her mind she saw a frazzled gold string trailing behind him. If this didn't tie things up, she could always kill Steel outright. But not tonight. She had dinner plans and didn't have time to change.

Steel finished the last of his fajitas. The chips lay untouched in their bowl, and Josh's eyes were turned out the window of the restaurant at the milling crowd in the mall. He had barely touched his enchiladas.

"See anybody?" Steel asked.

"Dude, it's Friday night. They should be here."

Steel watched the condensation run down the side of Josh's untouched glass of soda. "What do you know about Winston Poole?"

Josh turned toward him. "Why?"

"I saw him today at the police station. Lieutenant Kane thinks he had something to do with that murder/suicide."

Josh's face blanched, and he nervously poked at his enchiladas. "Really?"

Steel leaned forward and took the fork out of Josh's hand. "What are you not telling me, Josh?"

"Bro, I can't tell you right now. Okay?"

Steel studied the boy's angry features and the scared look on his face. "Did you know Armando?"

Josh touched the healing hole in his lip. "Where'd you hear that name?"

"At the police station."

"I only met the dude once."

"Is that why you dyed your hair?"

The air grew still. Josh's eyes drifted into the past. "Ila wanted me to." Josh seemed to recede within himself. "I never told Mom. Dude, I let Ila talk me into the black hair and the piercings."

Steel reached over and pushed the glass toward Josh. "Take a drink. Relax. It's over. It's in the past. You're a new creature now."

Josh took the soda and drank deeply. "A new creature, huh? Bro, I can't seem to shake the memory of the old creature. I know God is in my heart, whatever that means. I know I'm a child of God, whatever that means. But I still feel dirty, you know? Slimy. If I hadn't let Ila talk me into it—"

Steel interrupted him. "No more 'what ifs,' Josh. Dwelling on the past can't help you."

"Whatever. So, speaking of your past, what's up with this Raven? Is she after you?"

Steel glanced out the glass windows at the milling crowd. "I noticed a car following us tonight."

"Bro, being around you is dangerous. Makes Uncle Cephas look pretty tame right about now." Josh finished his soda.

They walked the length of the mall several times but saw no sign of Armando or his cult. As they left the mall, a shadow separated from the bushes next to the brick wall and moved toward Steel.

Instinctively he saw the movement and automatically categorized it as a threat. His heart rate accelerated and his senses sharpened even as he screened out Josh's voice. He whirled, and the shadow became a huge man. The man's arm rose up, and the parking lot light glinted off the pistol in his hand.

"Give me your money, man." The dark face glistened with sweat. Steel froze and Josh kept walking, oblivious to the threat. Something sizzled behind Steel's right eye, and he lurched forward. He slapped the gun out of the man's hand and shoved the man backward, driving his huge body up against the brick wall. His head bounced on the hard surface. The man's eyes widened.

Josh ran up beside him. "What's happening?"

Steel's gaze stayed riveted on the struggling man's eyes. "Pick up the gun." He heard Josh's shoes squeak on the wet concrete.

"I got it. You want me to go get security?"

The man whimpered and looked away in fear. Steel reached back while keeping his gaze on the man.

"Give me the gun."

Josh placed the gun in his hand. Steel tingled at the feel of the warm metal. His hands had held a gun before. "Why did you do this?"

"I just needed some money, man. I got to eat. My woman, she's hungry too."

Josh touched Steel's shoulder. "I'm going for security."

"Wait." His eyes bored into the man's. Behind them he sensed the desperate, lonely fear of a trapped animal. "Where is she?"

The man licked his lips. "At the crack house. By the Purple Ape Café. But the café don't care about us. Won't even give us their trash. We're hungry."

Steel pressed the gun into the man's nose. "Wrong answer."

The man's eyes crossed as he looked at the gun. "Chill, man. My woman, she needs some smack too. Soon."

Steel glanced around the parking lot. At the far edge of the mall parking lot he spied a fast-food restaurant. He turned back to the man and shoved him across the parking lot. "Let's go."

Josh dogged his heels. "Where are we going?"

"To get him something to eat."

Josh hurried up beside him as Steel pushed the stumbling man across the asphalt. "Bro, in case you're having amnesia again, he just tried to kill us!"

"He's not a killer."

Josh glanced at the man's sweat-soaked T-shirt and his wobbly legs. "Dude, don't tell me you feel sorry for this loser."

"I know what I'm doing."

"All right. Sorry I asked! Why don't you let me go down the street and gather up a few prostitutes and homeless while you're buying?"

Steel ignored him and slid the gun into his pocket. The burger place had an outside food court lit by harsh fluorescent lights filled with swirling moths. Steel took the man's arm and slid his huge bulk behind a table. He dug in his pocket and retrieved his wallet. He tossed it to Josh.

"Go get him something to eat."

Josh caught the wallet and sighed. "What do I look like? King Burger?"

Steel glared at him. "Please."

Josh rolled his eyes and disappeared into the store. The man leaned against the tiled surface of the concrete table. Steel tried to ignore the smell.

"I can't even rob nobody. What you going to do with me?"

"Help you," Steel answered.

"Say what?" The man's forehead furrowed in puzzlement.

"The way I see it, you don't use the smack. Only your 'woman.' Do you love her?"

The man's eyes widened in amazement. "I am not believing you, man. I just tried to rob you, and you asking me if I love my woman?"

"It's a simple question."

The man was silent, and he leaned back. "You serious, aren't you?"

Steel crossed his arms. "I'd like a straight answer."

The man looked away and rubbed his face with a meaty hand. He was huge, with slabs of muscle covered by a thin patina of fat. His face was covered with coarse stubble. His black, short hair was cut almost to the scalp. In the harsh light his dark skin took on a greenish tinge. "We hang together."

"Don't confuse love with need," Steel stated flatly.

The man's mouth fell open. "You are one strange dude. You a marriage counselor or something?"

Josh came through the door and placed a drink and a sack on the table. He held a half-eaten sandwich in his hand. Steel raised an eyebrow.

"What?" Josh sat at the table. "Dude, I didn't eat anything at the mall, but now I'm hungry. Being your errand boy drums up an appetite."

Steel ignored Josh and pushed the food toward the man. "Eat."

The man studied the sack suspiciously and cast one last look at Steel. He grabbed the sack and emptied the fries and sandwich onto the table. He devoured the food quickly, pausing to drain half the glass of soda in one gulp. His actions were quick and efficient, and he barely tasted the food. When he was finished, he wiped the grease from his lips and burped.

Josh took the last bite of his sandwich. "Dude, you were hungry."

The man nodded. Steel took the empty sack and sandwich papers and tossed them into the nearby trash. "What would it take to get you away from your 'woman' and back on your feet?"

The man leaned forward, and he glanced at Josh. "Where did you find this man? He a superman or something?"

Josh shrugged. Steel slid into the seat opposite the man. "Sometimes God tells me to help people. Even when they don't want it."

The man's eyes widened, and he glanced back over his shoulder toward the parking lot of the mall. He looked back at Steel. "You mean like an angel sent you or something?"

Steel raised an eyebrow. "Not this time. At least, I don't think so. What's your name?"

"Theophilus Nosmo King," he said, and he glanced over his shoulder again.

"Nosmo King?" Josh grinned. "No Smoking? Your mother named you after a sign, didn't she?"

"That's why I go by Theophilus." He blinked and studied Steel. "You be the one to help me?"

"Josh, go back in and buy twenty dollars worth of gift certificates."

Josh's mouth fell open. "Gift certificates? Dude, you've got to be kidding."

"I'm going to give you some gift certificates for food. If I give you money, you'll spend it on your woman's smack. Mr. King, for some reason, I think you can shake this. I think you can leave this woman and your lifestyle behind and find a purpose in life. What do you think?"

King studied his big, meaty hands. "I don't know. I pray, man. Sometimes I pray thinking maybe God might still hear me. I used to be a preacher, but I met Lydia, and we ran off together. God hadn't been too good to me. Can't blame Him, though. I ain't been too good to Him."

"If you were a preacher, then you know you can come back."

King looked at his hands and slowly closed them into fists. "You don't know what I've done."

"No, I don't. But God does. And God's capacity for forgiveness is pretty big." Josh appeared at his side with his hand clutched around four five-dollar gift certificates. Steel took them and handed them to King. "Take these. Leave your woman right where she is and go find a new life."

King slid the pieces of paper into his pocket and retrieved a torn bill. He held it up to the light. "I won't be needing this then." He tossed the bill on the ground and stood up. "I got to check on Lydia one more time. But I'll think about what you said. You said God told you to help me?"

"Yes."

King gazed at him with his tired, reddish yellow eyes. "Maybe God is still listening to the likes of me." He turned and lumbered off across the parking lot.

"Is there a problem?"

Steel turned around. A uniformed man was rolling up to them on a Segway. His voice sounded familiar, and as he eased into the light, Steel could see it was Sergeant Raffle.

"Dude, you're a mall cop?" Josh asked.

Raffle smiled and took off his helmet. "Only when I'm off duty. Times are hard."

"That man tried to—" Josh pointed to King's receding figure, but Steel shook his head and Josh fell silent.

"He was just hungry. I fed him."

Raffle studied him with his intense hazel eyes. "Good for you. The man deserves another chance. Look, I know you don't think Raven was after you at the mall, but you did see her face. I wouldn't be sitting out in the open beneath a street light."

"We're going home."

Josh's eyes widened, and Steel shook his head again. Raffle looked back and forth between them. "Something else?"

"No," Steel said.

Raffle nodded and put his helmet back on. He reached into his shirt pocket and pulled out a card. "My cell phone number is on there. You need anything, call me."

Steel took the card. "I will. Thanks."

As Raffle sped away, Josh threw his hands up in the air. "Why didn't you tell him about the gun?"

"Because then he would have to arrest him. Raffle's right. Everyone deserves another chance."

"Dude, I'm just glad God doesn't tell you to save animals. We'd have stray dogs coming out of our ears."

Raven watched the huge man sit at the table and begin talking to Steel. Steel glanced across the parking lot, and even from this distance his gaze seemed to paralyze her. She looked away and leaned back into the shadows.

"Idiot!" she said to her reflection in the rearview mirror. "You should have done this yourself! But no, you trusted a homeless man." She stopped and looked across the parking lot again. Could it be she didn't want the man with the turquoise eyes to die? She touched the silver amulet at her neck. A tap on her window startled her. She looked through the glass at a police officer. He motioned for her to put down her window.

"Is there a problem, Miss?"

As she opened her window, Raven studied the green eyes, and her gaze drifted to his nametag. "No, Sergeant Raffle. I was just checking my messages." She reached over and held up her cell phone.

"Well, you'd best be moving on. It's not too safe in the mall parking lot after it closes." He smiled at her.

Raven felt a strange chill at the sight of the man as he rode off on his Segway. She closed her window and glanced down at her watch. She had enough time to make her dinner date, and then she would pay a visit to the homeless man and his woman at the Purple Ape Café. He may not be able to identify her, but she never left loose ends.

Chapter 10

OSH RAN THE shower as hot as he could until his skin was red and puffy. Anything to distract him from the pain and emptiness he now found at home. After he toweled off, he stood in front of the steamed mirror in his bathroom and studied his face. He had a new zit just next to his nose, and his hair was still stubbly and short. He looked like he had lost some weight. He had never been much for exercise, but he decided it was time to start something. Maybe he could run with Jonathan every morning. He flossed and brushed his teeth and spit into the drain. When he looked up, a face floated behind his reflection. He dropped his toothbrush, shocked at the sight of the man with long, black hair. He whirled around, but the bathroom was empty. He looked back at the mirror. Only his reflection stared back. Shivering, he jerked the bathroom door open and screamed as he ran into a figure. Steel stood in the hallway, his arms filled with two pillows and a folded blanket.

"Are you all right?" He asked.

Josh calmed his breathing. "Dude, don't sneak up on me like that."

"I got these out of your mother's bedroom," Steel said hoarsely. "I'll sleep on the couch."

Josh studied the man's bright blue eyes, the simple lines of his face. He had forgotten that Jonathan had lost something too. There had been a growing fondness between the man and his mother. "Uh, yeah, I get it. I'm going to bed."

"Don't stay up too late with your new toys." Steel walked toward the den.

Josh gritted his teeth. He had forgotten about his new purchases still in the truck, locked up tight at the end of the walkway. For a moment he considered going out and getting them. Then he remembered the hovering face in the bathroom and decided to wait until morning. He stepped into his bedroom and closed the door behind him. Feeling his way across the darkened room toward his bed, he paused, aware of a presence behind him. He turned toward the closet. The door was closed, even though he thought he had left it open. He tiptoed to the light switch by the door and turned it on. The room was empty. Slowly he walked toward the closet door and reached out to take the handle. Quickly he jerked the door open and stepped back. Only his clothes rustled from the movement. Sighing tiredly, he crossed to the light switch, and the room plunged into darkness. He slid beneath his tumbled covers on the bed and pulled them up to his chin.

For a few moments Josh tried to fight off the blotches of black and yellow that played across his closed eyes. He rolled over in bed and saw a shape against the window. His heart raced, and he turned on the lamp beside his bed. Boobo, his stuffed monkey, stared back at him. He laughed nervously and reached out to pick up the monkey. His parents had given it to him on his fifth birthday. The hands had torn off of the stubby arms, and his right ear was missing. The bright blue eyes stared at him in lifeless humor. Josh glanced at the door, afraid Jonathan would see him with this relic from his childhood. He pulled Boobo up against his chest. He inhaled, and his mind unreeled the record of his life back to when Boobo was new, back to when both of his parents carried him to the playground on a cold, autumn day, back to when they were alive. He slept.

Steel stood outside Claire's bedroom and felt his heart race. He couldn't sleep in there. He kept seeing her eyes, hearing her voice. He strode down to the dining room and sat. His hands trembled as he pulled the gun from his back pocket. It was a Smith & Wesson 642 Airweight 38 special revolver with a stainless finish. The gun felt light as he watched his hands open the chamber. There were three bullets in the chamber. He knew nothing about guns, and yet he knew everything. It was the ultimate backup gun, easily concealed with a mechanism that was simple and effective. He also knew that it came with a laser guide as an add-on. He placed the gun carefully on the tabletop and then noticed the tiny black hangman's noose dangling from the trigger guard. He gasped and recalled the image of King eating his burger. There had been a black braided string bracelet around his wrist. Raven.

Steel jerked the card out of his pocket and found his cell phone. Raffle answered on the second ring. "Raffle? Where's the Purple Ape Café?" He had to find King.

Josh awoke with a gasp and sat bolt upright in his bed. He swung his feet over the side of the bed and studied the shadows moving against the curtain over the front window. Outside the wind thrashed from another thunderstorm. For a moment he tried to recall what had awakened him, and he thought he saw a figure move outside across the window. He hurried across the room and opened the door to the hallway.

A pale light shown from a small reading lamp on his mother's rolltop desk in the den. He walked up to the couch and glanced over the back. The pillows were stacked where Jonathan had placed them. The blanket was still folded. Where was Jonathan?

He walked into the dining room. Piled on the table sat the box and accessories of his new tablet. It had been plugged in so the battery could charge. He called out. "Jonathan?" Only the wind answered.

Josh went to the front door and pulled it open. A sudden gust of wind blasted him and made him stumble. He stepped out onto the front walkway. No truck. He walked out into the yard, and his feet slid through the tall grass. Where had Jonathan gone? He walked back to the front door and closed it behind him. Something moved on the couch, and he drew a deep breath.

"Jonathan?"

"I thought you would never let me in." A voice came from the shadows. Josh reached for the light switch, and suddenly the presence stood in front of him. Tall, dressed in a long, black overcoat, hair draped over his shoulders, the man from the mirror stood between him and the light switch.

"How did you do that?" Josh fell back.

"Magick. The magick of the vampire, Josh."

Josh felt a dread grow inside of him. He felt as if his heart were being squeezed. His breath quickened, and sweat broke out on his palms. He gasped for breath and backed up against the fireplace. "Winston? Dude, what are you doing here?"

"My name is Armando, Josh. I have a message from Ila."

Josh jerked when he heard her name. "What have you done with her?"

"Nothing more than invited her into my clan. She sent me here to get you. She misses you." Armando moved gracefully across the room, and the dread grew stronger as he neared. Josh pressed his back against the rough brick of the fireplace.

"Leave me alone."

Armando paused with his face just inches from Josh. He

noticed an odd, circular tattoo near the base of Armando's neck. Armando leaned closer, and Josh turned away. He felt Armando's lips close to his ears. His breath was as cold as ice.

"I saw you at the mall. We are waiting for you, Josh. At the Blood Klotz." Armando pulled back, and a smile played across his lips. "Ila is waiting."

Lightning suddenly flashed against the windows, and Josh squeezed his eyes shut against the brightness. Thunder rattled the walls, and he opened his eyes. Armando was gone, and the front door flew open as wind flung rain into the room. He searched the den with wild eyes before slamming the door against the horror of the night and collapsing onto the floor. Armando was no longer human. Armando had joined the legion of the damned. Josh had seen it in his eyes. More importantly, Josh had *sensed* it. He placed a hand on his tank top, now drenched with sweat, and felt the beating of his heart as it hammered beneath his breastbone. Where was Jonathan when he needed him?

Raven gazed out through the window at the city stretching out beneath her. Rain clouds were moving back into the area after the day's showers. Near the horizon three bright stars gleamed, and a three quarters moon was disappearing behind gathering clouds. She wore an ankle-length blue dress, off the shoulders with a deep cut down the back. Her natural hair was hidden beneath a flowing blonde wig. She had placed a few stray tresses over the right side of her face for effect. In her gloved hands she clutched a hand purse in which rested her knife. The silver amulet glittered on the blue twine around her neck.

"Ms. Poe?" Wulf said.

Raven turned and hid her revulsion behind a smile. Wulf's gray hair gleamed, and his perfectly tailored suit hugged his athletic figure. "Yes, I'm Victoria Poe. Thank you for accepting my invitation."

Wulf smiled and revealed perfect teeth. For a second Raven thought she saw two sharp fangs, and then she blinked and they were gone. "The pleasure, I am sure, will be mine," Wulf said in his heavy Eastern European accent and motioned with the wolf head cane for her to follow an attendant, who sat them at a table overlooking the city.

"Have you eaten here before?" he asked as a waiter handed them their menus. His hands moved deftly as they opened the menu. His perfectly manicured fingernails seemed to change into talons and then back. Raven swallowed and blinked slowly. It was just her imagination.

"Yes. I suggest the filet. The beef is excellent."

"Ah, yes, in Texas. Home of the cowboys."

Raven occupied herself perusing the menu and tried to clear the cobwebs from her mind. Maybe fatigue was clouding her thinking. She couldn't let it. Her plan was too complicated, and she had to be on her toes with Wulf.

The waiter took their order, and Raven took a deep breath, trying to compose herself.

"Ms. Poe, are you feeling ill?" she heard Wulf say.

She looked up and smiled as she gently shook her head. No fangs. But his eyes were so haunting. Gray with tiny flecks of red. She blinked. "I am just a bit tired. Jet lag. And please, call me Victoria."

"Victoria." The name rolled off his tongue, and the sound of his voice was hypnotic. "A regal name indeed." Their appetizers arrived, and Raven watched him sip wine, watched the red liquid paint his generous lips with moisture. She closed her eyes. What was happening?

"When you called my office this afternoon, you said you had an important business proposition." Wulf said.

"Yes. I'm a business associate of Vivian Ketrick." Raven tried to focus on the condensation running down the side of her water glass, anything but those eyes. She had turned down alcohol in the hope it would keep her senses clear for later when she paid a visit to the homeless man and his woman.

"What a tragedy regarding her late husband!" Wulf shook his head. "Vivian has rallied, however, and has assumed control of his business."

"That's what I understand. Now"—Raven leaned forward—"I have researched your company, Wulf Pharmaceuticals. I know you have large interests in Europe and North Africa. I think Ketrick Enterprises is primed for a takeover. I could convince Vivian Ketrick to submit to a merger."

"I encourage submission," Wulf said.

Before Raven could answer, the main course arrived. She studied her crusted sea bass with au gratin potatoes. Wulf remained silent as he cut into his filet. Rich, red blood pooled in his plate. He lifted a piece of rare beef to his nose and inhaled before he placed it in his mouth and chewed slowly, his eyes closed in ecstasy. Raven watched his mouth move, his neck contract, the muscles pushing the meat down his esophagus. She pressed her cold water glass against her cheek while Wulf dabbed at his lips with his napkin and wiped away blood.

"Ms. Poe, I find it startling that here in America so many of your citizens eat their meat practically raw." Wulf smiled.

Raven breathed deeply and let the cold tingle on her cheek. "I don't understand."

"In my country the act of drinking blood can earn you a stake through your heart. But here it is the preferred manner of cooking a fine steak. The world is full of such delicious ironies."

He placed another bite of the bloody meat in his mouth, and Raven fought to keep her gaze off of his lips.

"I respect your desire to help me with any acquisitions. But the fact is, Ketrick Enterprises is all but mine. Vivian and I worked out a deal this afternoon. She submitted."

Raven tried to stick to her plan. She had to turn his attention to Atchison. "Then you know about her problems with Charles Atchison?"

"Who?"

"The only member of the board not signed off on her promotion to CEO. Without his signature, Ketrick Enterprises will go into probate. The assets will be tied up for months."

Wulf chewed his meat, and his gray eyes did not waver in their stare. He swallowed. "Just what does this have to do with me, my dear Victoria?"

Raven stabbed at a piece of potato. "I know Mr. Atchison. I believe if you were to meet with him, impress him with the fact that an international businessman will be involved with Ketrick Enterprises, I believe he might be willing to sign the papers."

Wulf finished the last piece of his filet mignon and considered her offer. "An interesting proposition. And just what would you get out of it?"

"Satisfaction that I have helped my friend solve a problem. Not to mention the stock options I own. With a merger I stand to make a substantial amount of money. Of course, I would rather keep Vivian out of this. She doesn't need to know I'm pulling some strings behind the scenes. You know how proud she is."

With his fork Wulf dipped a piece of bread in the bloody gravy on his plate and tucked the reddened morsel neatly into his generous mouth. "How true. Let me consider your proposal, Victoria. It is very enticing. There is a saying in my country. Only a hungry wolf truly knows his prey."

The room swam, and she was dizzy. Her vision blurred, and she felt something warm on her cheek and touched it with a finger. Her finger was covered with bright, red blood.

"Oh, my." Wulf placed his knife and fork carefully on the table. "You seem to have a cut." He reached over and touched her cheek with his delicate finger. Raven felt a chill.

"A cut?"

"From earlier, when you were hiding beneath the desk at Vivian's office." Wulf's fangs were visible in his open mouth. "Will you submit, Victoria? Will you receive the mark of the wolf dragon?"

Raven's heart raced and she tried to pull away from his touch, but she couldn't move. Strings appeared out of thin air, purple and gray and black, wrapping around her throat, confining her arms. She gasped for breath. She saw the lamb cake, smelled the blood, saw her stepfather reaching out his nicotine-stained hand, saw the world tilt, and somewhere in the distance a shadowy figure with a crown of thorns waited. Bright crimson threads sprung from his wrists and feet, intertwining with the strings confining her, vainly tugging at them. He turned one eye in her direction, and she longed so desperately for Him, for peace, for forgiveness and she knew if she could just talk, tear the strings from her throat and speak His name... Then she screamed as Wulf leaned toward her with his wolf snout and his long fangs and sank them into the delicate nape of her neck where the mark of the wolf dragon glowed and pulsed!

Raven jerked and looked around her. Wulf was sipping his wine, and she was sitting quietly in the restaurant. What had just happened? Wulf's eyes filled with mischief. "Is something wrong?"

"No," Raven mumbled. What were they talking about? "That was just an odd remark."

"I'm from Romania, Victoria. Vampires and werewolves, you

know." He smiled and motioned to the waiter. "Perhaps I need to learn more about American humor."

Raven released her breath and smiled. Could he have seen her in Vivian's office? Even if he had, she had been dressed like a man and was under the desk. Still, his bemused look made her nervous. Was he playing with her like a cat plays with its intended meal? Or more like a wolf pursuing his prey?

The waiter brought the dessert tray. "Would you like something?" Wulf asked.

Raven shook her head and laid her napkin beside her plate with a trembling hand. "Just coffee."

Wulf looked over the tray. "What, no blood pudding?" He laughed, and the sound echoed through the restaurant.

Chapter 11

STEEL LEFT THE truck parked in the driveway of what had to be King's crack house and stood in the driving rain, studying the trash-littered front porch. Down the street a giant purple neon ape danced on the front of the Purple Ape Café.

Steel peeked through a window into the dim interior and made out several bodies reclining on the trashy floor, illuminated by oil lamps and candles. He glanced around the corner toward the back. A rickety set of stairs led up the side of the two-story house toward the elevated back porch. He watched a figure separate itself from the shadows and hurry up the stairs. The figure paused at the top of the stairs, and for a brief moment, lightning filled the night with light. Beneath the bill of a cap Steel saw Raven's eyes take in the territory as she eased through a screen door. It *had* been Raven behind the homeless man's attack, and now she was tying up loose ends.

He opened the front door and slid into the interior of the crack house. No one stirred. Body odor and the smell of burned rubber and candle wax filled the air. He moved down a hallway with peeling wallpaper and reached a kitchen. The sink was filled with dirty dishes, and the table was piled with food in various states of decay. From an open doorway at the far corner of the kitchen a stairway led up toward the second floor.

He paused. He could hear nothing above the sound of rain on the tin roof and the howl of the wind outside. Thunder shook the windows, and he slowly eased his way up the stairs. At the top a hallway stretched toward the front of the house.

He peeked around the corner. Raven stood over the body of a woman lying on a mattress.

Raven had changed from her formal attire into charcoal sweats. After making her way up the back stairwell, she had entered the upstairs and paused to survey the dark interior. Since the crack house had no electricity, the only light came from candles scattered around the hallway upstairs.

At the end of the house, away from the street, she glanced around the corner into a large sitting area. A greasy set of windows barely let the lightning flash through. Trash covered the floor, and the stench was disgusting. A stained sleeping bag stretched out over a trash pile, and curled up on her side was a woman wearing a threadbare T-shirt and black athletic pants. Her hands were tucked up under her head, and around her left wrist was the bracelet Raven had tied on the homeless man's arm.

So this is what he was willing to kill for. Raven pulled out her knife and knelt beside the sleeping woman. Deftly she slid the tip of the knife under the twine bracelet and cut it loose. She held it up against the candlelight and blinked. Candles. Strings.

Maybe it was the trash. Maybe it was the odor of putrefaction and rot. For certain it was the memory of the string and the candle, and suddenly in her mind the dark, sinuous twine emerged again from its memory cabinet, encircling her wrists and ankles and pulling her backward into an endless tunnel of frayed strings and knotted threads until she was once again in the front yard with her lamb.

Victoria pulled the knife from her lamb and felt hot tears run down her cheeks. How could Father do this? She thought he had changed.

So much for her prayer!

She hurried across the yard, red blood dripping down her pink dress. She stepped gingerly through the front door. One did not run in Father's house. The living room was filled with twine and string stretching from corner to roof to window to door. Thumbtacked to pictures on the wall of her mother. Stretching around door frames to more pictures of her real father lost forever in the deserts of Iraq. Strings of all colors and hues were knotted and tied. Some were attached to brass chimes hanging from the ceiling fan in the middle of the roof. Others were tied to empty cans strung along the corners. One false move, one errant step, one hasty movement, and the strings would tell Father she had come home.

Over the months since her mother had died Victoria had learned the crazy, twisted pattern of the strings. She had learned how to slide between the webs and traps to avoid waking Father, especially on Sunday mornings when, after a night "on the town," Father was very mean and made her do bad things.

She eased her way through the maze of strings and entered the kitchen. Here the strings were mostly strung along the cabinets and the refrigerator to alert Father if Victoria was trying to get a snack. Her stepfather sat at the table hunched over a bottle of beer.

"Why did you kill my lamb?" she whispered.

Father glanced at her obliquely and belched. "I told you why. You don't belong to your God. You belong to me. To me! And no one is going to tell me what I can and cannot do with you. Understand?"

Victoria stepped back and hit a string. Tin cans rattled above the stove, and in the far bedroom her stepfather's chimes clanged. "I hate you, Father. I hate you!" Her voice was barely above a whisper.

"Now, now, Victoria. Hate is such a strong word."

She glanced over her shoulder. In the doorway to the living room stood a tall man in a black, full-length coat. His bare head was as white as an egg. His eyes were a deep crimson, and a star-shaped scar marred his cheek.

"Who are you?"

"A friend." He reached over and took the knife from her. "My name is Lucas."

"Who are you talking to?" Father asked.

Victoria pointed to Lucas. "Lucas."

"An imaginary friend?" Father laughed. "Or your God?"

"Oh, I'm not your god, Victoria. Not yet, anyway."

Victoria felt her heart race and her stomach burned. "What do you want?"

Lucas pulled aside his coat, and on his bare upper chest tattoos seemed to move and come to life. He pointed to a tattoo of a black bird. "I wanted to show you something. It's a raven."

Victoria's eyes widened in amazement. "Is it alive?"

"It can be. Here." He touched the tattoo, and the raven flapped its wings and turned its head to look at the girl. "The raven is an interesting bird. It gathers bits and pieces of trash and makes something useful."

"Like all of Father's strings?"

"Don't talk about my strings." Father chugged more beer. "And stop talking to nothing. You're creeping me out."

"You don't have to listen to him anymore, Victoria." Lucas said.

She glanced over at the raven tattoo. "What do you mean?"

"I can help you with your stepfather. I can give you a raven tattoo just like this one. You can take all the trash in your life and turn it into something just for you. Wouldn't you like to see your wish come true?"

Victoria nodded. After all, God hadn't answered her prayer. Father hadn't changed. He was still the mean, nasty man she was growing to hate more and more every minute.

"What do I have to do?"

Lucas pulled aside his shirt and revealed the animated raven tattoo. "Just accept my gift. Touch the raven, and you will never have to put up with your stepfather's meanness again."

Victoria glanced back at her stepfather. He was still poised at the table, his eyes roving back and forth as if he was trying to see what she was seeing. In that moment she hated him more than ever. She reached out with her finger, her gaze fixed on Father, and touched the raven tattoo.

The white skin around the tattoo suddenly turned red and blistered, and Lucas's mouth opened in a scream. Blood burst from the blister as it ruptured. "You're one of them?"

Lucas shoved her hand away and disappeared. The knife he had been holding seemed to hover in the air. Victoria grabbed it before it could fall to the floor. She had no idea what had just happened. But she had made up her mind. She glared at her stepfather. "I'm going to go live with Katie. I'm tired of your meanness."

Father shoved the kitchen table out of his way and stepped toward her. "You're not going anywhere, sweetums."

Victoria turned and ran into the living room, deftly dodging the strings. But Father was too drunk to pay attention. He ran into the strings by the kitchen door, spun around as they wove their way around his face and neck. He stumbled and fell backward into the metal cans, and more strings pulled from the wall and the windows. Still he teetered and grappled with the twine as he stumbled around the room, wrapping himself more and more tightly in the strings. The ceiling fan churned away and the brass chimes clanged. Suddenly the strings around her stepfather tightened and pulled him into a web of multicolored threads, upward into the ceiling fan. It slowed and moaned under the man's weight, but he kept going backward and now up.

"The knife." He gasped as the strings tightened around his neck. "Cut me lose."

Victoria watched as the twirling, swirling figure of her stepfather swept the room clean of strings. She watched quietly as he was pulled upward into the spinning ceiling fan. She remained still and quiet as the fan groaned and sparked and smoked under her father's weight until the entire ceiling cracked and collapsed onto the floor on top of her stepfather.

She kicked aside sheetrock and broken glass with her pink slippers and stood over her father's figure. He was still tugging at the strings wound around his face and his neck. His lips gasped for breath just as her lamb had.

"The knife…" he whispered.

She held up the knife and then slid it into the satin belt of her pink dress. "God didn't answer my prayer, Father. But I still got my wish. I don't have to put up with you anymore. No more monsters in my life. I can stand up to you and watch as you die. And there are more like you out there, I just know. Maybe Lucas was right. I'll gather the trash like the raven and get rid of all of you."

Blood bubbled on his lips, and he grew still and silent. He was tied and trussed just like her lamb. She plucked a red string from her father's face and tied it around the base of the knife. That was one.

Raven shook her head as the memories retreated and was startled to see the woman looking up at her. But the eyes were empty, devoid of life. The drugs had done her job for her.

Steel drew a deep breath, ready to tackle Raven, when a roar sounded from the other side of the room. The door to a bathroom exploded in wooden splinters, and Theophilus King thundered across the bedroom floor like a rampaging rhino.

"What have you done to my woman?" he bellowed with his huge muscled arms pumping. Raven brought the knife up but couldn't use it before he barreled into her. They crashed through the window and out into the storm.

Steel ran across the room just in time to see the two struggling figures slide across the rain-slick tin roof and disappear over the edge. Steel glanced down at the woman. Her eyes were empty. Dead before Raven even touched her.

Steel ran back down the stairs into the kitchen and stopped, horrified, as Raven burst through the window over the sink. Glass and dirty dishes showered the room as she slid through the rotten food on the table and fell to the floor. King jumped to the sill of the broken window. Raven stood shakily. Her hair was wild, and her cap was lost somewhere in the stormy night. She turned and raced down the hallway toward the front door. Steel watched her trip over the sleeping people, and in the process, she overturned candles and oil lamps. The trash ignited, and fire leapt along the hallway. King jumped down onto the kitchen floor, and his feet slipped in the trash. Steel reached out and grabbed him.

"King. It's me, Jonathan Steel."

King stopped as his eyes focused on Steel. Tears streamed down his cheek. "I got to get her. She killed my woman."

"Your woman was already dead. Raven didn't kill her. But she was going to kill you." An explosion rattled the walls, and Steel glanced down the hall to see fire billowing along the rotten wallpaper. "Right now we've got to get these people out of here, Theophilus. Forget the killer."

King blinked and looked back at Steel. "Lydia?"

"She's dead, Theophilus. You can't save her. But we can save these people."

King nodded and pushed past him. Steel fought the stinging smoke and the heat from the growing fire. He watched King pick up three people at once and slide them out the front door. Steel helped more of them out. King ran up the stairs, and Steel followed him. The smoke was thick, and the rooms upstairs were empty. He found King perched on the trash pile, Lydia cradled in his arms. Already the flames were eating away at the floorboards, and the smoke was so thick he could hardly see.

"We have to go." He placed a hand on King's shoulder. King nodded and led the way down the stairway with Lydia in his arms. They hurried into the backyard, and King placed her gently on the wet grass. Rain fell on her face and washed away the ash. She looked clean and peaceful.

"She's at peace at last," King said. He crossed her hands over her chest and stood up. "It's all gone now. Everything I touched is trash. All gone. I got nothing." He turned his weary eyes on Steel. "You saved my life. You're a good man."

"Raven wasn't coming for Lydia. She was coming for you."

The lines on King's face hardened as he wiped the rain away. "She wanted me to kill you, didn't she?"

"Yes. You have to tell the police. Sergeant Raffle will be here any minute and…"

"No!" King grabbed his arms in a painful grip. "Not the police! I can't go back to the big house. I can't." He released Steel, and the light from the burning house played across his face. "You goin' after this Raven?"

"If I don't, she'll come after me. But I work within the law, King."

"Fine. Ain't nothing here for me anymore. You came here to save me, and maybe God is giving me another chance. I'm going with you."

Steel shook his head. "You need to talk to the police first."

King put his huge hand on Steel's shoulder. "I ain't going to blow this chance, Mr. Steel. This is a sign. God is calling me back. Why else would He have sent you to save me? Cops find out I had a weapon, I'd be breaking my parole. They make me go back to jail. All this for nothing."

Steel sighed. "I have a truck in the driveway. Can we get out of here?"

King nodded and pointed behind him. "There's a service road down by the interstate."

Steel blinked rain out of his eyes. What did God have in mind now? He saw red and blue lights whirl in the street on the other side of the burning house. He had to decide quickly what he was going to do. Raffle said King deserved another chance. Apparently it was time to give it to him. Steel ran toward his truck. The street was filled with people running in confusion as thunder rattled, lightning flashed, and the house burned like a furnace in the night. Raffle stood next to Steel's truck, and he was still wearing his mall uniform. He glanced past Steel at King standing in the backyard.

"Go. I'll take care of this," Raffle said.

Steel slid behind the steering wheel, started the engine, and drove down to where King waited. King ran around and slid into the passenger seat. Steel gunned the engine. They reached the service road just at the sirens neared. He turned down the narrow road and, minutes later, came out at the interstate. He drove onto the entrance ramp just as he sighted the blue car disappearing down the highway.

[Chapter 12]

OSH PACED AROUND his bedroom, glancing at the clock. Two in the morning. He replayed the feeling he had when Armando had entered the house. Evil. A demon had taken Armando. He should know. He had been taken by a demon once.

"You probably went after Theophilus, didn't you Jonathan?" He shook his head. "Dude, you saw somebody you could rescue, and you just couldn't resist." Josh slammed his fist against the wall. "But what about Ila? You can help a homeless crack head who tried to rob us but you wouldn't even help Ila!" Josh's face grew hot with anger. "If you had been here, Armando wouldn't have come in. But no, you had to go rescue a worthless lump of burned-out neurons and leave me with Captain Demonic!"

He had to do something about Ila. He crossed to his dresser and flipped on a small lamp. He opened the top drawer and pulled out an old cigar box. Inside the box a tube of black hair dye lay next to three pairs of pierced beads of different colors. Under the tube of hair dye he found the matchbox. In dark red letters the words "Blood Klotz" were written in what could have passed for blood. Ila had taken him to the bizarre coffee house and introduced him to Winston Poole.

"I should have taken you and walked out, Ila." And as far as he knew, Ila was damned and now controlled by one of Armando's demons. "My fault," He concluded. "And since Jonathan isn't going to do anything about it, it's up to me."

Josh took the box into the bathroom and turned on the light. Squeezing the black hair dye into the palm of his hand, he massaged it into his short, reddish blond hair. After the dye had stained his hair, he stripped and stepped into the shower and washed the unused dye from his skin. He walked dripping into his bedroom and pulled on the black jeans and T-shirt from that fateful night. Once dressed, he chose a lip bead from the cigar box.

The hole was almost healed, and he had a hard time pushing it through. Blood spurted onto the mirror, and his eyes watered with the pain. Finally, tears streaming down his cheeks, he felt the lip bead pop through his inner lip, and he sealed the stem with the holder. He wiped the tears from his face and studied his reflection, taking more studs from the box and reopening the old wounds in his ears and eyebrows.

Stiff black hair stood on end from his scalp, and the beads glittered in the light. If he didn't know any better, the last three weeks could have been a dream. But he felt different inside. Christ resided in his heart. He breathed a quick prayer for strength and packed up his new tablet and iPhone from the dining room table. Something glittered in the light as it tumbled off the table onto the floor. It lay there cold and impersonal. He had never shot a real gun. But he had never fought off a real demon before. He grabbed the pistol and tucked everything into his backpack and walked out.

The thunderstorm had finally let up. In the backyard his father's vintage car was still covered with a tarp. He had never been allowed to touch it. But there was something his father had prized beyond the car. Josh crossed to the empty garage and pulled a cover off of his father's motorcycle. He had been forbidden from riding it too, but he had fooled his mother. Once a week he had pushed the motorcycle down the street and hidden it under a bridge until his mother had gone to sleep. Then, sneaking out of his room, he had ridden it each weekend, always returning just after midnight on Sunday to put it back in the garage. He drew a deep breath, pulled on his father's helmet, and sat astride the black motorcycle. He kicked the starter, and the engine roared to life.

"Ila, I'm coming." He rolled down the driveway at the back of his house and roared off down the street. Soon he would be meeting Ila, and this time he would lead her away from the evil of Armando and his clan. He would do what Steel had refused to do.

Steel heard the sound of a motorcycle roar into the night but ignored it. He pulled the truck up in front of Josh's house and studied King's hulking shape. The huge man got out of the truck and slowly turned around, his vacant eyes searching the night. "Lydia is dead. Treece and Flossy gone. I got nobody left. Nobody. I done burned a dozen bridges." His eyes finally focused on Steel. "Lydia was all I had." He stumbled on the sidewalk and sat down heavily in the wet grass. Tears glistened on his dark cheeks. "You ever lost someone you love?"

Steel nodded and slid out of the truck. He sat down on the grass beside the huge man. "Twice."

King nodded as he pulled up his tattered T-shirt and blew his nose. "It hurts so bad."

"Yeah, it does."

"I had a dream. God sent an angel to me. Angel told me I had one more chance. One more. I think you're that last chance," King said.

"What are you going to do now?"

"Can't tell the police what happened. They'll put me in jail. I guess I'll try going home to my aunt. She's been praying for me for years."

"How are you going to get there?"

King wiped his nose. "I'll take the bus."

"It's three a.m. The buses aren't running."

"I'll walk."

"Where does your aunt live?"

"In Tyler."

Tyler was an hour and a half drive east of Dallas. Steel sighed. It was happening again—God using him for His plan. He didn't like it, but he knew he couldn't resist it.

"Why don't you come inside and get cleaned up. Get some sleep, and we can talk in the morning."

"No, man. I'm not fit for your house." King shook his head. He glanced over at the truck. "I'll sleep in the back of your truck. Me and God. We got a lot to work through. I got a lot of praying and confessing. And I got to deal with the pain. She's gone, and I got nothing left but God." He stood up and climbed back under the shell on the back of the truck. Steel shrugged and lowered the gate.

"Fine. We'll talk in the morning."

Steel made his way to the front door. He was exhausted, but he needed to check on Josh. He glanced down the hallway and saw the light on in Josh's bathroom, but Josh's door was shut. The kid must be asleep. He collapsed on the couch, not even taking his shoes off, and tucked the pillow under his head and he slept. The smell awoke him, and Steel opened his eyes to see Theophilus King bent over him.

"Ain't you got a boy with you?" King asked from the back of the couch.

Steel squinted into the morning sunlight coming through the kitchen window. "You scared me half to death. What are you doing?"

"I woke up about an hour ago and decided to go to the backyard to take care of my toilet. Your garage was wide open, and the back door was standing open. I came in looking for you or the little man, and you were fast asleep. You know that you snore?"

Steel stood up. "Josh isn't here?"

King pointed to the hallway. "His bed is empty, and so is the bathroom. And there's some stuff in the bathroom you ought to see."

Steel pushed past him and hurried to the bathroom. A cigar box sat on the back of the commode. Inside he found a tube of black hair dye and a lip bead. He looked closely at the sink and saw bits of black dye scattered on the white porcelain. What had Josh done? Steel hurried into Josh's bedroom. The floor was still damp, Josh's footprints impressed into the carpet. The closet was open, and Steel stared at the black outfits.

"No! He couldn't have!" Anger surged, and he swatted a stuffed monkey sitting on the end of Josh's bed. It tumbled across the bed and slammed against the wall. King squeezed through the door and stood quietly in the corner.

"What can I do to help?"

Steel looked up. "Where did he go? How?"

"I saw oil in the garage under a canvas. Probably a motorcycle."

The phone rang. Steel pushed past King and hurried to the kitchen, snatching the receiver off the wall.

"Josh?"

"No, this is Charles Atchison."

Steel glanced at his watch. It was nearly ten in the morning. "You're still alive?"

"Very funny. I have worked a miracle of biblical proportions. I managed to pull a few strings and got us a court date today, on Saturday of all days, with a juvenile judge. I know this is quick notice, but Dr. Lawrence wanted action, and I got you action!"

Steel drew a deep breath as his mind reeled. "When today?"

"Two o'clock. Dress nicely, Mr. Steel. This judge is very eccentric, and he is doing Grace Pennington a great big, enormous favor. We mess this up, and I'll be run out of the state on a rail, and you'll never see Josh again. Be at the courthouse by one thirty. I have a lunch appointment at twelve, and then I'll meet you there."

"I hope it's not at the mall again."

"Copeland's, if you must know. But I'll be inside. Does that make you happy?" The line went dead. Steel slammed the receiver on the phone. This was bad.

Why had Josh gone back to his old ways? Then he remembered Ila's mother. She had said that Ila had run away with some kids. Had Josh gone off to rescue Ila?

King's stomach growled behind him. Steel turned. "I've got to find Josh. He must have gone after Ila, his girlfriend."

"Maybe I can help, Mr. Steel." King said.

Steel looked at him. For the first time he noticed the man's face no longer carried sadness and despair. "Not unless you can find a vampire clan run by a guy named Armando."

King raised an eyebrow. "I know a lot about the street, Mr. Steel. I been there for years."

"How tall are you?"

"Six foot five. I used to weigh three hundred fifty in my days on the police force."

"Police?"

"Los Angeles. Before I became a preacher." He looked down at himself. "I lost a little bit of my muscle."

Police? Maybe there was more to King than he thought. Steel glanced at the dining room table. Josh had taken his tablet and iPhone. And the gun was missing. Alarm bells sounded in his head. Every passing moment things were getting worse. *God, what do I do?* He drew a deep breath and tried to clear his mind. A plan began to form. But it would mean trusting Theophilus King.

"Mr. King," Steel said, turning to look up into the man's eyes. "I need help with this, and I have to find Josh before two this afternoon. If Josh doesn't show up, the judge will put him in a foster home. This house belonged to Josh and his mother, and she died three weeks ago. I made a promise to take care of Josh."

King nodded, and his brow furrowed in concentration. "You ain't doing so well with the taking care of him part, are you?"

Steel felt like he had been slapped. "No."

"'Cause you came to help me."

"Yes."

"Why?"

"For some reason only the Lord understands, He decided to put me here on this earth to help people in need. When I saw your face, I knew you wouldn't kill me. I knew you needed help."

"And now, Josh is gone because you weren't here."

Steel nodded and crossed to the dining room table. He slumped into the chair. "That about sums it up."

King lumbered into the dining room and sat opposite Steel. The chair creaked from his weight. "I had a long talk with God. Lydia is gone, and I need to bury my past with her. Can't let God down this time. He told me to help you cause I owe you my life, Mr. Steel. I'm in your service. I'll do whatever you want me to do."

Steel nodded. He had no choice but to trust Theophilus Nosmo King. "Thanks. I'll get your back if you'll get mine."

"Deal," King said.

"Deal." He extended his hand, and King shook it.

"What do you want me to do?"

Steel reached into his back pocket and took out his wallet to get some cash. "Go get some clean clothes. Take the truck, and then stop on the way back and get us something to eat."

King took the money. "I don't have to kill nobody for this money."

"Let's hope not. Before you leave, unload the luggage from the truck shell. I'm going to take a shower."

King slid the cash into his dirty pants pocket. "Whatever you say, Mr. Steel."

"You can call me Jonathan."

King nodded. "Call me Theo." He walked out the front door. Steel went to Josh's bathroom and showered and shaved. He put on his nicest pair of jeans and a Hawaiian shirt. He hadn't brought any dress clothes. He hadn't known he would be appearing in court before a picky judge. When he came out of the bathroom, the rest of the luggage lay in the middle of the floor.

Steel began rummaging through the bags. He had grabbed Claire's equipment pack and put it in with some of Josh's clothes. Ah, there it was. He opened the backpack, and out slid Claire's laptop. He put it on the desk, hooked up the power, and turned it on. Once the main screen came up, Steel went to the e-mail program and began to compose a new message. In the address book he found Josh's name followed by his e-mail address. But what to say? If he made the message too blatant, Josh might get mad and ignore it. If Ila saw the message before Josh did, she might erase it.

"Need to talk. Man of steel." He typed and hit the send button. A window came up saying two messages had been sent. Two? Claire must have written an e-mail and had never sent it. Steel closed his eyes and gently pushed the sorrow back into a corner of his mind. He searched for Copeland's and found it located in the Lintonwood Mall parking lot. He memorized the map that appeared on the screen. Then he shut down the laptop and waited.

Theo appeared at the door at eleven thirty. He carried two bags of clothing and two sacks of food. "Got some good bargains at the store." Theo's face had come alive with a smile. "Now, you come over here and eat while I get cleaned up. Then I'll take the truck and go look for Josh while you go talk to the judge."

Steel crossed to the table. "We only have one vehicle, Theo."

Theo pointed to the garage. "Go look in the backyard. There's an old car under a tarp. The keys are by the back door. But I'm a little too big to fit behind the wheel. I'll take the truck."

Theo disappeared down the hallway into Josh's bathroom. Grabbing a burger from the bag, Steel walked through the garage into the backyard. Beneath a dark brown canvas tarp Steel discovered a gleaming, classic 1968 Mustang convertible. Why hadn't Josh taken the car? A motorcycle probably fit his dark image better.

Theo came out of the bathroom a man transformed. He wore a football jersey over silky red athletic pants and flashy high tops. "The only other man I ever respected as much as I respect you was my captain at the police station, and we all called him 'Chief.' So from now on, you the Chief. Got it? So, how do I look?"

"You clean up pretty good."

"The man's got to look good. The man has to fit in on the streets, Chief. And I found this." He held up a matchbook. Steel took it and read the name.

"Blood Klotz?"

"Yeah, a place for a bunch of strange dudes. I'll go check it out and bring Josh to the courthouse. I know where it is. Been there before."

"I'm going with you," Steel said.

Theo took the matchbook back. "Listen, Chief, you just a little too white and little too straight to go down to the Blood Klotz. You'd stick out like a sore thumb. Josh's friends see you get out of the car, and they'll disappear like a bunch of roaches. You want Josh back, you let me handle it."

Steel's heart sank, and he felt the anguish of loss. "I lost him once before. I don't want to lose him again."

Theo placed a huge hand on his shoulder. "We both done lost something today. So, you listen here, Chief. I owe you my life. I won't let you down. I got a new life here, and I ain't gonna turn my back on it. I'd march through hell for you right now."

Steel looked up at his deep brown eyes. "That's what scares me. You may have to walk through hell to find Josh."

"I been there before, and I come back. You said you were gonna look for that lawyer dude?"

Steel nodded and took the Mustang keys off the rack in the kitchen. "He said he was having lunch with some new clients. I'm going to try and catch him and see if we can postpone this hearing." He dug through one of his bags and pulled out Josh's old cell phone. "Call me if you find Josh."

Theo nodded. "Let's rock and roll, Chief."

Chapter 13

OSH SAT IN the darkness, shivering. The old cattle warehouse stunk of rotten meat and cowhide. He had gone to the Blood Klotz and found one of Armando's followers. He had passed on a message that he was ready to join them but wanted to meet them on neutral turf. The squirrelly guy had told him to meet them at the warehouse at 11:00 a.m. Josh glanced at his wristwatch. Ten after eleven. They were late.

He considered climbing back on his motorcycle and heading back home. His anger at Jonathan had cooled and, with it, his determination. Maybe Jonathan had a point about helping people. He couldn't help himself. Just as Josh couldn't seem to keep himself from always doing the wrong thing.

"How about a ride, boyfriend?"

Josh whirled, and Ila stood not ten feet away. She wore tight black jeans and a silky black blouse. Long, black gloves covered her arms up past her elbows. Her beautiful blonde hair had been dyed to a deep black. She wore pasty white makeup and black lipstick. Josh found her revolting yet strangely alluring as she walked across the dirt floor of the warehouse and leaned across the motorcycle and kissed him.

Josh swallowed and put the helmet down on the motorcycle seat. "Ila, I've come to take you home."

Her laughter echoed inside the warehouse, and far up in the dark rafters, birds were startled by the sound. "I'm not going back, Josh. And neither are you. You've come to join me, haven't you?"

Before Josh could speak, he felt them behind him. A dozen dark-clad figures materialized out of the shadows. Leading them,

Armando moved almost as if he were floating. "Has the mundane come to join the clan?"

Ila touched Josh's cheek. "He is but a child, but I will teach him the vampire ways, and one day he will pledge to this clutch."

Armando's eyes glowed faintly in the subdued light. "Will he be your thrall?"

"Yes." She smiled at Armando.

"I do not take his pledge lightly. Rasmussen, come here." Armando gestured to the group, and a tall, thin kid no older than Ila hurried to Armando's side. "You were supposed to bring Josh to me."

Rasmussen's face was pale, and his shock of black hair stood on end. "Yes, sir. But Josh insisted on meeting on neutral ground."

Armando held up a hand for Josh to see. His fingernails lengthened into razor-sharp talons, and he backhanded Rasmussen. The talons ripped gashes across the boy's neck, and spurting blood filled the air with a fine spray of crimson. Rasmussen choked, grabbed his throat, and fell backward. Armando's gaze never left Josh's face. "This is what happens when you disobey me, Josh. But I am not without mercy."

Armando knelt over Rasmussen. The gushing blood had stopped, and the boy's eyes were glazed over. "He is almost dead, Josh. But I have vampire magick. I can return his life to him. Behold!"

Armando ran a hand over Rasumussen's ruined throat. The flesh closed, and Rasumussen suddenly sat upright. He coughed, and Armando put a hand on the boy's cheek. "You will never disobey me again."

Rasmussen's eyes were wild with fear. "Never, master. Never!"

Josh remained absolutely still even though a drop of drying blood tickled his cheek. He was in dangerous territory, and he realized that Armando's level of power was great. If he and Ila were to escape with their lives, he had to play along.

"Dude, I came for Ila. If it is her wish, then I will try my best to join you. But I have a lot to learn."

"Yes, you do. Until you are one of us, I will refer to Ila by the name you are familiar with. I give her permission to be your sire, fledgling. Your first lesson regards our activities during the day. We sleep and rest and move about at night."

Josh looked back at Ila. "I am hungry. Why don't we go back to the Blood Klotz for some food, and you can begin my lessons?"

"We shall teach you of a new food. You will never hunger for mundane food again. She may accompany you," Armando said as he looked around the warehouse. "I like this place. The smell of old blood and dead meat is intoxicating. I think this will be our new home."

Josh sat astride the bike, and felt Ila snuggle up against his back. He felt her cold breath on his neck, and the deep, foreboding of evil surfaced again in his heart. He wanted to scream, to run, to flee from this unspeakable horror that surrounded him. If he could just get Ila out of this building, he could talk some sense into her. Starting the motorcycle, he peeled out, throwing the stinking dirt up into a cloud. When he looked behind him, the dozen or so vampires had disappeared. He headed for the open doorway at the far end of the warehouse, for the light that beckoned, for the sanity of the sun and daylight and normality. But clinging to his back was the one thing that could drag him back down into darkness.

Copeland's sat at the base of the hill next to Lintonwood Mall. Steel parked the convertible under a small crepe myrtle and killed the engine. He walked into the restaurant and scanned the tables for Atchison. A woman with blonde hair and dark sunglasses accidentally bumped into him, and he apologized as she disappeared out the door. He saw Atchison in a corner alcove as far away from the windows as possible, sitting with a man in a polo shirt. The man glanced his way, and Steel felt a shiver of recognition. He had seen him somewhere before. Atchison glanced over his shoulder.

"Mr. Steel? What are you doing here?"

"I had to talk to you about the hearing. We need to get it pushed back."

"Impossible. I went through a lot just to get someone right away! I'm not changing it now."

Steel sighed. "Josh...isn't here."

Atchison's face paled. "What do you mean, isn't here? Look, I stuck my neck out for the two of you. If we don't show up with Josh, you and Dr. Lawrence can kiss custody good-bye."

"We can't postpone?"

Atchison glanced at his watch. "It's one o'clock now. We have to be there in less than an hour, Steel."

The other man studied their exchange with a bemused grin. "Sounds intriguing."

Atchison looked at the man. "I'm sorry. Jonathan Steel, Rudolph Wulf."

Wulf? Steel's memory flashed back to the study of Robert Ketrick, overlooking Cross Lake. Pictures hung on the wall. One picture showed a silver-haired man. The testimonial written in the corner of the photograph was, "Best wishes, Wulf," and beneath it had been scrawled the number "12." For a moment the implications of Wulf's presence here began to stretch through his mind until he spied the purse sitting on the table.

"And who else is here?"

"Victoria Poe. A new associate of mine and prospective client." Wulf's voice dripped with power, sophistication, and control.

"Poe?" Steel said. His mind raced. "Quoth the raven, nevermore." He scooped up the purse and ran to the emergency exit. He shoved the door open, and the alarm filled the restaurant. Whirling the purse over his head, he tossed it across an empty stretch of grass next to Preston Road.

"What are you doing? She just went to the restroom," Atchison shouted.

"It's a bomb!" Steel screamed. The purse somersaulted through the air, and when it came to rest, it rolled across the grass and stopped. Nothing happened.

Atchison stood up. "Are you crazy? No one is trying to kill me…"

The explosion blew out the windows, and glass, dirt, and grass showered the interior of the restaurant. A patch of sod landed on top of Atchison's head.

Raven smiled as she pressed the send button on her cell phone. The air filled with the sound of the explosion, but the smoke and debris were *outside* the restaurant. She glanced back as the man with the turquoise eyes bolted through the door and stopped as his gaze met hers. She gasped and let out a loud curse. He tore across the parking lot toward her.

Raven's heart raced, and she fought down panic for the second time in a week. She hurried across the parking lot and into the mall. She had parked her car on the other side of the mall, reasoning she could get lost in the mall and emerge on the side away from the emergency vehicles that would converge on the restaurant after the explosion.

She raced along the walkway, dodging patrons and stumbling

over baby carriages, until she came to an empty elevator and pushed the up button. The man raced toward her, but he would never make it in time to stop her elevator. He glared at her as the elevator doors whooshed shut. Raven reached the second level and saw the man running toward an escalator. The up side was closed off, and he had to fight people crowding the down escalator. She bolted through the crowd as he reached the top of the escalator. She was getting sloppy, and it would get her killed. She had to focus. Survive. Kill or be killed.

Raven looked over her shoulder just as the man vaulted over an electric cart and landed on her back. They fell forward over the railing and into air. Raven reached for the knife hidden in the folds of her dress just as they hit water, crashing into the massive fountain at the center of the mall.

The blow took her breath away, but she managed to roll out from under the man's body and pin him down beneath the water. She worked the knife out of her belt and slammed it down. His hands flew out of the water and with an iron grip stopped her mid-plunge. She was astride his waist and pressing the knife closer to his chest, her weight keeping his face beneath the water. His bright eyes gleamed beneath the surface, and if the knife didn't kill him, maybe he would drown.

Suddenly her silver amulet fell out of her dress and dangled between them. It caught her eye, and the contents of it flashed through her brain. She hesitated for a microsecond, and suddenly a stream of water struck her in the side of the face. She tumbled off of the man as another jet in the fountain erupted in its predetermined sequence.

The man lurched up out of the water, gasping for air. She swung the knife at him once again. He tried to block it, but the knife cut a thin line along the inside of his forearm. Blood spurted into the water as another jet caught her in the back of the head. She tumbled forward onto him and pushed him over the edge of the fountain onto the hard, tile floor.

Raven's thoughts reeled, torn between memories of her past and the contents of the amulet. Why hadn't she thrown it away? She saw the strings of her past emerge from the shadows. One string led back to the man's heart, to his lips, to his soft voice, to his touch. She had loved him once, and *they* had made her kill him. Now he was alive, and she longed to just be with him.

Instead the other string that led to the power behind her very existence cried out for his death. She cursed the conflicting emotions.

Raven shoved him back down onto the tile and whispered. "Beware the demon of the spiral eye."

Steel fell beneath Raven's weight, and his head thudded against the tile floor. Light reflected from a silver amulet dangling around her neck. She tossed her blonde wig aside and spoke. He suddenly grew dizzy, and a sickening nausea burned its way through his system. Raven bent over him, water running from her hair and pooling on his face. "Having a flashback? Good. It'll give me time to get away."

Steel was somewhere else. Again.

Steel sat in a chair with his hands tied behind his back as the tall African man hovered over him like a giant.

"Americans love baseball." The man wore dark gray coveralls, and he carried a baseball bat in his left hand. He touched the bat to Steel's chin. The last six inches of the bat were covered by tightly wound steel wire held in place by metal studs and nails. "I can hit a home run out

of the park with your head, man of steel." The African laughed, and Steel jerked his head away from the touch of the cold wires.

"Enough, Mazi!" Another man stepped into the room. He wore a khaki shirt and dark pants. He glared at Steel and reached out one hand to push the bat away from Steel's face. "The Captain said not to kill him, you fool."

"Mr. Kito, perhaps a base hit, then?" Mazi grinned and exposed brown teeth. Before Steel could react, Mazi swung the bat and hit him in the knee. He screamed in agony.

"Stop!" Kito grabbed the bat and tore it from Mazi's grip. His black eyes gleamed with malice. "Take him to the operating room."

Steel's vision swam with the aftermath of the pain. He felt the skin over his knee swell, and he could barely feel his right leg. Mazi pulled him up from the chair and pushed Steel through the door of the grimy room. They passed into a corridor of what looked like a hospital or clinic. Steel smelled antiseptic and fought the urge to vomit. Mazi pushed him into a brightly lit room with an operating table in the center.

Two people stood in the room. A short woman in surgical scrubs pushed her dark hair up into a surgical hair cover. Her olive skin seemed perfect, but the malice in her eyes marred the external beauty. The other man turned around. Bright, turquoise eyes gleamed from the shadows beneath the Panama hat he wore. He was dressed in khaki shirt and pants, and he put a meerschaum pipe into his mouth.

"No smoking, Captain." The woman barked at him. "We have pure oxygen in this room."

The Captain raised an eyebrow and glared at her. "Dr. Monarch, I am not a fool. I will not light the pipe."

Steel blinked in disbelief, and his heart raced. Here was the man he had been searching for. Just weeks before a tip had led him here. The Captain stood before him with his horrid pipe. On one side of the pipe an angel was carved into the white bone. He knew that a demon was on the other side.

"I knew you were here!"

"I told you not to try and find me." The Captain motioned to the table. "Please sit."

Mazi shoved Steel onto the table, and the Captain pointed to Steel's hands. "Remove the bindings."

Mazi glanced over at Mr. Kito. "I need my bat. He will try to escape."

The Captain shook his head. "Why should he try to escape? He has found what he has been looking for. Right, son?"

Steel continued to glare at his father while Mazi removed the cord from his wrists. Mazi took his bat from Mr. Kito. "Just in case," he muttered.

The Captain took the pipe from his mouth and paced back and forth. "I told you to stop looking for me, or you would have to pay the price. Do you know where you are?"

"Somewhere in North Africa," Steel whispered. "Some kind of biological weapons facility."

The Captain stopped pacing and pointed the pipe at Steel. "No, son, this is a prison camp. You're lucky the militia didn't cut your head off. It cost me a lot to get them to spare your life."

Steel looked around at the surgical suite. "This looks like a hospital. More of your experiments?"

The Captain smiled. *"Oh, no. Not my experiments. Dr. Monarch has made some impressive advances. For instance, this."*

The Captain reached to a nearby surgical stand and picked up a plastic envelope. Steel tried to focus on the contents.

"What is it?"

"A marvelous technological advancement. Dr. Monarch is going to let you be one of the first patients to experience it."

Steel pushed up away from the surgical table and started toward the door. The blow came hard across his back and knocked the wind out of him. He thudded onto the floor, gasping for breath. Mazi turned him over onto his back and picked him up like he was a rag doll. He placed Steel on the surgical bed, and Steel finally caught his breath.

"Mr. Kito, please take Mazi's toy from him before he kills my son." The Captain leaned into Steel's vision. *"Let me tell you what your future holds. You will undergo this surgery. And then, one day, you will escape from this prison camp and come after me again. On that day I will whisper something in your ear, and your life will end. Everything you hold dear will disappear in a puff of smoke. Think about that. Your devotion to your precious God will vanish. Your 'transformation,' as you call it, to your new life will be forgotten. You will have nothing left but an empty page. Do you want that? Do you want to forget your God? That is what will happen if you come after me again. Do you understand?"*

Steel gasped for breath and whispered. *"Nothing can separate me from the love of God."*

The Captain clamped his pipe in his teeth. *"We shall see."*

Dr. Monarch appeared in his view with an oxygen mask. *"Don't fight it, and it will all be over in no time."*

Steel tried to raise his hands to ward off the mask, but he couldn't find the strength. He struggled against the mask as it clamped down on his face, and all faded to darkness.

Steel blinked water out of his eyes and tried to sit up. A group of shoppers were huddled around him, and he heard the approaching sound of a siren. He slowly climbed to his feet and stumbled out into the parking lot, but Raven was long gone. Why hadn't she killed him when she had the chance?

[Chapter 14]

UDGE BOLTON SAT behind his desk and glared down at Steel and Atchison. He was an older man with gaunt features and short white hair. His mouth was turned down in a perpetual frown. He leaned forward to glare at them.

"What happened to you?" he growled.

"A minor altercation," Steel said.

"He saved my life," Atchison added.

Bolton's frown deepened, and he glared at Atchison. "Saved your life? What'd you do, drown?"

"No. A woman left a bomb at my table. Mr. Steel threw it away and chased her down. They fell in the fountain at the mall."

Bolton sat absolutely still. "At the mall?"

"She tried to shoot me yesterday at the Galleria. And today she pretended to be a new client and met me for lunch," Atchison said.

Still no movement. Bolton blinked. "I'd advise you stay away from shopping malls, attorney. Why was she trying to kill you?"

"I don't know." Atchison shrugged. "But I want police protection."

Bolton finally raised an eyebrow and looked back at Steel. "You just happened to recognize there was a bomb in this woman's purse?"

Steel looked at Atchison and shrugged. "I know how Raven works. She couldn't get him with the rifle, so she tried a direct approach."

"Raven?"

"Her code name."

"You know the assassin?"

"It's complicated."

"Yes, it is. But you're going to make it simple for me."

Steel drew a deep breath. "I have amnesia. I don't remember my past. I recognized the woman, but I don't know from where."

"That's why I thought she was shooting at him and not me," Atchison said. "But I guess he was right. I need protection, Your Honor."

"Mr. Atchison, will you please stop babbling on about these attempts on your life before I shoot you myself? I'll make sure you have a police escort until this assassin, what was her name?"

"Raven."

"Until Raven is apprehended. In the meantime, you might want to find out who hired this assassin to kill you." Bolton leaned back in his chair and shuffled through some papers. "I have at my disposal some interesting documents submitted by Mr. Atchison, Grace Pennington, and Lieutenant Kane. I'm not totally ignorant of yesterday's events, Mr. Steel. I pride myself on being informed when it comes to the welfare of a child. Speaking of which, where is Josh Knight?"

"On his way," Atchison answered at the same time Steel said, "I don't know."

Bolton's face bobbed back and forth as he looked at both of them, "Well, which is it?"

"We don't know," Steel answered.

"Theo found Josh."

Steel turned around and watched Josh come down the aisle, followed by Sergeant Raffle. He glared at the boy as he saw the dyed hair and the lip bead. "Where have you been?"

Josh stopped and his fists clenched. "Helping someone."

"Ila?" Steel felt his face grow hot.

"Someone had to save her. You were off saving Tubby the Crackhead. Dude, he showed up at the Blood Klotz, picked me up, and carried me out to the truck." Josh's eyes were wide with anger, and the veins stood out in his neck. "I went after Ila. Because you wouldn't."

"Oh, and what about you? Who saved you when you were possessed by the thirteenth demon?" Steel shouted back.

"The same guy who just stood by and let my mom go into the fire. It should have been you!" he screamed.

Steel saw crimson, and he lashed out with his hand, striking Josh across the cheek. Josh's head snapped, and spittle flew in the air. He wiped at blood at the corner of his mouth before throwing a punch at Steel. Steel caught his fist in midair.

"Stop it, the both of you." Raffle pushed in between them.

"Who are you?" Bolton asked.

"Sergeant Raffle with Dallas PD."

"Judge, I can explain—" Steel started.

"Explain what? Why you hit a minor? In my courtroom?"

Steel flushed and glanced over at Josh. "I have a problem with my temper."

"I'll say he does." Josh stepped up beside him. "I told him once, 'For someone who wants to help people, you sure are violent.'"

Steel closed his eyes and fought down the anger. "I had a troubled childhood, Your Honor."

"I've heard that excuse too many times. Well, you won't be taking care of Joshua Knight."

Josh glanced at Steel, and he felt his heart drop. "Then I can go? Good! You promised my mother you would take care of me. Instead you went after Mr. Nosmoking and left me alone with a demon-possessed vampire!"

"What are you talking about?"

Josh crossed his arms. "Dude, Armando came by the house last night while you were out rescuing the homeless. He threatened me."

"Armando? At the house?" Steel looked away, deep in thought.

"Look, let's calm down and see if we can work this out with the judge. I can call Cephas, and you can come with me."

Josh stepped closer to Steel, pressing his face close to him. "Bro, I don't want to stay with you. I'm leaving."

"You are going nowhere, young man." Bolton slammed his gavel. Steel flinched. Josh glared at the judge.

"I am putting you in the custody of the state until I can sort out all of this mess and find you a foster home."

"No!" Josh screamed.

"Your Honor?" Steel began.

"Not another word, Mr. Steel, or I will gladly and without hesitation throw you in jail for contempt of court."

"I'm not going to a foster home," Josh said.

"Yes, you are." Judge Bolton pressed a button on his desk and spoke into an intercom. "Bailiff, please come to courtroom five."

Josh's eyes grew wide, and he looked at Steel. "Josh, don't…" Steel said.

Josh shook his head and ran. He hit the back doors just as the bailiff was trying to come in. The door collided with the bailiff's head, and he went down. Steel ran after Josh and chased him down the halls of the courthouse. Josh disappeared into an open elevator. The doors closed just as Steel reached them. He was surprised to find Theo waiting outside the doors.

"Stairs right over here. I used them before."

They both ran for the stairs, and Steel took them three at a time. He heard Theo's thundering footsteps behind him. They burst out into the foyer of the courthouse just as Josh disappeared through the front glass doors. Steel followed just in time to see Josh disappear around the corner on the motorcycle. There was no way he could reach it in time. He fell to his knees, gasping for air, and felt Theo stop just behind him.

"I lost him. Again," Steel gasped.

[Chapter 15]

EPHAS LAWRENCE GLANCED at the screen above the airline counter. His flight to Dallas had been delayed again. Thunderstorms in the area had practically shut down air traffic into and out of Dallas Fort Worth Airport. His cell phone rang, and he pulled it out of his pocket, sliding his tiny reading glasses down to study the readout.

"Jonathan, good to hear from you," he said as he lifted the phone to his ear. "When will you be going to court?"

"I just left," Steel said.

Cephas frowned at the sorrow in his voice. "What happened?"

"I lost Josh again."

"Tell me about it." Cephas crossed to a bench and sat down. It took a while, but Steel told him everything. "So you think this Rudolph Wulf is possessed by the twelfth demon?"

"I saw his picture in Ketrick's office. I can't help but believe that he has something to do with Armando. Cephas, I don't know what to do."

Cephas glanced again at the airport departure board. No flights out to Dallas tonight. He sighed. "Jonathan, you remember I told you about the manuscript with the twelve illustrations around the edge of the circle? The number twelve is associated with the figure of a wolf. You have stumbled onto something very dangerous. It would seem that this demon is trying to consolidate his power, perhaps by claiming the old hunting grounds of the thirteenth demon. Don't get in its way."

Cephas heard Jonathan breathing heavily on the other end

of the phone line. "Cephas, you've got it wrong. It's the twelfth demon who better not get between me and Josh."

"Jonathan, do not do anything rash and impulsive. Remember your anger."

"I already have."

"Jonathan, my flight has been delayed until tomorrow. I am trying my best to get there. I am afraid my old foe, Satan, is working on me. I fear something huge is building, Jonathan. It is no coincidence that you and I have been drawn together in this conflict."

"Cephas, you take your time. I'll handle the situation here. I'll find Josh no matter what demon stands between us. I don't want you or anyone else to get hurt."

Cephas saw a destination listed at the bottom of the board. An idea began to form in his mine. "Very well, Jonathan. I will arrive as soon as I can. My prayers go with you, my friend."

"Thank you, Cephas. I will be in touch."

The line went dead, and Cephas snapped the cell phone shut. He stood there surrounded by the bustling, hurtling masses of people and smiled. If he couldn't get to Dallas, he could get close!

Steel slumped into the seat in Bolton's chambers where he had been waiting for most of the afternoon. His face throbbed and his head hurt. But most importantly, his heart was torn. He should be out looking for Josh, but when he and Atchison received the "request" that they wait for Judge Bolton, he couldn't pass up the possibility of gaining custody.

The secretary's phone buzzed, and when she picked up, she listened a moment before responding, "Yes, Your Honor," and hanging up. She led them into Judge Bolton's chambers. Bolton had taken off his robes and sat behind a regular-sized desk. He motioned for them to sit.

"Mr. Steel, it seems that we are not finished after all."

"Your Honor, please. I know I should have controlled my temper with Josh, but—"

Bolton leaned forward and silenced Steel with a hard glare. "This is Saturday, and my wife and I make it a ritual to have my grandchildren over. Bear my sacrifice in mind, Mr. Steel. I am keeping score. I didn't ask you here to discuss the custody issue. I've made my decision."

A light tap interrupted, and the door opened to usher in Lieutenant Kane and Agent Ross.

"It has come to my attention that you are wanted for questioning by the police. They asked that I hold you until they arrived. Hello, Sue. It's been a long time." Bolton scribbled something on his legal pad.

Kane nodded and pointed to Ross. "FBI Special Agent Ross, Your Honor."

Ross settled into a seat beside Steel and smacked at his nicotine gum.

"Two teenagers on opposite ends of this city were found with their throats torn out. Looked like they had been attacked by some kind of animal. Any ideas, Mr. Demonbuster?" Kane asked.

"Maybe you should be looking for Armando."

Kane looked like she had swallowed a bad oyster. "All I know is that you withheld information. And then there was the bomb at the mall today."

"Raven was trying to kill me!" Atchison said, and Kane looked at him as if realizing for the first time he was in the room.

"I guess you were right, Steel," Kane said.

"Atchison was with Rudolph Wulf." Steel looked at Atchison.

"It was a business meeting." Atchison pushed his glasses back up onto his nose with a shaky hand.

Steel glanced at Ross. "I saw Wulf's picture at Ketrick's house."

"We took all the pictures as evidence, Steel. I don't recall a Mr. Wulf."

"Check with your people. He signed it, 'Best wishes, Wulf.' And he put the number twelve in the corner."

Ross froze and then suddenly laughed. "Let me guess. You think Wulf is the twelfth demon?"

"It explains his connection to Ketrick."

"His connection to Ketrick is purely business," Atchison said. "Wulf Pharmaceuticals is interested in buying out Ketrick Enterprises. Ms. Poe arranged a meeting for us to discuss the matter. I was surprised Vivian didn't show up…"

Steel felt like he'd been slugged. "Did you say Vivian?"

"Vivian Darbonne Ketrick is the head of Ketrick Enterprises. At least she wants to be."

"What do you have to do with Ketrick Enterprises?"

"I'm on the board of directors. Last week Vivian shows up with some documents claiming she's the heir to Ketrick's business, that the two of them had gotten married and he left everything to her. I told her she was crazy. I wasn't about to vote in favor of making her the new CEO."

Steel turned and glared at Ross. "Did you know Vivian was involved?"

Ross shrugged. "First I've heard of it. Wouldn't surprise me. She's very resourceful."

"I'll say." Steel looked at Kane. "Vivian hired Raven to kill Atchison. Can't you see? Atchison must have been the only member of the board she couldn't sway."

Atchison jumped to his feet. "I want this Raven stopped before she kills me!"

"Stay away from malls," Judge Bolton said.

"Was she trying to kill Wulf too?" Steel asked. "Why?"

"Because she wants to be number twelve?" Bolton said. Steel glanced at him, and the man smiled.

"It would fit Vivian's style. Take out both threats in one fell swoop. It makes perfect sense."

"It doesn't make any sense at all!" Bolton screamed. "This whole afternoon feels like a scene out of a horror movie. You're all nuts!"

"Your Honor." Steel leaned against the desk. "I know you feel overwhelmed by what is going on here. I promise you it is all related. Even down to Josh's disappearance. Please give me a week to clear it all up. One week. Cephas is trying to get here as quickly as he can." Steel paused and drew a deep, shuddering breath. "Josh's mother died protecting us from Robert Ketrick. It's there in those reports you read. As she was dying, I made her a promise I would take care of Josh. I'm going to find him. No demon, no human, and no legal institution is going to stop me."

Bolton sat back in his chair. "You promised his mother, while she was dying?"

"Yes. And I always keep my promises."

Bolton frowned. "You slapped that boy right in front of me."

"Josh didn't deserve that." Steel sighed and looked Bolton in the eyes. "And I will not let him down again."

Bolton frowned and rubbed his chin. "I don't know why, but I'll give you a week from this coming Monday. I want you, Dr. Lawrence, and Josh in this courtroom at two in the afternoon."

"Thank you, Judge Bolton," Steel said and reached forward with his hand. Bolton looked at the blood-stained hand and reluctantly shook it.

"Just don't bring any demons with you. Now, get out of my

chambers, all of you. There's still time for me to go see my grandchildren."

Steel stood up. "And I'm going to see an old friend."

[Chapter 16]

IVIAN LUXURIATED IN the feel of the silk kimono on her skin. She stood on the balcony of her penthouse apartment just above the corporate offices of Ketrick Enterprises. The sun was a fat ball of fire squatting on a long string of thunderclouds. Lightning lit up the clouds from beneath, and the sun burned them from above. Inside of her one of the three demons she controlled writhed in pleasure, and she closed her eyes.

"Patience, my little darling. Patience."

"Who are you talking to?"

Vivian glanced over her shoulder into her apartment. Two men sat on her couch. Both men were identical in size and proportion. Huge muscles rippled under their tank tops. One man had long, bushy hair around his thick face. The other was bald. They were sharing a snack, a dove that had landed on the balcony.

"Don't get feathers on my new couch." Vivian said. The two men had once belonged to Armando's clan. But they had proven too "violent" for Armando's taste.

"I was talking to my demons," she said as she stepped back into the living room.

She turned and walked across her newly redecorated apartment and found the leather pouch on the coffee table. The image of the wolf dragon on the cover tantalized her. After having read Wulf's notes, she understood the significance of it. She opened the pouch and took one of the vials out of its slot. She held up the red liquid and watched it refract the light into a crimson rainbow.

"With this blood we will conquer this country, one fool at a time." She heard the elevator door ding outside her front door.

Vivian motioned to Fang and Spike. "Somebody's here. Both of you go out on the balcony and wait."

Fang licked his bloody lips. "Bloody sweet! Can we have 'em?"

Vivian shook her head. "You two need to calm down. You can't kill everybody that wanders by. It might draw too much attention. Go out onto the balcony."

The two brothers disappeared, and Vivian slid the vial back into the leather pouch. She crossed to the foyer and placed the pouch on a table beside a vase of black roses. She touched a red fingernail to a doorplate. The door opened, and Jonathan Steel stood on her threshold.

"Well, look what the cat dragged in." He had a red gash on his arm, and his face was swollen. "And I'd say you've been in one dickens of a cat fight. Come in, Jonathan Steel."

Steel's brilliant turquoise eyes held barely contained rage. She knew he had a problem with his temper. It pleased her to taunt him about it. "Cat got your tongue?"

"Why are you trying to kill me?"

Vivian opened her mouth in surprise. "Kill you?"

"Raven."

Vivian felt the dawning of genuine surprise, and she smiled as she stepped aside to allow Steel into the room. "You were the man from her past? Oh, my, honey child, I had no idea."

"You had no idea?"

"Obviously not. If I wanted you dead, I would take care of it myself."

"What about Charles Atchison?" Steel asked.

"Atchison is a fool. He knows I would make a killer CEO for Ketrick Enterprises."

"But he wouldn't sign off on the decision."

"I had no leverage over him." Vivian turned and walked into her living room. "How do you like my new living arrangements?"

Steel followed her, and she watched his gaze travel over the deep red velvet coverings of her couches and the maroon carpet. His gaze focused on the painting of Vivian in a red dress above the fireplace. "When did you give up black?"

"Black is boring. But Robert liked it."

"And you got him out of the way, didn't you?"

"He took care of that himself. Here. Read this." She picked up a letter and handed it to Steel, who took it gingerly, as if it might contain poison. "Atchison is no longer on the board of directors. The new ballot went out today to the stockholders. He's off the list, as you can see. The other board members voted on it."

Steel handed the letter back. "So now what? You're after bigger game, aren't you?"

Vivian felt surprise again and studied his alluring eyes. "What game?"

"The twelfth demon?" Steel said.

Vivian stumbled and turned away from him to hide her surprise. "I don't know what you're talking about."

"I'm talking about today, Vivian. Raven tried to kill Atchison and Wulf at the same time. Arranged a lunch with them under the guise of merging Ketrick Enterprises and Wulf Pharmaceuticals. But..." She felt him draw closer. She felt the heat of his body, smelled his sweat. "I just happened on the scene just in time."

Vivian turned and brought her hand around to slap him. He caught her wrist in his hand. She studied the bruise on his left cheek and then saw the thin red line down his arm. "You chased her, didn't you?"

"Then you admit you hired her to kill Atchison." Steel still held her wrist.

"I admit nothing. It's obvious this Raven is worthless. If I had hired her to kill anyone, I'd be disappointed. So disappointed, I would terminate her services." Vivian leaned close to him. "With an emphasis on 'terminate.'" She watched Steel flinch, and he released her wrist.

"What are you up to, Vivian? Get rid of number twelve and move up the list?"

Vivian rubbed her wrist. How had he figured out about Wulf? "You don't understand all there is to know about demons, Jonathan."

"I want Josh back."

Vivian raised an eyebrow. "The brat? Don't tell me you lost him again."

Steel's face twitched with irritation, and Vivian felt a small tingle of pleasure. Steel studied her with his steady gaze.

"A man named Armando came to Josh last night and offered to take him to see Ila, his old girlfriend. Josh said Armando was possessed. I imagine Ila is too. Since you seem to have cornered the market on demons, you probably know something about it."

Vivian tried to hide her smile. "Armando? How sweet. How fitting. He actually went to see Josh?" She laughed. "He has more initiative than I thought."

Steel grabbed her shoulders. She almost unleashed one of her three demons but controlled him at the last minute. "If you have anything to do with this, Vivian, I'll—"

"What? Kill me? That's not very Christian, Jonathan. Besides, Armando doesn't serve me."

Steel backed away. "Wulf?"

Vivian led him back into the foyer and leaned against the table with the huge vase of black roses. "Let me give you a word of advice. If you thought the thirteenth demon was bad, wait until you meet the twelfth. They get stronger the higher up the 'corporate ladder' you go."

"They're still not as strong as my God."

Vivian laughed as she reached out to take a rose from the vase. She held it to her nose and inhaled the dusky fragrance. "I know the Bible well, Jonathan. You are familiar with the unpardonable sin?"

Steel's forehead furrowed in puzzlement. "What does that have to do with anything?"

"Josh surprised me on the mountaintop with that angel. But next time I will fill him with such desire he will denounce God. He will blaspheme the Holy Spirit. He will commit the unpardonable sin. And when he does, he will be mine."

Steel's face filled with surprise. "The mountaintop? Sandia Peak?" Steel had taken Josh to Sandia Peak just two weeks ago to spread his mother's ashes at her favorite spot. He had never mentioned being visited by Vivian.

"Josh never told you? Never mentioned the seven fine demons I brought with me?"

"He withstood you, didn't he? He defeated you."

Vivian slapped the rose against her leg and felt the barbs tear into her skin. "The angel caught me off guard!"

Steel stepped toward her. "Next time you meet Josh, you need to beware. He has the power to send your demons to hell."

Vivian reached out and pushed him away as she raked the rose briars across his neck. Steel stepped back and wiped at the blood on his neck.

"The unpardonable sin, Steel. Look it up." Vivian opened the door and motioned out to the foyer. "I suggest you stop worrying about me and start worrying about the twelfth demon."

Vivian watched him walk to the elevator before she closed the door. She leaned against the rich wood panel and laughed. Raven had been trying to kill Jonathan Steel? He was the person from her past? How delightful it would be to explore his past, to resurrect those dark memories. Ketrick had told her Steel suffered from amnesia. She really should look into refreshing his memory. The recalled memories would be so painful.

As for Raven, Vivian realized her usefulness was at an end. She had a better person in mind to destroy Wulf—the same person she had manipulated into destroying Ketrick—and he had just walked out of her living room.

She returned the rose to the vase and glanced down at the tabletop. The leather pouch was missing! Baring her fanged teeth, she let forth an inhuman scream of anger that rattled the windows.

"You are dreadfully incompetent!" Vivian heard the voice whisper behind her.

"Who's there?"

Wulf stepped in off of the balcony. "You let him take the vials." His face was twisted in anger. "I should kill you where you stand."

Fang and Spike appeared behind Wulf. They seemed different—taller and more muscular. Then she saw the mark of the wolf dragon on their necks. Wulf had taken them for his own! "Why didn't you stop him yourself?"

Wulf wore a long, dark coat that billowed as he moved and a maroon colored turtleneck shirt that hugged his frame. His eyes gleamed with unholy light. He stopped just inches from her and brought up the cane, touching the wolf's snout to Vivian's chin. "I am relying on you to take care of mortals, Vivian. You let me down. Are you familiar with the inferior and superior vena cava?"

Vivian shrugged. "What does that have to do…" Suddenly her throat closed down, and she felt like the top of her head was about to explode. Her face began to swell and grow warm. Her eyes pulsed with every heartbeat. Wulf lifted his hand. "The cavas empty the blood from above and below your heart into the right atrium. If you occlude the cavas, then the blood begins to build up. With every beat of your heart, more blood is pumped into a closed system. Your head swells. Your abdomen distends."

"It's like she's going to bloody explode!" Fang licked his lips.

"I want 'er liver." Spike bared his teeth.

Vivian felt her vision fading, felt blood trickle from her nose. If she had the power, she would teleport, but the trip to New Mexico had cost her. It had taken two weeks to recover. Through a haze of dark clouds she watched Wulf's animal face materialize. His clawed hand reached forward *through* her chest, and she felt one of her demons constrict in fear. Wulf wrenched it from her. It was a struggling, black insect shape. She felt herself being torn asunder as Wulf stuffed the demon into his fanged mouth. Wulf flourished his clawed hand, and the pressure released. She stumbled to her feet, and her strength abated as the two remaining demons within her writhed in agony. "What have you done?"

Wulf became his human self and wiped his lips. "Taken your dung beetle demon for safe keeping. You can have it back when you retrieve the vials. I give you until Friday. If you don't succeed, I'll take another. And if that isn't good enough"—his eyes blazed beneath his mantle of gray hair as he leaned into her face—"I'll take the last ones, drain you dry, and claim your soul for the master. Now, I must get ready for the Bloodfest." He rammed his cane against the wood floor, stood up, and disappeared from sight.

Vivian collapsed onto the floor, hugging her arms around her partially empty torso. Her sobs filled the silence with despair. Fang and Spike crossed the room and glared at her.

"Master Wulf gave us a new power, love." Fang smiled, and suddenly his face changed. His hair writhed with power, and he became a man wolf with a long, distended snout and huge teeth. His hands grew claws, and he hunched over her.

Spike smiled and revealed vampire fangs. "He gave me vampire magick. Bloody sweet, it is! Now he told us we could help you."

Vivian wiped tears from her eyes. Perhaps she could still salvage this situation. "You'll help me recover the vials from Jonathan Steel?"

"Yes," Fang muttered through his muzzle.

"You will have to obey my every command. Without question." She straightened.

"As long as it does not violate Master's will," Spike said.

"You heard him. He wants the vials back." Vivian smoothed down her dress and wiped blood from her nose. Using Steel to defeat Wulf had just become a casualty of her need to survive. "You boys want to taste some blood? When the time is right, you will get those vials back for me, and then you can kill Jonathan Steel."

Interlude

"How was your weekend?"

"Excellent."

"Good. After our last session you seemed so weak I thought you would benefit from a break. Now that you have succumbed to my voice again, I will ask you one question."

"Please ask."

"Do you want to return to your distant past?"

"Of course. Why not?"

"It is just that it seems so..."

"Violent?"

"Yes, that is one word for it. Do you think it is wise to recall such violent behavior?"

"I am a peaceful man. My past will make me free."

"Of course."

"You told me it would."

"I did."

"Then let us continue."

Near the Danube River
From the annals of Zamolxis
Translated by Rudolph Wulf
Circa 430 B.C.

With his dying breath the chief priest relinquished his power, and it flooded into me. It filled me with awe and a sense of greatness. My fingers relaxed from around the old man's throat, and he fell back onto his bed. Within me I sensed the new power swell, filling me with knowledge and memory. And purpose.

"Cescal, what has happened?" I heard the voice behind me. I whirled and watched as Roffan entered the room with his ever-present aide, Asclan. Roffan wore the simple tunic of a soldier in the army of Thrace. His dark hair was pulled up into a tight knot upon his head, and his smooth features were twisted in disgust. His hazel eyes glittered in the torchlight.

"I am Saitnoxis now. I am no longer Cescal." I listened to a hoarse voice within me and obeyed. Soften your voice! Be filled with sorrow!

"It is with great sadness I assume the duties of our departed chief priest. See to the arrangements for his cremation." Asclan's eyes grew wide with horror as he looked at the old man's body. Would he see the handprints on the man's neck? "Is there a problem?"

Roffan looked back at me. "For long I have watched you, Cescal. I have seen your scheming and devious ways lead you ever upward in the cabal of the priesthood. I do not think the death of our chief priest is of natural causes."

Asclan glared at me but said nothing. He was a strong and formidable man. He wore his hair in ringlets, and he carried a spear of the army. I had no doubt that Roffan had turned him against the priesthood.

Smile, the voice within said. Ignore Asclan. He is but a man. Roffan is now your greatest enemy. I smiled. "Roffan, you are a good man. And Asclan, you have shown great promise as an advisor to the king. I would never stoop to killing the chief priest. I do not desire the weight and responsibility of this office. It is a holy responsibility thrust onto the unwilling. Would you don these robes and take his place?"

"I do not know how you did this, Cescal." Roffan stepped toward me. "But I shall see to it that the chieftain knows of your treachery. For now horrible things have happened, and the king's sanity stands on the edge of a knife. In spite of my advice, our chieftain, Sitalces, has sent for Saitnoxis."

"Then I shall go to our chieftain. Asclan, call Sancles and have him organize a fitting memorial for our departed master. You can handle that simple task, can't you?" I let my new source of power lend thunder to my voice.

"Of course, Ces...Saitnoxis." Asclan spat the name and turned to leave the chamber. Roffan stepped closer to me.

"I know what you are up to, Saitnoxis. I could not stop you that night in the banquet hall, but I did keep your precious underlings from breaking free of their chamber. On that night the battle went to my master. This night it will not go your way."

I felt the anger build within me as my power writhed in fury. I wanted to lash out and destroy this creature of light before me. But, as always, the consequences of our actions were governed not by our choices but the men around us. "I made the choice to accept this power, Roffan. Now go to the chieftain and tell him I am coming. Spin your webs against me. But know that I will slash them down, and the victory tonight will be mine."

Roffan turned quickly and left the room. I removed the dead man's white robe and golden sashes. After donning my new apparel, I hurried from the chief priest's quarters to the main hall.

I marveled at the clarity of the night and the brilliance of stars I had never so appreciated. It was as if my senses were tripled. Distant, ancient memories surfaced from the former hosts of this mighty power within me. I saw the three planets aligning and the moon eclipsed. But the starry night above me was empty of this miracle, and it would be over two thousand years before the Event would be available again to free my army of darkness. I cursed the name of Roffan and his master.

In the distance I could hear the cadence of the war drums. The outer clans were still quarreling and threatening to overthrow Sitalces. We must not let that happen. I nodded at the sound of the inner voice.

At the threshold of the main hall blood ran in an irregular trail up the stone stairs and into the fire-lit interior. What had happened here? I hurried into the chamber. Smoke curled in the flickering torchlight. Servants were prostrate on the floor, and from the far throne I heard sobbing.

Sitalces, dressed in a flowing robe and his golden peaked helmet, held his face and blubbered like a child. At the foot of his throne a grotesque, bloody mass lay in a tangle. Roffan stood beside the chieftain with a hand on his shoulder. I grimaced at the sight of the self-righteous fool who thought he could stop the influence of the power that throbbed within me. It was a power that had held the hand that ruled these nations for decades.

"Master, what has happened?" I stopped short of the throne.

Sitalces looked up at me with tear-filled eyes. "Where is Saitnoxis? I sent for him, not his assistant."

I bowed and inclined my head. "I regret to report, your lordship, that your former chief priest has perished. I have assumed his duties and now am called Saitnoxis."

Good, good! The voice laughed within me. I felt a tingle of pleasure.

"Then you shall have to advise me. Look what these barbarians have done." Sitalces stood and motioned to the bloody heap at his feet.

I looked up and examined it. The head of a wolf. Not just any wolf, but a large, gray-haired wolf. It had been Sitalces's constant companion.

"My lord, they have slain your companion wolf," I said.

Sitalces descended from his throne and wiped tears from his face and his dark beard. His eyes glowed with anger. "Yes. Would they had taken one of my wives, or even one of my servants. But Dragon has been my companion since I was a child."

Roffan followed the chieftain down from the throne. "Your lordship, surely you do not mean this. Human life is far more worthy than that of a beast. We are created in God's image."

"Are we?" Sitalces shouted, spit flying through the air. "What tragedy then is life. What horror awaits my every waking moment. Do not speak to me of a god who would take my most innocent and devoted companion!"

I listened to the voice whisper within and curiously realized it had become my own voice. I and the power within were becoming one being with one purpose. I stood up slowly and surveyed the somber interior of the chamber. Servants still quivered in their fallen positions. Soldiers stood guard around the chamber with their eyes averted. Far off in the cloistered darkness of Mount Kogain my loyal ones waited. You will have to continue to be patient, my lovelies. Sitalces had to be the focus of all my energies. I looked down at the wolf head and then up at the bright, crimson banners that hung behind the throne. Perhaps this incident would become a defining moment.

"My lord, it is time to send a message to our god," I suggested.

Sitalces looked at me with confusion etched on his face. "It has not been three years since the last messenger was sent."

"I am aware of that, my lord. But these are dangerous times. The clans threaten to overthrow your new kingdom. They have killed your closest companion. They seek to dishearten you. I have a message I would like to send to Zamolxis. If the message is received, then there will be a new plan for your kingdom that will bring you unprecedented power and will bring the clans to their knees."

Roffan stepped between us. "My lord, do not consider this—"

Sitalces pushed him aside as his maddened gaze locked onto mine. He smiled, and drool ran down his face. He motioned to a nearby soldier. "Very well. You, go and choose a man, a just man with no guile from the village."

I lifted a hand. "A moment, my lord." I crossed to the soldier and whispered in his ear. He rushed out of the throne room, and I motioned to the remaining soldiers. "Bring forth the sacred spears."

Three soldiers snapped to attention and hurried from the room. Sitalces motioned toward the doorway. "Shall we move to the public area? There are scant viewers for the ceremony, but I trust you to bring me good news and a plan to avenge this night's tragedy."

I nodded and motioned to the porch off the throne room. "After you, my lord."

Behind me Roffan closed his eyes in defeat and disappeared into the shadows. The choice had been made. Sitalces was mine!

By the time we had made our way onto the porch, the soldier had appeared with a delicious surprise. Asclan stood in the torchlight. His face was red with anger, and his ringlets shook with fury.

"You have put him up to this, Cescal. Admit it," he shouted.

I stepped forward and motioned for the chieftain to have a seat in his outside throne. "My lord agrees it is time to send a message to our god. You have been chosen as the most suitable messenger. You would not blaspheme your own god by refusing this honor, would you?"

Asclan looked about him wildly. Perhaps he was looking for Roffan. But he was at the fate of all humanity and its freedom to choose. Asclan's fellow soldiers stood to the side with impassive faces. A crowd of sleepy villagers gathered on the slope in front of the great hallway, carrying torches and lanterns. Asclan looked down at them and found no pity.

"I cannot refuse this honor, Your Majesty. But I beseech you to reconsider the words of Cescal as our new high priest. He is not ready for the job."

Sitalces opened his mouth to speak, and I laid a hand on his shoulder. "Your Majesty can rest assured I am well aware of my shortcomings. That is why I seek the wisdom of our god. If you will allow me to proceed, we will send the message."

Sitalces looked at Asclan, then back at me. Specks of the wolf's blood dotted his tunic and beard. He nodded. "Proceed, Saitnoxis."

I motioned to the three soldiers standing at one side. They planted the butts of their spears on the ground and assumed the position with the spear points slightly angulated outward to catch the thrown body. I walked slowly across the open porch as the stars glittered above me and the torchlight cast dancing shadows on the man's face. I leaned into Asclan and whispered into his ear.

"There is no message. There is only your death. I am an evil as old as man itself."

I stepped back, and Asclan regarded me with sudden fury. "No!"

But before he could protest, his body was swung backward by the two huge soldiers at either side, and he was tossed upward in the air. His body arched across the open porch and thudded down onto the spears. He tried to hurl one last curse in my direction, but the life drained out of his eyes even as his blood spilled onto the ground.

I turned to Sitalces. "Zamolxis has received my message. Shall I tell you what needs to be done?"

Sitalces's bright eyes were fixed upon Asclan's dead body. "Yes," he whispered.

I hurried inside and stepped up onto the throne. With a jerk of supernatural power I pulled down the two crimson banners behind it. When I turned, Sitalces stood in the door, his face clouded with confusion. "What are you doing?"

"A new banner shall fly over your legions, my lord. This night, your companion shall not have died in vain." I walked into the shadows to Roffan. His gaze burned with righteous indignation, but he was powerless. I jerked the pike out of his hand and turned back to Sitalces.

"You shall show your people that your resolve shall not be broken by this incident. You shall show these clans that you embrace their treachery, and you shall exceed it." I lifted the head of the wolf from the floor in front of the throne. With one powerful thrust I mounted the head on the end of the pike and secured the crimson banners at the base of the head. Pushing past the confused Sitalces, I hurried out onto the porch. By now hundreds of restless, sleepy villagers had gathered in the open courtyard. Already the faint glows of dawn crept over the horizon.

"People of Thrace, your master this night has been dealt a great blow. But he shall embrace this hatred, and he shall send forth his forces to subdue this world in his name. From this day forward, Zamolxis has decreed that you shall follow him. You shall put hand to sword without hesitation. You shall laugh at death, for your soul knows no end. You shall fight for your king under the banner of the Thracian Wolf Dragon." I thrust the pike upward into the early rays of the morning sun. A wind caught the crimson banners, and they fluttered and gyrated behind the wolf head like a serpent.

The people roared with approval, and their voices resounded with praise as Sitalces stepped up beside me. He looked up at the wolf head and serpentine banners curling in the morning breeze.

"What have you done?"

"Made you a king." I smiled.

Chapter 17

STEEL DROVE THE Mustang up onto I-635 and dialed his phone. For the second time that day he called Cephas Lawrence. When the man answered, his voice was almost drowned out by the voices of many people.

"Cephas? Where are you?"

"In the airport in…" His voice crackled with static. "Bad connection."

Steel sighed. "I found out that Vivian Darbonne Katrick is involved in this entire affair with the twelfth demon. I paid her a visit tonight. She had a leather pouch with three vials of blood in it."

Cephas's voice quickened. "Blood? Listen, Jonathan, Wulf Pharmaceuticals is based in Romania." More static. "…ties to the old Communist regimes of Eastern Europe. You may be dealing with a biological weapon."

Steel slowly glanced at the leather pouch on the seat beside him. "Is that his plan? Release a biological agent on Dallas?"

"I doubt it, Jonathan. These demons are subtler." His voice disappeared for a few seconds. "…turn the vials over to the government."

"Where it will be tied up for months in analysis. I have to find Josh now! Especially if this blood is toxic!"

Cephas grew quiet on the other end of the line, and Steel heard garbled voices in the background. "I know someone in Dallas…working with biologic agents."

"Good. Can I meet this person tonight?"

"I will make some calls and get back…" The line went dead.

Steel had to know how the blood was involved. Josh's life was in danger. His phone warbled, and he picked it up. But it wasn't a call. It was an e-mail reply from Josh.

"Trust me. It's not like I'm going to Transylvania!"

Steel typed in a quick reply. "The judge gave us a week. Let me help." Steel hit the send button.

Suddenly the phone rang. He jerked in surprise and drew a calming breath as he answered. "Hello?"

"Mr. Steel?" a female voice answered.

"Yes."

"Meet me at Eastwood mall food court in fifteen minutes. Bring the vial."

"Who is this?"

"Dr. Lawrence called me." The line went dead.

Steel pulled back onto the interstate. Cephas didn't waste any time.

Steel sipped bottled water and studied the dwindling crowd of shoppers grazing in the food court. The woman walked out of their midst. Her small, athletic body was obvious beneath her workout pants and tank top. Her blonde hair was pulled back in a short ponytail, and she stopped in mid-stride as she saw him. He watched her swallow and saw her dark eyes dart around the food court before she continued on.

"Mr. Steel?" She paused in front of him.

"Yes. And you are?"

"Renee Miller. Mind if I sit down?"

"Please." He motioned to a chair.

Miller sat and glanced once more around the area.

"Are you expecting someone?" Steel asked.

"Just making sure I wasn't followed. Do you have the vial?"

Steel leaned back in his chair. "First, how do you know Cephas?"

Something dark passed across her gaze, and she looked away. "I'm not here to discuss my past. He asked me to come get some blood from you. Said it might be helpful."

Helpful? Steel pulled the vial out of his pocket. "Here it is."

Miller took it gingerly and held it up to the light. "It's blood all right. Wonder what's in it?"

"I'm hoping you can tell me."

Miller slid the vial into her pocket. "If Rudolph Wulf is involved, you can bet it'll be something dangerous. Good night, Mr. Steel." She stood up to go, and Steel reached out and grabbed her hand. She whirled back toward him and jerked her hand out of his grip. A look of panic clouded her features.

"Get your hands off of me!" she barked.

"Sorry." Steel stood away. "What did you mean helpful?"

Miller rubbed her hand and backed away. "I'll call you as soon as I know something."

Steel stood up. She was hiding something. He reached into his pocket and touched the memory card he had found in the pouch. He should give it to her as well. But a quiet inner voice told him to hang onto it.

"Cephas's nephew may be in danger. I need to know quickly."

Renee Miller studied him for a minute, and a profound sorrow drifted across her face. She looked away and sniffed. "I'm going to the lab now." She turned and disappeared into the crowd.

"Where's the walking mountain?" Lieutenant Kane asked as Steel sat at the table in the coffee shop the next morning. Kane had summoned him to an impromptu meeting, mainly to find out what he had learned from his visit with Vivian Ketrick. "Raffle said you'd acquired a pet."

"Theo? He went to church. Said he hadn't been in three years."

Kane wore khaki pants and a denim shirt. Her hair was still wet from her shower, and she was sipping at a cup of coffee. "Good. I don't want Nosmo anywhere around me. Understand?"

"Theo. He prefers Theo." Steel glanced over at Sergeant Raffle seated at the end of the table in a T-shirt and jeans. Ross completed the group in his usual dress shirt, red tie, and overcoat. At least he didn't have to spend much money on a wardrobe. "Any word on Josh?"

Kane opened a portfolio. "Nope. We've been canvassing the usual neighborhoods and haven't found hide nor hair of him."

Ross popped some nicotine gum in his mouth. "How was your visit to Vivian?"

"She all but admitted to hiring Raven to kill Atchison. Atchison is blocking her from taking over Ketrick Enterprises."

"Do you have proof?" Raffle asked.

"No. My word against hers."

"Then we can't touch her." Kane studied her notes.

"What can we do?" Steel asked.

"We can find our friend Armando. If what Josh said is true, Armando is involved in all of this. Even to the point of having something to do with Vivian Ketrick." Kane looked up at Steel. "Do you always complicate matters like this?"

"Yes," Ross said. "With Steel nothing is simple."

"If you've finished bashing me, can we talk about a plan to find Josh?" Steel asked.

Kane sipped at her coffee. "Armando is up to something. Something big. We had another dead teenager last night. That makes three. All with their throats ripped out and drained of blood." She pulled a sheet of paper out of her folio and handed it to Steel. "One of my informants picked this up."

Steel studied the sheet. It showed a huge splatter of black meant to be a splash of blood. Etched across the black were shaky white letters inviting all "vampyres and monsters" to a "Bloodfest." "What is this?"

"It's sort of a rave party for vampires. Part of the vampire lifestyle. Armando is resurrecting the clans and bringing them out of the woodwork." Kane leaned back in her chair. "They have these lavish balls where they expose their 'true vampire souls.' The invitation is sent discreetly so that mundanes don't show up."

"Mundanes?" Ross picked at his teeth.

"Normal people." Kane finished her coffee. "We need to infiltrate this Bloodfest and find out what's going on. Armando knows Raffle and me. Ross, you have any agents who could go in?"

Ross leaned forward. "I'm here after Raven. I don't care about Armando or Vivian. I've been building this case against Raven for two years. I'm not about to abandon the chase to dress up like Dracula. You're on your own." He stood up and walked out of the room.

Kane looked like she had swallowed a roach. Her eyes shifted to Steel. "Looks like you're elected."

"Where do we find this Bloodfest?"

Kane gazed off into the distance and then smiled. "We'll pay a visit to my informant. But," her eyes twinkled with mischief, "we'll have to wait until sunset."

Steel drove beneath the huge water tower emblazoned with a giant bee above the name "Ferris." Kane sat in the front seat in silence. She pointed to a burger restaurant. "Take a left at the DQ, and go under the interstate."

Steel drove beneath the interstate and out under an open sky filled with stars. Near the horizon he spied three bright stars so close together, they were almost one. Nearby the full moon was dusky and dull orange. Around them the land stretched flat and treeless. A cluster of houses in an unfinished subdivision glimmered in the darkness.

"First house on the corner over there." Kane pointed.

Steel pulled up in front of a brick house shrouded in ankle-deep grass. Most of the front yard was barren, cracked clay. Kane rang the doorbell and squinted when the front porch light came on. The door opened, and the thick odor of incense wafted into the night. The shadowy figure standing in the doorway seemed ghoulish in the dim light.

"Suzie Q, what brings you to my front door?" a raspy voice asked. His hair was stringy, pale blond, and hung about his face in matted strands. His watery blue eyes were rimmed in red, and he wore a sleeveless red T-shirt with a smiley face with fangs.

Kane stepped unhindered into the man's house. "I need a favor."

Steel followed her into the warm, redolent atmosphere of the man's living room. The floor was covered in dirty shag carpet. A huge, black velvet painting of a matador being gored by a bull hung above a dirty couch.

"You came at a bad time, Suzie Q," he rasped.

"This is Jonathan Steel." Kane motioned to Steel. The man glanced at Steel as he threw his hair back out of his face. Only then did Steel notice the man's teeth. He had three sets of fangs. One set on the bottom row of his teeth and two sets on the top, one on the incisors and another set where the bicuspids should be. The man smiled and motioned to the couch.

"Mr. Steel? Nice name. Sit."

Kane shook her head. "I haven't had my shots, Bile."

"Bile?" Steel asked.

"Yeah. My name. Like it?" The man laughed as he collapsed on his couch. "So, why are you here?"

Kane motioned to Steel. "Mr. Steel needs some help. He's trying to find a runaway." She paused and glanced at Steel. "Seems he has wandered off with one of your vampire clans."

Bile raised an eyebrow and ran a pink tongue across his teeth. "I'm not in the clan anymore."

"Yeah, but you're a fangmaster."

Bile nodded and ran a long fingernail across the tips of his fangs. "The best in the South."

"Then why did you leave the clan?" Steel asked.

Bile shrugged. "I couldn't stand the taste of blood. Made me sick every time. You got to be either a drinker or a donor."

"Donor?" Steel glanced at the bleeding matador.

"Most of the vampire wannabes do nothing but give blood. They enjoy being the entrée." Kane said.

"Why?" Steel glared at Bile.

"You're needed by another human being." Bile suddenly stood up as if he could remain still no longer, "So who's this kid?"

"I'm his guardian until his uncle gets here."

"Guardian? You're not doing a very good job, are you?" Bile wiggled his eyebrows and grinned. Steel clenched his fists, and Bile flinched.

Kane stepped between them. "Don't kill him yet. We still need him." Kane held a picture in front of Bile. "Recognize this person?"

Bile stepped back, and his face grew paler. He tore his gaze from Steel and glanced at the photo. "No."

"Gloria Sanchez. You made her a set of fangs about a month ago."

Bile laughed nervously. "Yeah. That's right. Sure did. I made her a double incisor set. I remember now."

"She's dead, as you can see in the picture. And I'm still looking for suspects. You wouldn't do very well if you went back to jail, would you?"

"Look, I made her a set. That's all. She came over, and I did her impressions and shipped her teeth. I can show you the invoice."

"You help us out, Bile, and I'll make sure your name is taken out of the investigation."

"Sure."

Steel pulled the Bloodfest invitation from his pocket. "How do I get in?"

Bile licked his fangs. "You would stick out like a nun at a rave."

Kane looked Steel up and down. "We could get Bile to make you a set of fangs. You can go as Bile's thrall."

Bile shook his head. "Now, wait a minute. Some of these vampires and vampirettes don't take kindly to the fact I left the clan."

"You still make fangs for them," Kane said. "Look on it as a business opportunity."

"And you would cover all my expenses?"

Kane sighed. "Yes. And drop you from the Sanchez investigation."

"You're going to turn me into a vampire?" Steel asked.

Bile rubbed his hands together. "I know. Good for me. Sucks for you."

Chapter 18

OSH RUBBED SLEEP from his eyes and sat up in the darkness. His right cheek ached. He touched the bruise and winced. He had finally pushed the big man over the line. It was probably smart not to do that again. Seeing King at the Blood Klotz had pushed him over the edge. The anger just seemed to flow out of him. All of the rage over his mother's death had welled up, and he had turned it on Jonathan. And now he was on his own.

A thin ribbon of light fell from the metal roof onto the floor of the warehouse office. Ila lay next to him. She had curled in upon herself with her eyes closed in sleep. Armando had sent them to this room while he met with the rest of his clan. Why he didn't include Ila, Josh couldn't figure out. But he had enjoyed being alone with her again. He ran a hand through the edge of her black hair, and she shifted in her sleep.

"I came for you, Ila," he whispered. "There's so much I wish I could have said to my mother. And now I can't. But you can still make things right with your mom. I'm going to save you. I promise." Ila sighed in her sleep, and Josh pushed aside the musty blanket and stood up. Far up in the top corner of the room a broken skylight revealed three bright stars, glittering in the night.

Josh walked across the dusty interior of the office and out onto the stairway high above the warehouse floor. What would he do now? He didn't feel the presence of evil around Ila, so she wasn't possessed. He just had to talk her into going home. That was, if they could get away from Armando.

Light flared from beneath the walkway. What was Armando up to? Quietly Josh eased down the metal stairway. The flickering light cast eerie shadows across the warehouse floor from an office. Dust motes swirled in a dizzying pattern in the slats of light. He eased up to the nearest window and peered through the blinds.

Armando stood shirtless in the center of the room surrounded by a dozen flickering black candles. His clan stood opposite him in a semicircle.

"My children, I offer you a new power of incredible beauty." The words flowed off of Armando's lips with hypnotic power, his lip bead glittering in the candlelight. "I offer you true vampire magick. Tonight you shall drink my blood, and you will find the will and the desire to grow beyond your meager powers." He glanced around the circle of men and women. Eleven in all looked back at him, some with eager anticipation, others with trepidation. Armando reached down to the table before him and lifted a razor blade in each hand. Showing no signs of reaction to the pain, he crossed his arms and cut a thin line through each side of his chest. Then he cut a line on the inside of each forearm. Blood trickled from the cuts, and he laid the razor blades aside.

"Who shall be the first?"

Some hesitated while others stepped forward. Josh watched in horror as they pressed their lips against the cuts. This was insane! How could he have ever wanted to be like these people?

"Enough, my children. There are more to feed." Armando pushed the people roughly away to give room for the other eager members of the clan. When the last had fed on his blood, Armando put on a black shirt. The eleven had taken their places back in the semicircle but seemed listless and slack eyed.

"Good!" Armando spoke as he walked up to the first woman. "The new blood still runs strong in my veins. Would you like to invite in the magick? Would you like to become a true vampire?"

The woman nodded slightly, and her lips barely moved. "Yes."

Armando smiled and leaned down to bring his mouth close to hers. He exhaled a long, moaning sigh. Josh sucked in a deep breath as he saw the thing come out of Armando. It swirled in dirty particles into the woman's mouth. She tried to jerk away, but Armando held her face while the mist thing streamed into her. She blinked and smiled. Armando nodded and moved on to the next person in line.

Josh backed away in horror. Armando was filling his clan with the power of demons! He had to get Ila out of here as quickly as possible. He turned into the darkness and ran head-on into Ila. She screamed, and he clamped a hand over her mouth.

"Quiet!" he whispered.

Ila's eyes shimmered in the meager light. "What's wrong with you?"

Josh's mind raced. "Let's just say I'm having second thoughts about joining your clan."

"Too bad." He whirled, and Armando stood behind him. "You're not going anywhere."

"Bro, what did you do to those people?" Josh asked.

"I did nothing to them. They feasted on my blood."

"Did it work?" Another voice from the darkness was followed by the appearance of a woman dressed in dark red. Josh's breath caught in his throat, and he stumbled back.

"Vivian?"

"Hello, sweetie." Vivian smiled. "You look better in black."

Ila squealed. "Vivian!" She hurled herself on the other woman, and Vivian accepted her with open arms.

"My sweet, precious Ila. Has Josh been bad to you?"

Ila pulled away, and her face was plastered with a ludicrous smile. "No. He's going to join us. Just like you tried to get him to do on the mountain."

"Oh, he is." Vivian sauntered over to Josh and ran a finger along his bruised cheek. "Did someone hit you?"

"That man did." Ila frowned. "Tell her, Josh."

"You mean Steel?" Vivian raised an eyebrow. "He hit you?"

Josh looked away. "I pushed him too far."

Vivian raised an eyebrow and glanced over her shoulder at Ila. "Ila, honey child, would you be so kind as to give me a moment of privacy with Josh?"

Ila nodded. "Yes, Miss Vivian." She walked off into the darkness.

"Josh, let me lay it out for you. I know what you're up to. You want to save little ole Ila. You want to be like Steel. But I have other plans for you."

Vivian stepped closer to Josh, and he tried to step back away from her. Armando had moved behind him, and he bounced against the man's chest. Vivian stepped closer to him and pressed herself against his body. "I see you had no qualms about becoming what you were before." She touched his lip bead with a red fingernail. "You could still join us. You could reject your God and become one of us, and I'll fill you up with something sweet and powerful." A circular tattoo seemed to move on her collarbone. "You can have the mark of the wolf dragon."

"Get out of my face! I'll—"

"You'll what?" Vivian only smiled. "You're a pathetic weakling, Josh. You have no power over me. If you cooperate with me, I'll let Ila go when this is all over. She'll be untouched by our vampire magick. But if you don't cooperate"—her eyes filled with menace—"Armando will drain her."

Josh squirmed as he felt Armando's iron grip on his arms. "No!"

"Promise me you will cooperate." Vivian's eyes were fixed on his.

Josh relaxed and sighed. "Fine! I'll cooperate as long as you leave Ila alone."

Vivian smiled. "Good! You've made the right choice. Now, think about my other offer. Say 'ta ta' to God and join us."

[Chapter 19]

I DON'T LOOK SO hot in the daytime." Bile squinted at the noonday sun streaming in through his dining room window. "Old habits die hard."

Kane pulled the drapes shut on the bay window. "I agree you look better in the dark. And the darker it is, the better you look."

Bile blinked and rubbed his eyes. "Funny girl. Ready to get started?"

Steel glanced at his watch and tried to suppress his growing impatience. He and Kane had returned so Bile could transform him into a vampire for the Bloodfest.

"I'm not too happy about this, Bile. I could be out looking for Josh."

Bile pulled his wispy hair back and secured it in a ponytail. "If you want to go to the Bloodfest, you have to look the part. Come on. Let's go to my lab."

Bile led them past his small kitchen and through a door into an enclosed two-car garage. A dentist chair sat in front of a bench covered with dental equipment. Bile motioned to the chair.

"Have a seat, seeker."

Steel sat in the chair and cast a curious look at Kane. She perched on a stool, her face plastered with a sardonic smile.

"A seeker is someone who has an interest in vampires," Kane said.

"You've got to learn the lore, man." Bile turned to his bench and began mixing something in a bowl. "First we make the impressions of your teeth so I can make sure the fangs set well on your incisors." He paused and reached for a sheet of paper and handed it to Steel. "Choose your poison."

Steel looked at the pictures of various sets of fangs. Double fangs on the top row of teeth and single on the bottom. Double fangs in the middle. Even quadruple fangs. They all had distinctive names, and the top of the sheet said, "Fangs by Bile, the Fangmaster."

"Just give me something simple." Steel tossed the sheet on the bench.

Bile turned around holding a metal mouthpiece filled with bluish goop. "Where's your sense of adventure, Mr. Steel?"

Steel opened his mouth to answer, and Bile shoved the mouthpiece in. "Bite down and hold it for about five minutes."

Steel almost gagged on the cold, slick substance. His eyes watered, but he refused to give in to the gag reflex.

"Bile, tell Mr. Steel how you became a vampire." Kane tried to wipe the smile off of her face. She was enjoying this way too much.

Bile pulled up a stool and sat on it. "I drowned when I was six. My mother threw me into the deep end of the pool to teach me how to swim. Sink or swim, she said. I sank. Took twenty minutes for the medics to revive me. When I woke up…" He paused, his gaze fading into the distance, his face becoming pale. "I was different. I could read people's thoughts. I could see the future. At first I was scared. Then I found books about clairvoyance and…"

"The occult," Kane said. "That's where it always begins."

Bile checked his timer on the bench and wiped sweat from his forehead. Steel felt the cold goo oozing down his throat, but he kept his attention on Bile. "I'm not a Satanist, Suzy Q. But I had to figure out this new life I had. So I went to my weird uncle Tremayne. He told me when I died, an ancient spirit had moved into me, and I was now a vampire. When I was twelve, he initiated me into his vampire clan."

Jerome moved through the cold, brittle branches of the barren forest toward the top of the hill. It was almost midnight, and a full moon bathed the leafless woods with cold, silver light. He breathed deep, trying to suppress the fear he felt. His uncle said it was up to him to come alone to the hilltop. He had slipped out of his bedroom, leaving his sleeping mother and father unaware of his intentions.

In the distance he made out the gleam of a lantern through the tree trunks. He rounded a huge tree and came upon a circle of rough stones about twenty feet in diameter. In the center of the circle the lantern and a silver goblet sat on a large stone. He stepped into the circle, his breath steaming on the cold air. Twigs cracked behind him, and he turned.

"Welcome, latent one." Uncle Tremayne stepped into the light of the lantern, dressed in a black coat. He had white hair and pale blue eyes that gleamed in the lantern light. Four others moved quietly into the stone circle. "It is time for your awakening. Do you seek to become one of the Kindred?"

Jerome drew a deep breath and felt the world grow distant and ethereal around him. The moon seemed to take on a brighter shade of silver that he could taste as well as see. He felt the presence of the others as they encircled him. He wanted this—more than anything he had ever wanted in his life. "Yes."

Uncle Tremayne smiled, and Jerome felt a chill at the sight of the man's fangs. "Then it is time for the Bloodletting."

Uncle Tremayne walked into the light of the lantern. A flash of silver in his right hand revealed a small, ornate knife. Jerome watched in eager anticipation as the knife blade nicked the man's wrist, and blood flowed into the goblet. Uncle Tremayne handed the knife to another member of the group, and each person contributed blood to the goblet. When the last was done, he handed the knife to Jerome.

"Your turn."

Jerome glanced at the bloody knife and felt a growing sense of fascination and revulsion. He plunged the tip into his wrist, and blood gushed. He watched the bright, red blood grow purple in the light of the full moon. Uncle Tremayne's finger pressed on the wound.

"You've hit an artery. In time you will learn how to be more careful. For now, drink of the goblet, and you will be transformed."

Jerome accepted the silver goblet in his free hand and brought the cup up to his lips. He could smell the coppery scent of fresh blood, and when the first drops touched his lips, he felt nauseous. He sipped at the salty fluid and dropped the cup. Blood splashed onto the dead leaves of the forest. He fought to keep the blood down. He felt Uncle Tremayne's hand on his neck.

"Don't worry, fledgling. In time you will grow to love the blood. Welcome to a new world order."

Jerome looked up at the people in the circle, trying desperately to cling to new sensations he had felt that night, but all he could think of was keeping his stomach from heaving.

"Like I told you, I never could get used to drinking blood." Bile finished his story and pulled the mouthpiece from Steel's mouth.

It made a sucking sound, and Steel swallowed quickly to keep from retching.

"These powers you acquired, where did they come from?" Steel said as he picked flecks of dried goo from his lips.

Bile began working with the mold, mixing chemicals and pouring them into the hardened dental material. "Several schools of thought. There are those who think the world is filled with the spirits of the old gods. One of these gods will inhabit the body of a human and transform him into a vampire. I lived that lie for years in order to stay part of my old clan."

"Old gods? Sounds like your demons, Steel." Kane got up and filled a cup with water from a sink against the wall. She handed the cup to Steel. "Some people who claim to be vampires believe they are immortal and no longer human. A new species of animal."

"Yeah, but most of them are only playing games." Bile stuck the new mold into a ceramic oven. "The Bloodfest is nothing but a huge role-playing game. For every hundred 'wannabes' there are a dozen real vampires."

Steel sipped the water and washed the taste of the goo from his mouth. "And they actually drink each other's blood?"

"Sure." Bile wiped his hands on a towel. "About five years ago…"

Bile stepped into the darkened room filled with the odor of hot wax from the dozens of black candles sitting on low tables. He wore his lose fitting "pirate" shirt, and he automatically began to loosen the strings at his neck. Four people sat on the floor before the candles, two men and two women. A tall figure in black materialized from behind a screen set against one wall. His long hair was pulled back into a dark ponytail that dangled like a long snake along his back. His chiseled features resembled a skull, and his bright, green eyes

glittered in the candlelight.

"Welcome, Bile. I understand you want to join our clutch?"

"Yes, sire. But I am a donor."

The man smiled. "Then you are not a childe, an inexperienced one?"

Bile swallowed nervously. "No, sire. I come from the clutch of the Black Hand."

The man took Bile by the hand and led him into the center of the room. "Why did you leave them?"

Bile felt the hands pushing him downward to the floor where he sat on two pillows. "They broke their own blood oath of secrecy. I could not remain a faithful member."

The man's hands danced at his neck and pulled the shirt off of his shoulders. "And you have been certified clean of disease?"

"Yes," Bile whispered, his nervousness growing.

"Here is the blade." The man's breath played across Bile's neck as he took the razor blade. He felt the sting of alcohol on his right shoulder, its pungent odor filling the air. The four people sitting in front of him seemed eager, anticipating the ritual. He reached over Bile's shoulder and made the three, quick incisions on his skin. He felt the warm blood trickle down his back and then the man's lips as he drank the blood.

Steel handed the cup back to Kane. "That is so wrong."

Bile's eyes came back into focus. "I know that now. Some vampires use butterfly needles, little needles and tubes used in the medical field. You just stick the needle in and suck on the straw."

"How much blood are we talking about?" Steel asked.

"Only a teaspoon at a time," Kane answered. "It's not the amount of blood that matters. It's the ritual."

Bile nodded. "Yeah, it's the clan that matters. People like me, we don't fit in very well. Vampire clans, goth clubs they all attract people like me because we can become something we're not. We can glow! We can shine! No inhibitions. No rules. No morals. Total freedom to be and do whatever you want." Bile's smile faded. He shrugged. "At the time it was the lifestyle I wanted. You know, intimacy, friends, belonging. I stayed with that clutch about a year until Zilo disappeared."

Steel felt a chill. "Zilo?"

"Yeah, our sire. But I think he became a black swan."

"A person who turns his back on the vampire world and becomes an enemy to it," Kane said.

"This man called himself Zilo?" Steel sat forward.

Bile nodded, taking the mold out of the oven. "Yeah. It was short for Huey Zilo Pockets or something like that."

"Huitzilopochtli?" Steel breathed the name.

Bile popped the new mold of Steel's teeth out of its hold and onto the bench. "Yeah, that was it."

Steel looked at Kane. "Robert Ketrick used that name. Claimed it was the name of the thirteenth demon."

Kane raised an eyebrow. "Well, we thought he was tied to vampire clans somehow. Now we know for sure."

Bile began working with the mold of Steel's teeth. "Last night I checked with some of my contacts. There's rumors of a mysterious new Grand Master at this Bloodfest. It wasn't easy getting that info. Even if you're a fangmaster, you're still an outcast."

"Who is it?" Steel asked.

"Don't know. Vampires are secretive," Bile said.

Steel rubbed his chin and looked over at Kane. "All of this is legal?"

"Consenting adults can do whatever they want. Unless you're

dealing with murder. I worked a case once. A small clan got into Satan worship and killed an entire family."

Bile held up two fanged teeth. "Wait a minute. Not true. Real vampires don't believe in Satan. According to the vampire creed there is only pleasure and fulfillment, no God, no Satan."

"So, if you tried to invite a spirit into you, say a demon, and you were a real vampire, as you call it, you wouldn't be able to?" Steel asked.

Bile turned to his bench and pressed the two fangs onto the mold, adjusting their position carefully. "Right. You can't invite in what you don't believe in. That's the catch. If real vampires, not just role players, admit there is a Satan and there are demons, then they could be accused of practicing the occult and indulging in criminal activity just like Suzy Q is talking about. No demons, no crimes. So they don't believe in anything but themselves and pure pleasure."

Steel raised an eyebrow. "Then where does this new Grand Master play into things?"

Bile smiled. "Word is he's been a vampire all of his life. Traveled the world. He has power. Calls it vampire 'magick.' Psychic power, man! You don't need spirits and demons to tap into that immortal, psychic power of the mind. Now, if this vampire magick were for real and he could give me, let's say, *real* fangs, I'd follow him anywhere." He held up the fangs. "Now, let's see if these babies fit."

Steel ran his tongue over the sharp points of his fangs. They felt unnatural and uncomfortable. When he spoke, his voice had a lisp. But worse than the fangs was the huge, white wig Bile handed him and the scratchy, Baroque-era clothing he put on. Lace cradled his neck, and an ascot was tied around the whole mess. It was tucked into a waistcoat of deep azure. Bile wore a dark maroon coat with frilly lace bunched at the throat. His wispy hair was pulled back into a ponytail. He turned his red eyes toward Steel as they drove down the street toward the hotel.

"You really should have worn a pair of my contacts. Those eyes will give you away." Bile said.

"I don't know where those contacts have been. At least I watched you make the fangs."

"Hey, I run a clean business. I'm licensed. And I expect to get paid."

From the backseat of the car Kane leaned forward. "You will get paid, Bile. Just submit the invoice to my department. We'll cut you a check. Sometime."

"Now, Steel, man, just be cool. Don't talk unless someone talks to you. Follow my lead. And"—Bile turned his red eyes toward Steel as he pulled into the hotel parking slot and stopped the van—"keep your anger in check. Got it? Vampires are cool." He pulled a pair of tiny, blue sunglasses out of his pocket. "You might want to put these on to cover up those baby blues."

Steel donned the sunglasses and felt Kane's hand on his shoulder.

"Here's your earpiece. I'll be here in the van. And Raffle will be right outside with an assault team if you need it. If you find Josh, grab him and get out of there. If you get into trouble, I can have backup in two minutes."

Bile flashed his fangs in a grin. "Let's go be one with the night."

The old hotel looked as if it should have been condemned. Maybe it had been. Steel followed Bile across the street and into the seedy entrance.

"Man, you have got to loosen up your step," Bile said. He handed

Steel a walking cane. "Use my cane. Move like an animal, a huge cat. Be stealthy and languid. You're a vampire, one of the children of the night."

Steel took the cane and tried to slow his cadence. He moved his legs in fluid strides as they went deeper into the musty interior of the hotel. Down a long hallway with peeling paint, toward the thundering sound of electric rock. The hall ended in a courtyard with huge, wooden doors opening into the ballroom. Mist curled from within, and Steel made out the movement of bodies in the far distance illuminated by pulsing strobe lights and the odd counterpoint of hundreds of candles.

A tall, willowy blonde in a low-cut dress met them at the main door. Blood trickled down the corners of her mouth. Her eyes were rimmed in black. Two red blotches on her neck trickled fake blood. "Good evening, gentlebeings. May I see your invitations?"

Bile pulled the invitation from his waistcoat. "Of course, my dear. Bile and his companion for the night."

The blonde glanced at the invitation and pointed to the open door. "You may enter at your own risk."

Steel swallowed and stepped into insanity. The ballroom was filled with a mass of moving, writhing people. To call them people was a stretch, for they were only human beneath their ghastly façades. Women were dressed in translucent gowns that moved with ghostly, ethereal breezes and barely concealed their bodies. Men with long hair, no hair, short hair, with piercings of all kinds wore everything from Victorian era clothing to leather. Leather and chains adorned androgynous figures that moved and swayed to the music. Throughout it all there was the pervasive fragrance of incense and the undeniable scent of blood. Steel felt his heart race with anxiety, and he tried to slow his breathing. The presence of evil threatened to drown him.

"My God," he whispered, "where are You tonight?"

Bile was instantly recognized by some of the women. They moved with languid ease to him with sultry questions about his absence from the scene. Men hovered around him to see his fangs. He glanced over his shoulder at Steel, and his face was flushed with excitement. It seemed he had missed this madness after all.

Steel cleared his mind. He grasped the cane and imagined himself one of the things moving around him. He tasted the blood on his lips. He inhaled the feral odors. He became a predator stalking the pulsing flesh around him. He stepped into the heaving mass of humanity and moved among the restless people like an animal. His senses grew more acute as if he had been on the hunt before. Diaphanous-gowned women leered at him with their fanged teeth exposed. Men glared at him with jealousy, recognizing him as an alpha male moving in on their territory. In one corner a group of men with long hair and wispy beards glared at him with yellow eyes. Werewolves? Their glares held a mixture of hate and grudging respect. He felt oddly at home on the hunt. He blended in with the mass of people and adopted their stances and their body language. Nearby an Asian woman stared at him and spoke to her friend in French. The lyrical words rolled over Steel like a wave of cold water, and he faded into the past.

"Can I have him now?"

Steel opened his eyes. He tried to rub them and found his hands bound to the side of the table.

"I suppose so." Dr. Monarch stepped into view, and Steel blinked tears away. She came into focus. "Just don't hit him in the head, or my surgery will be pointless."

Steel looked over at Mazi standing in the door of the room. His baseball bat protruded up over his shoulder; he wore it on his back in some kind of holster. "Good morning, Rouille."

Steel shook his head, and the pain took his breath away. "What?"

"That is your name from now on. Rouille. It is French for rust." Mazi laughed out loud until tears ran from his eyes. Mr. Kito pushed into the room and glared at Mazi.

"That is enough, Mazi. Good morning, Rouille."

"That's not my name," Steel said.

"It is from now on." Kito placed a backpack on a table next to the bed. "Beginning in the morning, you will be punished if you speak English. From now on you must speak French."

Kito opened the bag and removed a handful of clothes. "These are your clothes from a former life. They will be burned." He tossed them into a trash can. He reached into the bag and removed a pistol. "Ah, a gun. Would you like it, Rouille?"

Steel tried to sit up, but the cloth restraints pulled him back onto the bed. His head bounced on the pillow, and pain exploded behind his eyes. "If I had that pistol I would—"

"What? Kill me? How would your God like that, Rouille?" Kito handed the pistol to Mazi, who tucked it into his belt. Kito pulled out a leather notebook bound with elastic bands. It was stained and tattered. "Well, what have we here?"

Steel blinked away the pain as he looked at the notebook. "My notes."

Kito smiled and tossed it into the trash can with the clothes. "Then, like the rest of your past, it will be destroyed."

"No!" Steel shouted. "That has everything I've collected about my father. You can't destroy it. Look, let me go, and I promise you—"

"Rouille, you do not yet understand that there is nothing you can offer that will cause me to let you go. My job is to destroy the old you. My job is to convince you there is no God in your life. My job is to show you that all hope is lost."

"Votre Dieu vous a abandonné," Mazi said.

"Your God is dead," Kito said.

"Votre Dieu est mort," Mazi echoed in French.

"Minister Goimi is your god," Kito said.

"Goimi est votre dieu," Mazi smiled.

Steel swallowed. He now knew where he was. Youssouf Goimi was the defense minister of one of the many warring northern African states. He had led an armed insurgency against the president.

Kito reached into the bag and removed a leather-bound book. "Ah, and here we have something of interest. A Bible. How precious is your Word of God, Rouille?" Kito stepped closer and held the Bible close to Steel's face. "You can smell the leather. How old is this Bible?" Kito opened it. "To my wonderful son on his fifteenth birthday. Love, Mother."

Steel jerked against the restraints and suddenly found the tip of his own gun against his temple. Mazi shoved the cold metal harder against his head, and pain blinded him.

Kito closed the Bible. "How sentimentally sweet, Rouille. But it is part of your former life. From now on there is no God."

"Votre Dieu est mort." Mazi shoved the gun against his head.

"There is no hope." Kito held the book against his chest.

"Il n'y a pas d'espoir," Mazi whispered and laughed.

Kito handed the Bible to Mazi. "Mazi, would you like this book? Perhaps you can find some use for it."

Mazi pulled the gun away from Steel's temple and took the book. "I can use the pages for my smokes." He smiled at Steel.

Kito closed the backpack and placed his hands behind his back. "So, Rouille, we will take you now to your new home. Every day you will recite the phrases you have just heard in French. If you speak in English, you will be punished. There will be no books or signs or any written material available to you in English. You are now a citizen of this republic."

He turned to leave, and Mazi tucked the small Bible in his belt. "Votre Dieu vous a abandonné." He laughed.

The sounds of the crowd and the dusty odor of powdered wigs brought him back, and Steel blinked. Another flashback. His soul was gripped by the sensation of despair, and he had to shake his head to clear away the fog.

"I can't take these new vampires." Bile pointed to a cluster of incredibly beautiful women with pale skin and bright lips. Hovering around them were tall, handsome men in modern dress. Steel squinted through the blue sunglasses. Did their skin glitter?

"Why?"

"They don't even have the good sense to wear fangs! It's the twilight of our vampire era. Whatever. Forget 'em. That must be the new Grand Master." Bile pointed toward a stage set up at the far end of the banquet hall. Huge red banners fell from the ceiling behind the stage. The center banner carried the image of a wolf's head. At the foot of the stage stood Rudolph Wulf dressed in a long, gray cloak with a red ascot at his throat. He was talking to Vivian Darbonne Ketrick. Vivian glanced his way, and their gazes met, but she did not register recognition.

"Do you know him?" Steel asked.

"Never met him."

Wulf made his way through the crowd toward the wine table. "Let's pay our respects," Steel said as he pressed his way through the crowd toward Wulf. He shouldered aside white-faced vampires, dark-skinned vampires, and three girls in tall Marie Antoinette wigs. But Josh was nowhere in sight. He felt the evil emanating like waves in a pond as he grew closer to Rudoph Wulf.

"You must be the new Grand Master," Steel said in a slightly tenor voice.

Wulf surveyed him with a withering gaze, but his eyes filled with interest as he studied Steel. "Yes, I am. Have we met?"

Steel shook his head and kept his voice high pitched. He threw in a slightly perturbed British accent. "You haven't had the privilege."

"I have not, Mr...?"

The name floated up from oblivion. "Jeremiah. Just call me Jeremiah. I'd like you to meet my friend, Bile. He is a Fangmaster." Steel motioned behind him. Bile stepped forward and shook Wulf's hand. Bile's eyes widen at the man's touch.

"Rudolph Wulf. I see you are an empty spirit, Bile. Unlike your friend here, who seems to be a shining light in the darkness. Too bad. Jeremiah doesn't know what he is missing." Wulf released Bile's hand.

"You could give me vampire magick," Bile said eagerly.

"Be patient." Wulf turned his gaze on Steel. "I sense the spirit of good within you, Jeremiah. Poor choice. But it is not too late to rectify that mistake. You can join me tonight and embrace my vampire magick."

Steel remained calm. Did Wulf know who he was? "I am

considering a change, Grand Master Wulf. That is why I'm here. Bile agreed to introduce me to new friends tonight. I'm hoping I can become someone's thrall. I've been away from the life too long."

"Living among mundanes can be tiresome." Wulf smiled and exposed perfect teeth with fine, small fangs on each upper bicuspid. He lifted a goblet of red wine from one of the many tables and sipped.

"May I ask who made your fangs, Mr. Wulf?" Bile motioned to Wulf's face.

"No one. They're quite natural."

Bile sighed. The man was in vampire heaven!

"Bile, before this night is over, you will see vampire magick that will make such a feat seem like child's play. I can take your pitiful existence and give you true meaning and power. I can transform your miserable mundane life into one of grandeur and majesty. For you see, Bile, I am the most powerful creature on the face of this planet. For instance, it is now time for me to address the cattle around me from the dais. As you can see, it is across the room. But for me, it might as well be right here." He smiled and disappeared.

Bile drew in a sharp breath, and Steel stepped forward into the empty space where Wulf had been standing. A mighty rush of wind sounded from the stage area, and he turned to see a tornado of white mist materialize in a cone of light shining from the roof. The crowd gasped at the sudden wind rushing through their midst, and all eyes turned to the stage. Wulf materialized in the center of the whirlwind. His cloak flapped in the breeze, but his steel gray hair was unruffled.

"Welcome, my children." His voice boomed out over the audience as the wind died down. "I am your new Grand Master, Rudolph Wulf." He raised his hand and gestured through the air. A crimson flame materialized in his hand and swirled into the shape of a fiery orb. He let the orb roll around onto the back of his hand. The orb circled, defying gravity, and became a dark, pulsing object of deep crimson.

"I have ancient power, skilled in potions and ancient magick. There are those among you who are here because of your fascination with a fiction. Some of you have found meaning in the pages of books or the flickering images of film. When you leave this place, you will return to your mundane existences."

The dark red orb rolled up his arm and down his chest. It came to rest over his heart, pulsing with a dangerous rhythm. "But tonight, there are those among you who will take the first step away from your ordinary existence into the world of vampire power." Wulf's eyes blazed with demonic power as he leaned forward toward the audience, now pressed against the stage in anticipation. "I am here to give you true vampire magick."

A wave of awestruck wonder passed over the crowd as the fiery orb flowed through the cloak. Its pulsing rhythm grew louder as a reddish light glowed beneath the fabric. The sound of the beating heart grew stronger, and it pressed upon the skin of Steel's face, bouncing along the cortex of his bones and penetrating to his marrow. Steel grimaced at the subsonic pulse and resisted the urge to be mesmerized by its heady rhythm. Wulf gestured to the curtains behind him, and they dropped. Steel gasped at the sight of an upright coffin. A young woman lay motionless, only her eyes moving in panic, paralyzed. Wulf leaned in to her. Suddenly his face changed, his lips enlarged, and his face became that of a wolf. His fangs gleamed in the pulsating light, and he ravaged the girl's throat. Blood sprayed into the air, and the girl's scream was muffled by Wulf's transformed face.

Some in the crowd screamed; others gasped in wonder. Wulf pulled away, and the girl's head slumped to the side, barely attached to her motionless body. The snout disappeared, and Wulf turned to the audience. Blood dripped from his silver hair and ran down his chin. For a moment Steel saw the beast within, and then Wulf smiled and wiped his mouth with his sleeve. "Some of you are horrified. But as easily as I have taken life, I can return it." He passed his hand over the girl's torn throat, and blinding, red light blossomed. Steel blinked, and when he looked up again, the girl was awake, restored and smiling.

"Master," she said as he offered his hand. She stepped out of the coffin, and the crowd murmured in amazement. Wulf handed her off to Armando.

"For long you have supped of each other's blood." Wulf's hand reached toward the ceiling. "But I will give you a new blood filled with power and vampire magick. Many of you will flee this night. Do not return to this lifestyle. For I desire only those who would give themselves totally to my cause. Behold!"

With a final gesture toward the ceiling, Wulf's eyes glowed with fire, and the heartbeat became all encompassing. With its final beat the ceiling exploded in a shower of red. Steel looked up at the fire sprinkler system. Each spout gushed with blood. It showered down upon him, warm and copper scented. The crowd went wild as the blood covered them. Steel stepped farther back into the alcove, only then remembering the earpiece.

"Sue, it's raining blood in here," he shouted.

"We're coming in," she said. But the sound was drowned out by the roar of the crowd, which had split in two. One group pressed toward the stage; the other tried to flee. In the confusion Steel was shoved backward. Bloody handprints covered his coat. Blood coated his hair and ran down his face.

"Steel, we can't get in!" Sue's voice echoed in his ear, and then the earpiece was knocked out of his ear as he fell beneath the rushing crowd. Steel struggled to get away from the stomping feet. His blue glasses were crushed. The cane rolled away. He crawled through sticky, coagulating blood beneath a table.

Soon the fleeing crowd thinned, and about two hundred people were left. He glanced out from under the table at the crowd, whose faces were turned upward toward the falling blood. They were enthralled by Wulf's magick, forever given over to his cause.

"Silence!" Wulf's voice thundered above the sound of the crowd. Crimson-streaked faces beneath blood-clotted hair hovered above drenched clothing. Like one creature the crowd turned to Wulf. "I can take it away as easily as I give it," he said as he stood in his cone of bright light, untouched by the falling blood.

The blood falling from the ceiling thinned and drew clear. It became water. The crowd milled, and their voices grew hushed in reverence. "Would you like to have vampire magick such as this?" Wulf asked the crowd. A thunderous wave of assent answered him. "Then we shall journey to a sacred place where I will bestow on all true believers this power."

Vivian and Armando stepped out onto the stage behind him. "My assistants will give you further instructions. Divide into your clans, and we shall tell you how this power can be yours. Seek among you for the unbelievers, and turn them over to me. Go out and find true believers, and recruit them for my cause."

Steel crawled out from under the table and looked down at himself. His clothes were soaked with water, not blood. It had all been an illusion. Steel heard his name above the crowd. Bile stood on the stage beside Vivian and was pointing in his direction. He ran.

Steel shoved aside vampires and frightened men and women. All the while he eagerly scanned the faces for Josh. But Josh was not here. He emerged through the open doors into the night air. Kane had several squad cars parked near the entrance screening the panicked patrons.

Steel tugged off his soaked wig and tossed it aside. "It's a mad-house in there. I couldn't find Josh. Did you see him?"

"No sign of him."

"You promised me we would find him. You let them all get away." He shouted as his anger took over.

Kane pointed a finger at him. "Hundreds of people poured out of there, Steel. We're lucky no one died in the stampede. We couldn't stop anyone! And there wasn't a drop of blood in sight! Do you realize how many men I mobilized for this? How many wasted man-hours went into this raid? Can you imagine how this is going to look downtown? Steel, you've just made a fool out of me."

"Lieutenant Kane, you've got to believe me. Wulf is capable of manipulating dimensions of space and creating illusions. He turned the water into blood and then back again. Josh must still be in there somewhere."

Kane fumed and sputtered as she pointed to her earpiece. "My men are inside now, Steel. The ballroom is empty. The only people left are the ones who panicked after you screamed it was raining blood. Wulf isn't there. And there's no sign of Armando. I imagine Josh is still with them. The night was a total waste."

Steel opened his mouth to protest, and Kane poked him in the chest with a finger. "If I hear one more mention of demons tonight, I'm going to skin you alive. I'll call you if we get any leads on Josh." She turned and stalked away.

[Chapter 20]

IT WAS LONG after midnight when Steel pulled into the backyard. He climbed out of the Mustang and put the convertible top back and secured the tarp over it. He leaned against the car and stared up at the sky. Where was Josh? He hadn't been at the Bloodfest, and the idea of Josh in the hands of Wulf made him clench his fists. He pounded the fender in frustration. When he stopped, the pounding continued. He raised his fists before him. Where was the pounding coming from? The wooden fence in front of him exploded in splintered wood, and he threw his arms up.

Something huge hurtled across the yard and thudded against the car. Steel looked up into the face of a wolf man. The thing grabbed him by the shoulders with taloned hands and lifted him off the ground.

"Where is it?"

Steel saw another man climb through the hole in the fence. He was similar to the wolf thing but had glowing red eyes and fangs.

"I'll go inside and find the vials, love," the vampire said. "Save me a bite."

Steel struggled in the thing's grasp and kicked out at his groin. It was like kicking concrete. "I'm wondering, mate, if like your name, your blood is full of iron. Let's find out!"

The thing opened its mouth, and yellow fangs dripped with saliva. Suddenly the vampire twin rocketed across the yard and collided with them. The twins tumbled into trash cans, and Steel rolled as he hit the ground. Theo appeared at his side.

"Where'd they go?"

"Over there."

Theo went after the twins, and the three huge shapes came together with the sound of flesh and muscle impacting. Steel stumbled to his feet, and Theo bounced past him into the fence. He suddenly found himself in the grasp of the vampire twin.

"You'd best bloody well tell me where they are." He lifted him bodily and hurled him across the yard. Steel landed on the roof of the Mustang. The blue plastic tarp ripped, and the weight of his body tore through the old fabric roof. He fell into the car's interior into the backseat of the convertible.

Against the blue tarp he watched shadows dance around the car. He had to get out and help Theo, but the tarp was tied around the base of the car and prevented him from shoving the doors open. He had to climb out through the tear in the roof. He smelled gasoline. A bright light flared, and the tarp exploded with fire. In seconds the entire car was engulfed in flames.

Steel slid through the gap behind the backseat into the trunk. He pushed against the trunk, but it wouldn't move. The air grew hot and stifling as smoke filled the car. "Help!" he screamed. He pressed his feet against the interior of the trunk lid and kicked with all his might, but nothing happened. Suddenly he heard the ruffle of canvas, and the trunk flew open. A hand reached through the smoke and grabbed his arm. He was pulled bodily from the car and led through the smoke into the nearby bushes.

The explosion drove them both to their knees. Steel looked back through the bushes as the Mustang was engulfed in a huge ball of fire. Burning tarp and metal showered down around the backyard and onto the roof of the house. Steel stood up and saw Theo slumped in the grass, surrounded by burning debris. Who had pulled him from the car?

"Are you okay, son?"

Steel turned and looked into the face of Cephas Lawrence.

It took most of the rest of the night for the fire department to put out the flames. Theo was bruised but unhurt. The fire had burned up the garage, the kitchen and most of the living room. Parked in front of the house was Steel's RV, unblemished. Inside, Steel collapsed at his computer table and looked at Cephas Lawrence's tired eyes.

"You have fangs." Cephas said as he brushed ashes out of his huge mustache.

Steel sighed and popped the fangs out of his mouth and tossed them in the sink. "So did those twins. Your timing is perfect, Cephas."

Cephas's bushy white hair was filled with flecks of dirt and ash. "All the flights into Dallas were delayed, but there was one flight that could get me to Shreveport. Aha, I said. I can get my good friends in Lakeside to loan me a car. Imagine my surprise when Dr. Washington showed up at the airport to pick me up in your repaired RV. So I wasted no time driving over from Shreveport."

"Liz is in Lakeside?" Dr. Elizabeth Washington had helped Steel with the thirteenth demon and had promised to return to the site of the church with a state order to study the Inca connection. The church had been built on a huge mound civilization that had been conquered by the thirteenth demon centuries before.

"She has returned to the missionary house to oversee the excavation of the church site. She has several college students helping, and I would say she is quite happy. The repair shop had returned your RV just yesterday. I'm afraid I owe you the money it took to fix it. I was the one who suggested to Claire that she ram it into the jail." He fell silent, and tears came to his eyes. "Why in the world did I suggest she come and help you, Jonathan? It is my fault my only niece is dead."

"No, I should have listened to you. I should have walked away from this one." Steel drew a deep breath. "I promised Claire I would keep Josh safe. Now, he's gone again."

Steel looked over Cephas's head to a picture hanging on the wall. April Pierce and her father, Richard, smiled back at him. They had been happy until he came into their lives. Now, both of them were dead. Claire and Josh had a normal life until he came into their lives. "Cephas, what have I done? Why do these things keep happening to the people I care about?"

Cephas reached over and patted his hand. "Do you realize what you just said?"

Steel shook his head. "What?"

"The people you *care* about. When I first met you, your only motive was revenge. You were a man driven by fury and violence. Now look how far you have come.

"Followers of Christ are often asked how our God can allow so much suffering. Why doesn't He stop it? But the truth is, God gives us the ability to choose. We are not robots, Jonathan. And in those choices rests the possibility of good and evil."

"Evil I get. It's always there." Steel's fists closed. He felt the righteous indignation build, felt the anger surge. "They keep coming at us and coming at us and I keep trying to stop them and they keep hurting us." He pounded the tabletop.

"They do not sleep or rest, Jonathan. But neither does our God. And here is where you must find your strength. For in these episodes of evil, God has grown you. God has changed you. You are a better person now, a stronger person, a person who cares. God uses people for His purposes, and sometimes it is the processes He uses that confuse us. Jonathan, God can use evil for good. He used the greatest evil ever when Christ was nailed to the cross. And out of that has come the greatest good ever. Take comfort in the fact you now *care*. Take comfort in the fact that you can see beyond your own selfish needs to the needs of others. Let that righteous fury give you power, and, with God, nothing will stop you from defeating this twelfth demon. You will find Josh again. And when you do, you must not be angry with him. You must *care* for him."

The RV rocked as Theo stepped in. "So, you must be Jonathan's pop."

Cephas chuckled. "Dr. Cephas Lawrence. And you must be Theophilus King. You know theophilus means one who 'loves God.'"

Theo nodded. "Well, I ain't done too well with that, but Jonathan helped me find a second chance." He leaned against the sink, his sweaty skin caked with ashes. "Chief, I don't know what those two things were. But if I had been in better shape, I would have taken both of them."

Steel glanced at the huge man. "I think you made your presence known. They were after the vials of blood. Which means that Vivian sent them."

"Vivian?" Cephas leaned back in his chair. "Perhaps you should tell me everything."

Raven stood in the darkened hotel suite, one sliver of light from the barely opened curtains painting a stripe down her face. She remained as still as possible while her mind reeled with confusion. She had always been on top of things, but now her carefully planned life was crumbling. She had botched the Atchison job. And then she had failed with Wulf. At least he wasn't human.

But Steel was a different story. Her hand went to the amulet around her neck. She lifted it into the light and studied the round silver surface. Why she kept it, she didn't know. But with the arrival of Vivian and Wulf, her moral free world was crumbling around her. Her carefully constructed walls of denial were falling down brick by brick.

Steel had returned from the dead, and it reminded her of someone else who had returned from the dead. There was a time when all of her allegiance had been to Him. But then Lucas had showed up in her life and pointed her down another path. Her devotion to a Savior was buried deep beneath her desire to maim and destroy anything that reminded her of her stepfather.

The phone rang, and she jerked in the darkness of her room. She stared at the blinking red light on the hotel phone as it rang and rang until it fell silent.

Even with the lights off, she knew where she had placed each string in her room. The intricate web of colored twine gathered all the loose threads of her latest endeavor. Pictures of Atchison and Wulf were tacked to one wall. Hotel stationary with one word scrawled on it, "Steel," hung beside the picture of Vivian Ketrick fixed above her bed. When Raven came to Dallas, she had been in control of these strings. Now she felt like a marionette at the hands of an unseen puppeteer. She deftly slid through the strings without touching them and pressed the message button.

"Raven, you know who this is. Do I need to speak the phrase? I hope not. I know you have run into my son. I know you want to kill him. Forgive me for never telling you that he lived. But I have my reasons. I am instructing you to leave him alone. Do not kill him. I will deal with my son in my own way."

Raven listened to the crisp, clear tones and shuddered. How had the Captain found her? But then, did she really need to ask that question? He was always there, lurking in the background with his intense gaze fixed on those he owned, yet another string to snare her in the web she was growing desperate to break loose from. She stood in the midst of all her tangled strings, and her gaze settled on the white paper with Steel's name. It wasn't his true name, and even he did not know this. Should she tell him? She ran a finger through the dark, blue twine that held the amulet to her chest. She slid between the strings until she stood before his name. Truth was, she was relieved. She did not want to kill the man. She drew a shuddering breath.

"I hate you because I still love you," she whispered. He had come back into her life and had brought with him a love that threatened to destroy her carefully constructed world.

"Walk away, Victoria," she whispered. "Walk away, and don't turn back." But the words couldn't stop her from reaching out to touch the name.

Someone knocked at her door. She quietly eased through the strings and peeked through the peephole. The face of a hotel bellhop looked back at her. She stepped back from the door and glanced at her watch. It was four in the morning. Why would a bellhop come to her room this late? She eased quietly across the room to the window and paused long enough to pick up her backpack. Everything that was important to her was in the backpack, except for her rifle tucked away somewhere in an evidence locker.

Outside the window hung an old-fashioned fire escape. She had chosen the old hotel just for that reason. She pulled back the curtain and reached for the latch on the window. A shadow passed across the window, and she looked up into the hideous face of a massive man. He plunged through the window, sending shards of glass showering over Raven's head.

Raven rolled backward across the floor just as her door

exploded inward and filled the dark room with light from the hallway. The bellhop fell face forward into the room as the same massive man who had burst through the window now stepped over the bellhop's body.

Raven rolled away just as a huge fist passed through the air where her face had been. She kicked out with her foot and felt like she hit rock. The first man exhaled air, stumbled back, and tangled himself in the strings. Papers pulled from the wall and floated in the air. The first man, blindly swatting at the strings, crashed into the second man. They spun, entangling themselves even more, and Raven hurried through the door leading to the adjacent hotel room, locking it behind her. She always rented adjacent rooms. She hurried to the window. This window did not open onto a fire escape, but she had set up a thin bungee cord as an escape from just such an attack.

She opened the window and snared the harness just outside, stepping into it just as the two killers banged on the door behind her. Raven fell through the open window and passed into the shadowy darkness cast by an adjacent building that eclipsed the almost full moon. She could no longer be seen from the window. The thin bungee cord became taut, and she felt it slow her descent. She looked down to grab the edge of an awning and keep from bouncing back upward. Secured against the dark embraces of the awning, out of sight of the roof, she triggered the release mechanism. The cord fell away from the window and into a drainage ditch filled with dirty water.

Raven glanced over the edge of the awning back toward the roof. One of the men leaned out the window and looked down toward the drainage ditch.

"Think she's dead, love?" he growled as huge hands tore at the strings around his body.

The other man leaned out of the window. "Bloody sure. No one could have survived that fall."

"We could have, love."

"Too bad we couldn't take her head back to Vivian. Think she'll believe us?"

The first man shrugged and tossed a wad of strings into the air. "Don't care if she does, love. We done what we came to do."

Vivian had wanted her dead? And to think, just moments ago, she was toying with the idea of giving it all up. But now Vivian was fair game.

[Chapter 21]

OSH LOOKED ACROSS the hangar floor at the huge airplane on the tarmac. Already more than two hundred followers of Rudolph Wulf were on board and waiting for their journey to somewhere. And Ila was with them.

"Penny for your thoughts?" A voice whispered in his ear. Vivian stood beside him swathed in a flowing, diaphanous red dress. "I wish you could have been at the Bloodfest."

"I couldn't. I'm your prisoner."

The morning breeze ruffled Vivian's hair, and she studied him with her dark eyes. "You know, if you turn to our side, you could still save Ila."

"Save her from what? You?"

Vivian's face paled, and she glanced around her. "From Wulf. He is the twelfth demon. And he wants Ila for a special ceremony Friday night. Midnight. In Transylvania."

"Another sacrifice like the one in Lakeside?"

"What Wulf has planned makes that sacrifice look like a tea party. Now, you can renounce your beliefs and commit the unpardonable sin and join me, and I will see to it Ila is freed."

Josh shook his head. "Unpardonable sin?"

"It's in your Bible, Josh. There is a sin from which you can never be forgiven. But you must do so willingly. Now! Hurry!"

"Why are you in such a hurry?"

Vivian looked around her. "Because."

"You have your own agenda, just like you did with that Ketrick dude."

Vivian glanced away. "Do you want to save Ila or not?"

"Save Ila from what?" A deep voice boomed from behind. Josh watched Vivian's face blanch, and he glanced over her shoulder. A man dressed in a gray cloak stepped up behind her.

"I was just filling Josh in on our plan."

The man gently pushed her aside, his menacing gray eyes fixed on Josh. He emanated a sense of ancient power. "And you must be Joshua Knight come to rescue the fair maiden from the evil vampire clan."

"Dude, I came because Ila asked me to join the clan. I've turned my back on the world." Josh tried to sound convincing.

"You can't fool me, Joshua Knight. I am Rudolph Wulf, though you would know me better as the twelfth demon. I understand that for a while, you were graced with the presence of the thirteenth demon. Is that true?"

"Look, it wasn't graceful—" Josh stopped talking as Wulf drew closer. The memory of the fire in the church basement filled his mind, and he closed his eyes. "I just want to help Ila."

Wulf smiled, and Josh was shocked by the fangs. "Vivian, I think our little hero came here to emulate Jonathan Steel. To be the knight in shining armor. So pure, so righteous. He is a man without guile." Wulf cocked his head as he studied Josh. "Yes, he will do. He will be the one. Fitting, don't you think?"

Vivian's eyes shifted from Wulf to Josh. "He will be the messenger?"

"Of course. He is perfect." Wulf turned back to Josh. "You've been chosen for a very special task, young man. And if you do not cooperate, I will make certain your little girlfriend suffers a very painful fate. Do you understand?"

"Yes."

Wulf nodded and tapped a cane on the floor, and then disappeared. Josh blinked in confusion, searching the dark shadows of the hangar.

Vivian shook her head. "You fool! Now I have no other choice but to play along." Before Josh could ask her why, he heard footsteps scratching on the graveled roof. Two hulking figures came into view.

"Hullo, love," Spike said. "Sorry about your house, mate."

"Sorry about the car too. Bloody explosion," Fang said.

Vivian glared at the two men. "I sent them to retrieve a package Steel had stolen from me, and they inadvertently blew up your father's Mustang with Jonathan in it."

"Would have loved to taste that iron-rich blood. Bet it was bloody tasty," Fang said.

Josh gasped for breath. "I don't believe you."

"Doesn't matter. You'll die knowing you managed to do what you set out to do. Saving sweet little Ila." Vivian turned her attention back to Spike. "What about the other target?"

Spike shrugged and handed a leather pouch to Vivian. "Right out the window, love. Six stories up."

Vivian smiled and opened the pouch. Several vials of blood were tucked inside. Vivian ran a finger over the inner lining.

"Seems the memory card with Wulf's life story is missing." She smiled. "Too bad!"

"If Steel had it, it's nothing but melted goo," Spike said.

Vivian seemed to relax even more. "I have already accessed that data. No problem. Now, Josh, Fang found this in your backpack." Fang held up Josh's tablet. "I'll go over this with a fine-toothed comb to see what you've been writing in your little diary. And I gave the pistol to Wulf. Let's go."

"Can I have a few moments alone? Please."

Vivian leaned into him. "You should have listened to me. I could have gotten you out of this. But I'll give you a moment of silence with your God. He won't help you, I'm afraid. Soon we leave for Transylvania. We're on a tight schedule."

Vivian walked away, and the twins followed her into the shadowy hangar. Josh turned to gaze at other airplanes coming and going in the sky. In the east the horizon began to glow with the light of a new morning. Jonathan couldn't be dead. They were lying. What was he going to do? He patted his pants pockets and felt the iPhone. He slid it out and turned it on. He opened the e-mail program and discovered he had a connection. Quickly he put in his mother's old e-mail address, glancing over his shoulder. The twins were coming his way. He had time for only a quick message. His fingers danced over the virtual keyboard, and he touched the send button before he dropped the phone in his pocket and turned.

"I'm ready to go."

Spike blew foul breath in Josh's face and grinned. "Didn't put up much of a fight, love. Your friend."

Josh swallowed and prayed the man was lying to him.

[Chapter 22]

Interlude

LEASE, SIR, I think we should end these sessions."

"You have no choice in the matter, doctor."

"But these memories you're recounting can't possibly be true. You must be delusional. I can give you a medication—"

"Doctor, how is your daughter?"

"My daughter? She's fine. She's at school."

"Would you take a look at this picture?"

"It's my daughter. Who is this man?"

"He is my assistant, doctor. He will make sure nothing happens to your daughter as long as you continue to help me recover my memories. Do you understand?"

"You fiend!"

"I've been called worse. Shall we continue?"

"Very well. Listen to my voice, and continue to find your lost memories."

From the Annals of Saitnoxis
Translated by Rudolph Wulf
The forests of Sibiu
Wallachia, medieval Romania
Circa 1457

I watched the knight's nose wrinkle in disgust at the smell of death that drifted on the forest breeze. Amusing? Yes, and soon to be his undoing.

"My lord, do you find the food sufficient?" I asked the man sitting at the table. Eyes of liquid black turned in my direction. His slash of a moustache dripped with wine.

"It is merely sufficient, my good Saitnoxis. Perhaps if I had something fresh to drink." He held up his goblet. I clapped my hands, and a servant scurried to the table, which sat among the beautiful ferns and greenery of the forest.

"Take the master's cup, and bring him something fresh," I commanded.

The servant's eyes widened, but he dared not disobey. "Yes, Lord Saitnoxis." He took the goblet from the hands of Count Vlad and headed off toward the distant bodies of men, women, and children writhing on their stakes. I had tried to keep count of the dying, but the numbers were overwhelming. It was the festival of St. Bartholomew, and thousands of people thronged the city. Vlad had decided to let them celebrate the holiday at his own, unique outside feast. Only they weren't meant to dine with him, but to die for him.

"And why did you choose these people to die?" I asked.

"They are bourgeoisie, and they do not deserve to live. Are you getting squeamish?" He picked at his teeth with the point of a knife.

"My lord, it was I who introduced you to the art of impaling. I am the one who told you about Zamolxis and the ritual of his messenger. Although, my lord, you have elevated the process to an art." I reached for a goblet and drank of the wine. It was indeed stale. I spat it onto the ground, and Vlad laughed.

"See yon stake? The large man wriggling in pain. He is in charge of the winery here at Sibiu. He should not have let his wine grow stale. Ah, Saitnoxis, you have been a long and faithful friend, and you have taught me much of treachery. And to think that I almost listened to that coward, Rufen. He suggested I show mercy. Can you imagine?"

Ah, yes, Rufen. My old nemesis had tried to intervene early in Vlad's reign. But Vlad's soul was far too stained with bloodshed and malice. He had passed over a fine line into the realm of utter darkness. His soul was truly evil.

Rufen had been easily defeated. A thousand years of heinous acts by man had almost erased the faint glimmer of goodness that Rufen had seen in those few souls who surrounded Zamolxis. Yes, the battles had been won, and even more handily in recent centuries. We only had a few more centuries before the Event would come round again. And this time we would let nothing stand in our way.

Vlad belched. "You really saw an impaling to the god Zamolxis?"

"I was there." My vision faded into the distant past through the many hosts to the writhing, anguished army buried at Kogain awaiting their redemption. "You remember I am an old soul."

"In a young body," Vlad commented. The servant appeared with a goblet stained with crimson. He set it carefully on the table before

Vlad. Vlad took a piece of bread and dipped it into the red fluid. He slurped it, and the blood stained his teeth. "Very good. It is still warm. You may go."

The servant fell over himself getting away from his fiendish master. I must admit I was proud. Never had I so corrupted a human. Never had any human even begun to approach the level of evil and corruption that was Vlad the Impaler. I studied his pale features and the red pendant at his throat. On the pendant a red dragon was crucified on two crosses.

"You are of the Order of the Dragon—like your father. I was there when the banner of the Wolf Dragon was first hoisted over the Dacians. How things have changed and evolved over the centuries. I met with Clavius and saw to his ascendency in the Roman Senate. I was there when the carpenter was crucified. Speaking of which, I find it amusing that you wear a pendant representing your devotion to the church's order to eradicate all heathen, and yet you practice such heinous acts."

Vlad turned his dark eyes in my direction. Had I pushed him too far? His lips suddenly transformed from a scowl to a smile. "I am filled with contradictions, Saitnoxis. My father was of the Order of the Dragon. I carry on his work in my own just ways." His gaze shifted suddenly to the knight. "You, knight, are you troubled?"

The knight I had seen earlier jerked as he heard his name called. He stood at attention at the corner of the feasting area, but he had been careless. "My lord?"

Vlad arose and strode across the clearing. He motioned to four men at the other corner of the feasting area. As they hastened toward him, Vlad studied the knight's face.

"You wrinkle your nose. Do you mock this situation?"

"No, my lord. I would never mock you."

Vlad motioned to the thousands of bodies impaled on stakes scattered down the hillside and across the valley toward the gleaming city of Sibiu. "These who have died deserve their fate. I am the hand of their justice. How many are there?"

The knight began to sweat, and the whites of his eyes showed. "Upward of twenty thousand, my lord."

"And their odor, so pleasant to my nostrils, offends you?"

"No, my lord. My stomach churns, but—" He swallowed hard and fought for control. "I am not of the stout heart that my prince be."

The other men had reached them by now, and Vlad motioned toward the distant stakes. "Why would I want in my service a man who cannot look at death without vomiting? Death is a soldier's livelihood! You will join the others, but because you have been loyal until today, we will hoist you higher than the rest that you do not have to smell your company!"

The knight fell on the ground, groveling and pleading for mercy. The four men began to drag him, screaming, toward the distant stakes. Vlad returned to the table and tossed aside the coagulating blood in his goblet. He drew a deep breath and sat in his throne.

"The weight of leadership is great, but its rewards are even greater. Who could ever have such power as this, eh, Saitnoxis?"

I shrugged. "None, my lord."

Vlad watched as the knight was stripped and impaled on a high stake towering far above the others. "What will they say of me one day, Saitnoxis? Will they call me a butcher? Will they call me a madman?"

"There will be those who will see your brilliance, my lord," I said.

Vlad smiled and exposed sharp teeth stained with the remnants of his victim's blood. In the distance the sun was setting behind the stakes. It was a moving and glorious sight. "Thanks to you, Saitnoxis, I will be one of the most famous leaders ever to reign. You have made me great."

"I have made you a monster," I whispered. But Vlad had not heard me, as his ears were cocked to the wind.

"Do you hear that?"

In the distant depths of the forest, the bay of wolves echoed eerily into the coming evening. Could there ever be a more wondrous moment than this? The wolves, the dragon, the beast…all in one place surrounded by sweet, delicious bloody death.

"I hear them, my lord."

Vlad leaned back in his chair, and a tear rolled down from one eye. "The children of the night. What glorious music they make!"

Theo had cooked up a fine breakfast in the RV, but Steel chewed his pancakes mechanically, his mind focused elsewhere. Cephas held up the tiny computer chip Steel had taken from the pouch. "Where did you get this?"

"It was in the pouch with the vials of blood. Vivian will find out soon enough it's gone, and then she'll freak out. I'm hoping it may have some information on it that will help find Josh." Steel pointed to Claire's laptop. It had survived the fire. "I tried to access it. It's encrypted."

Cephas sipped at his coffee, then rubbed his huge moustache in thought. "While you were in the shower, I managed to get Liz to download the contents to her computer back in Lakeside.

One of her students is an expert in codes and encryption. We'll see what they come up with. Now, what was this about the unpardonable sin?"

Steel leaned back in his chair and glanced at Theo hunched over the tiny stove. "Vivian said Josh could commit the unpardonable sin, and then she could claim his soul."

Theo chewed on a piece of bacon as he leaned against the counter. "Ain't gonna happen, Chief. I should know. I was a preacher once."

Cephas nodded. "I need a piece of paper and a pencil."

Theo retrieved a notebook and handed it to Cephas. Cephas opened the notebook to a blank page and drew a line across the center. Cephas pointed to the left end of the line. "This is based on the excellent work of Dr. Hugh Ross. Have you heard of him?"

Steel felt a tug at his heart. "He was one of Claire's favorite authors."

"Exactly. He wrote an interesting book called *Beyond the Cosmos*. It's about the extra-dimensional nature of God. Specifically he talks about the tug of war man feels between his free will and the will of God versus the will of Satan."

"Here at this end of the line, imagine evil." He wrote the word in big letters. Then he pointed to the other end of the line. "And at the other extreme, good." He wrote the word in bigger letters. "Man lives on this spectrum between evil and good. The concepts are there from the moment of birth. So every choice we make with our free will moves us along this line between the two extremes."

Cephas wrote "Satan" above the word *evil* and "God" above the word *good*. "There are two other forces that affect our will. Satan's will pulls us toward the evil end of the spectrum. God's will pulls us toward the good end of the spectrum. We all know that God's power is far greater than Satan's, but God loves us enough to give us free will. So there are three forces at work. If our will joins in the direction of evil, then we move closer to Satan's will. If our will joins with God's, then we move closer to the good end. And the closer we get to either end, the stronger is the influence of that will."

Cephas marked a perpendicular line across the line close to the word *good.* "This is a point of no return. It is the threshold of salvation. As we draw closer to God by the increasing power of His Spirit and will in our lives, we make a conscious decision to give everything over to His mastery. We become transformed into a new creature. We cross this threshold, and now, we belong to God."

Cephas pointed the pencil at Steel. "It is my opinion that once we pass this line, we can still move back and forth between it and the better goodness of a closer relationship with God. But we can never pass back through the threshold to Satan's end of the line. Once we belong to God, He will never let us go."

Cephas pointed to the end next to Satan. "At the same time, there is also a threshold at this end of the line." He drew a second line across the longer line. "As the Holy Spirit works in our lives to try and move us back toward God, our will and Satan's will draw us closer and closer to this line. When we cross this threshold, God realizes that we have totally rejected the workings of the Holy Spirit within us. Jesus talked about this in the Gospel of Matthew. He said to blaspheme the Holy Spirit was the unforgivable sin. That means total rejection of God's urgings to move back toward Him. Now, what you must realize, Jonathan, is that God makes the decision to remove His will from your life. He gives that person over to the deepest, most horrid depths of evil because that is what the person desires. Once the person moves beyond this line, they are unforgivable because they have repeatedly and finally rejected God's mercy and forgiveness."

"Where would Ketrick be on this line?" Steel asked.

Cephas pointed to the space between the unforgivable sin line and the word Satan. "In this area. So, it would seem, is Wulf."

"Vivian?"

Cephas rubbed his moustache. "It is not my place to judge, Jonathan. But it would seem Vivian is still struggling."

"Then she hasn't crossed the line yet."

"Who is to say? Only God can say." Cephas shrugged.

Steel studied the other end of the line. "Then Josh has nothing to worry about?"

"If he belongs to God, then he will be fine. That doesn't mean he is incapable of doing wrong. Remember, he can move back and forth within the range between the salvation threshold and the perfection of God."

"Could he kill?"

Cephas's eyes flew open. "What?"

Steel looked at the line, his mind seething with an unwanted thought. It wasn't Josh he was thinking of now. It was Raven. Why, he couldn't begin to fathom. Why would he think that Raven belonged on the good end of the line? The woman was an assassin. His skin grew cold. Where was he on this line? How close had he come to committing the unforgivable sin in his past? A new memory seized his mind, and he was somewhere else.

"My friend, if they hear us speak in English, they will punish you again."

Steel glanced over his head toward the small hole in the wall of his cell. A hazel eye gleamed from the other room. The hole was his only communication with the outside world once the iron door was locked. "Rafe, I cannot be punished any more than I am."

The eye blinked. "You must not give up hope, my friend. God has not abandoned you."

Steel felt the anger stoke within him. "Hasn't He? I've served God for years. I have searched the world over to stop this madness. And this is how I am rewarded?"

The eye moved away from the hole. Steel watched the man's dark hair pass across the hole. Rafe sat in profile in the next room. His face was covered with a heavy, black beard. "How long have we known each other?"

Steel laughed. "All I know of you is what I can see through that hole in the cinder blocks."

"You know my voice."

Steel blinked and turned his gaze away. "Yes, I know your voice better than your face."

"It is not the voice that is important. It is the words," he whispered, "and you must not forget the words we have spoken. You must not forget the promise that waits for you outside these walls."

Steel felt despair settle over him. "I'll never see the outside of these walls, Rafe. I'll die here. My only friend a disembodied eye and a gentle voice."

"He is coming, my friend. Do not give in to the hopelessness." The hazel eye flashed for a second behind the hole and then disappeared. The sound of a bat tapping against the cinder blocks alerted Steel, and he sat up abruptly as the iron door opened. Mazi eclipsed the light in the hallway as he stepped into the cell and hunkered over Steel.

"Get up, Rouille," he said in flawed French. In the past six months Steel had learned to understand the man. He never let on that he knew French very well.

"Mazi. Go away," he managed to say in halting French.

Mazi swung the bat, and it caught Steel in the left shoulder. He slid off the cinder-block bed and fell onto the floor. "I will be back in one hour with a new job for you. It is time for a promotion, Rouille." Mazi laughed, and Steel retched with the pain in his shoulder. He had lost weight and muscle mass, and the bat had bruised the bone in his upper arm.

Mazi slammed the door to the cell, and Steel groveled on the floor. For months he had not heard a single word in English outside the few snatches of time in which Rafe spoke to him from the other cell. If Steel was caught speaking English, he paid for it with a blow from Mazi's bat.

Every day he was taken to a room with dozens of other prisoners. There they were forced to read Marx and Engels. They were forced to listen to speeches by the glorious leader of the rebellion. There were daily diatribes against God. God was dead. God had abandoned him. He was alone. In that room Steel searched the empty faces for Rafe. He was there somewhere, but they were to keep their eyes averted from anyone else. Eye contact was punished with more beatings.

Steel fell back onto the slimy floor and felt his body quiver with sobs. Tears ran down the sides of his face. He looked up at the dark ceiling and felt nothing. Five years before he had given his life and heart to Jesus Christ. He had changed. True, he had done some things in the past few years that were unsavory. But it was because of his quest.

Now, he felt empty. He felt abandoned. He tried to look beyond the dark ceiling. He tried to recall the beauty of the stars and the majesty of the heavens. He had not been outside in months.

"God…are You there?" he sobbed. Silence answered him. "If You are real, give me a sign."

Mazi threw open the door and pounded the bat against the wall. Steel jerked with the sound of the blow and sat up.

"Rouille"—he pointed to the bucket in the corner—"you get to clean the latrines."

Steel sank deeper into despair. This was God's sign? Mazi pulled him to his feet and pointed to the bucket. "Take your filth with you. There will be no prisoner coming by to empty your bucket tonight. Instead you will empty the buckets on this hallway. Then you will go outside and clean the latrines."

Steel picked up his bucket, and the odor washed over him. He retched, and Mazi shoved him through the open door. Noxious liquid splashed from the bucket across his chest. He emptied twenty buckets into a huge barrel. Then Mazi directed him to roll the barrel out the door. Steel did not even notice the sky above as he was led across the prison yard to the latrine house.

It was a low-lying structure of cinder blocks with a tin roof. Inside, wooden toilet seats rested on beams suspended above metal troughs filled with excrement. At one end of the room Mazi motioned to a hole in the ground.

"This pipe leads to an underground stream. Dump the barrel into the hole. Then scrape out the contents of each of the five latrine troughs into the barrel and dump that into the hole." Mazi lifted Steel's chin up with the end of the bat. "Then rinse, lather, and repeat."

He laughed and shoved Steel backward across the wooden beam. Steel tumbled in slow motion and landed face first in the trough. Human excrement filled his nostrils and his mouth. He wallowed in the filth and managed to upright himself, spitting and retching. He sagged over the beam, and Mazi was laughing so hard, his eyes watered.

"The only good thing, Rouille, is that you get to take a shower when the latrines are clean. You have two hours. Now, get to work." Mazi walked outside and left Steel to his misery.

By the tenth day Steel was a broken man. He moved through the paces of cleaning the latrines like a zombie. He heard nothing. He smelled nothing. He felt nothing. He realized God had finally and completely abandoned him. He was almost finished with the last trough when something white caught his eye. Buried in the pile of filth, a piece of paper surfaced. He glanced at it in disbelief. He glanced around to make sure that Mazi wasn't watching, then plucked the paper. It was stained and hardly readable, but in the darkness of the latrine house he could see enough to know the words on the paper were in English. A spark of hope flickered deep within his despair. Mazi bounced the bat off the doorframe, and Steel hid the paper in his coverall pocket.

"Find anything, Rouille?" Mazi asked as he came toward him. "A snack?" His laughter rattled the tin roof. Steel averted his eyes and went back to work on the trough. He hoped he had hidden the piece of paper before Mazi had seen it. Even as the thought dawned on him, he marveled at the word: hope. He thought he had lost all hope.

Steel stood beneath the outside showerhead and rinsed the filth from his body. He did the best he could to wash the dirt from his coveralls without completely soaking the paper. Mazi stood a distance away in the shadow of one of the prison houses. Steel carefully withdrew the piece of paper. In the darkness he couldn't make out what the paper said. Carefully he tucked it back into his coveralls and then pulled the wet clothing over his body. Mazi poked him in the back with the bat.

"Move it, Rouille. Or it will be time to start tomorrow's cleaning already."

Steel shuffled across the yard toward his prison house. He turned his head upward and for the first time noticed the far, distant lights of gleaming stars.

Hours passed, and he curled on the cinder-block bed waiting for the other prisoners to fall asleep in their cells. Mazi had gone long ago. A small slit in the door to the hallway let in a feeble ray of light. Slowly Steel eased off his bed and crawled across the floor. He reached out a hand and placed it in the light as if to catch the glimmer with his fingers. He listened. No one stirred in the hallway. Faint snoring echoed outside. Steel crawled over to the hole in the wall.

"Rafe? Are you there? I found something."

Silence came from the other cell. Steel leaned up and tried to look through the hole. Something had been placed across the hole. Rafe was gone!

Steel felt the growing pain of despair but recalled the paper in his pocket. Rafe had given him hope. Now the paper would give him hope. He reached into his pocket and pulled out the paper. Gingerly he placed it on the floor and carefully straightened it out. He smoothed away the wrinkles before leaning over to read the words in English.

> Who shall separate us from the love of Christ? Shall tribulation, or distress, or persecution, or famine, or nakedness, or peril, or sword? As it is written: "For Your sake we are killed

*all day long; we are accounted as sheep for the slaughter."
Yet in all these things we are more than conquerors through
Him who loved us. For I am persuaded that neither death
nor life, nor angels nor principalities nor powers, nor things
present nor things to come, nor height nor depth, nor any
other created thing, shall be able to separate us from the
love of God which is in Christ Jesus our Lord.*

Steel gasped as he read the words. His heart raced, and he collapsed onto the floor. "Thank You, God. Oh, thank You, God," he whispered as he sobbed and sobbed.

Mazi opened the door, and Steel sat waiting on the bed. He had hidden the passage from Romans in a crack of one of the cinder blocks of his bed. Mazi stopped and did a double take.

"You awake, Rouille?"

Steel nodded. "I am awake," he said haltingly in French. "I like my new job. Is it time to go to work?"

Mazi's mouth fell open, and he shook his head. "Yes, the latrines wait for you."

Steel stood up. "Who is in the next cell, Mazi? Can he help me in my job?"

Mazi glanced over his shoulder, and his yellowish eyes filled with confusion. "No one, Rouille. It is a storage closet."

Steel gasped as Mazi unlocked the door and opened it. Only an empty room filled with broken chairs and desks greeted him.

Steel watched the door slam in front of him. Rafe was gone. That is, if he ever existed. But it did not matter if he was real or not. He had kept Steel alive this long. And he had given Steel tiny glimmers *of hope in spite of his despair. He followed Mazi down the hall to the latrines.*

In the next four months Steel collected the rest of the Book of Romans, the four Gospels, and part of Acts. The pages had come from his Bible. Mazi had not used it for tobacco rolling. He was using his Bible for toilet paper.

"Jonathan! Are you all right?" Cephas touched his shoulder.

Steel shook his head. He drew in a deep breath and stood up. "Yes. I just had another flashback." He reached out and patted Cephas's hand. "Thank you, Cephas. You have given me hope. And that is something I was running short on."

Steel's cell phone rang. He glanced at the caller ID. "It's Renee Miller. She must have finished analyzing the blood."

Chapter 23

R. RENEE MILLER met Steel at the entrance to Ingenetics. It was a modern building nestled near the campus of the local medical school. The sign just inside the door listed her as the owner and CEO. And below it was the name of another company, Miller Avionics, also listing her as owner and director.

Miller's appearance was far different from the night Steel had met her in the mall. She wore a dark gray skirt and blazer over a light blue blouse.

"This way, Mr. Steel." Miller led them inside to the elevator.

"Dr. Lawrence said you own this building."

Miller glared at him for a second. "What does that old man have to do with this?"

The sudden venom in her voice shocked Steel. "He contacted you to see me. And he's in town."

Miller sighed. "Well, I don't care to speak to him. We have some disagreements from the past."

"That didn't keep you from seeing me," Steel pointed out.

"It's a love-hate relationship, Mr. Steel." Her voice was suddenly cold and clinical.

"And you own Miller Avionics too?"

Miller looked at him slowly. "Mr. Steel, I acquired Miller Avionics from my husband in a bitter divorce settlement. I took it so I would have the ability to travel anywhere at any time throughout the world as part of my work with Ingenetics."

Steel followed Miller out of the elevator onto the tenth floor of the office building. They were greeted by a young receptionist seated behind a glass desk.

"Dr. Miller, I tried to call you. Your brother is in your office."

Miller tensed and nodded. "I'll deal with him." She led Steel back through a long hallway. Offices branched off on either side, and at the far end he saw laboratory equipment through an open door.

"So, what do you do here at Ingenetics?"

Miller motioned to an open door that led into her office. "Ingenetics occupies nine floors, Mr. Steel. The two floors above this are all lab space. The lower floors are clinics and treatment facilities. But our main focus is on genetic archeology."

"There you are!"

The man was Steel's height, but there the similarities ended. He was thin and wore a khaki shirt and shorts. His long blond hair touched his shoulders. His face had a regal appearance, and Steel swore he could see makeup on the man's skin. His eyes were lavender.

"Malachi, what do you want?" Miller stepped past him into her office. Malachi followed her, and Steel paused in the doorway.

"I have to be in the studio in less than an hour, and you promised you would give me an update on that blood." He ran a hand through his hair, and his tanned face reddened. "As a major stockholder in this business, not to mention your brother…"

"Malachi, shut up." Miller gestured to Steel. "Meet Jonathan Steel."

He turned and threw him an impatient look. "Malachi Sebastian," he said and turned back to Miller. "Is he the overseer of your latest dig?"

Miller glared at him. "A client, Malachi."

Malachi glanced at Steel. "She won't let me on site. A new find in the Negev desert. I'm looking for a new season opener."

Renee shook her head. "Malachi, go do your show. When I find out something, I'll let you know."

Malachi straightened and drew a deep breath. "Fine! I'll speak to my attorney, Renee. You can't hide this from me."

He glared at Steel and hurried down the hall. Steel stepped into Miller's office. "Sibling rivalry?"

"I guess you really do have amnesia if you don't recognize my brother. He has the number one show on one of those science channels, *Artifact Hunter*. Heard of him?"

Steel shook his head. "No. What do archeology and genetics have to do with each other?" Steel studied her office as he spoke. It was generous, with a large window looking out over downtown Dallas. Shelves filled with scientific books covered both walls on either side of the window. A model of DNA sat on the desk beside a picture. In the picture a younger Renee Miller held a smiling baby. Steel studied the baby. Something wasn't quite right about the baby's head, but he couldn't put his finger on it. Another picture showed Renee in a wedding gown with a tall man in a dress military uniform. He seemed very familiar.

She motioned to a chair. "Malachi has a small division of Miller Avionics in the Nevada desert devoted to ancient devices. He calls it his archeological Area 51. He wants something sensational for his show. But I study ancient DNA. There's lots of potential in locating the DNA, for instance, of famous people. Or studying how genetic information has changed and mutated from the past. We even try to locate DNA from mythical creatures and extinct species from all over the globe. We use that information to help people with genetic diseases. Malachi uses it to promote his career." Miller moved around the desk and sat down.

"Lavender eyes? Is that the product of genetic engineering?"

Renee rolled her eyes. "Contacts. A product of his publicity department."

Steel glanced at the photograph. "I was looking at that picture, and I believe I might have met this man before."

Renee Miller tensed in the chair as she glanced at the picture. "That's my ex-husband, Mr. Steel, and you better hope you weren't one of his associates."

"I don't know if I know him or not."

"Amnesia, right?" Miller studied him for a long time. "Look, he worked for a government operation that was classified. We've been divorced for years, and I haven't seen or heard from him since."

"You have a child?"

Miller reached for the picture and turned it facedown on the desk. "She's in a special school. She's handicapped. Mr. Steel, if you want to find out about the vial of blood, I suggest you drop your interest in my ex-husband. And my daughter."

Steel drew a deep breath. The tantalizing memory of the man in the picture hinted at a deeply buried secret from his past. Once again he was being forced to choose between more knowledge of his past and helping the ones he cared about. "Sorry. What did you find out about the blood?"

Miller leaned forward and turned a laptop computer to face him. "Watch."

An animation played across the screen. It showed a tubular object floating among flattened spheres.

"Blood cells from the sample in the vial." Miller pointed to the flattened spheres. "This rod-shaped object is attached to the blood cells. Once the blood cells enter the digestive tract and are broken down, the rod is absorbed quickly by the small bowel."

The rod bumped up against a pink surface and quickly made its way through into a blood vessel. "Once back in the bloodstream, it hitches a ride on the victim's blood cell until it gets to the liver. In the liver the rod adheres to a hepatocyte." The rod moved away from the blood cell and entered what looked like a cell within the liver.

"The liver is the manufacturing center of the body, Mr. Steel. It makes most of the important substances of the body. This rod is a prion. It's a protein molecule that is not alive, but it can induce replication of itself. It serves as a template for making more protein molecules just like itself." The rod within the cell suddenly exploded into hundreds of duplicates until the cell ruptured. "Fortunately the process is self-limiting, and only a few thousand liver cells are damaged. The immune system responds quickly." The multitude of rods quickly disappeared under the onslaught of white blood cells. A few escaped back into the bloodstream.

"But enough escape to reach the blood brain barrier, a membrane that separates the contents of the bloodstream from the brain cells. It's a barrier that prevents dangerous chemicals from getting into the brain substance. But the prion is designed to quickly cross this barrier and migrate to one specific part of the brain, the prefrontal cortex."

The prion rods slid through a membrane and migrated across the screen to a tangle of nerve cells that looked like stepped-on bubble gum. "There they have a short-lived effect on the nerve cells until the glial cells that protect and maintain the nerve cells gobble them up, and the prion disappears from the brain." Miller turned the laptop back to face her. "What's interesting is that a small group of prions stay attached to the blood cells and effectively hide from the immune system for several hours. The unusual shape of the blood cell makes them very susceptible to ingestion by the spleen, which cleans up dead blood cells. The remaining few prions get broken down in the spleen and disappear from the body. The whole process is amazing. Their behavior in this case is unprecedented and no doubt the product of biogenetic engineering."

Steel shook his head as he tried to digest what he had just heard. "So Wulf designed this as a weapon?"

"This prion is hardly a weapon. It has a short life span and has a limited effect on one part of the brain. Then it disappears."

"How did you find all of this out?"

"That's proprietary."

"How would you get this prion into your system?"

"Ingestion. It has to enter through the mouth. It's not found in any other body excretion. Just blood."

Steel felt a chill. "You would have to drink the blood?"

"Exactly. See why it wouldn't make a very good weapon? You'd have to make your enemy drink blood. I'd say Wulf has a dead end here. Probably something he worked on, and he's trying to pull the wool over some buyer's eyes."

Steel watched the prions attack the nerve cells. "What effect would they have on the brain?"

"A flattening of emotional affect. Extreme apathy. A loss of will."

"Would a person be very susceptible to suggestions?" Steel asked.

Miller's eyes sparkled, and she sat forward. "Yes. That is a possibility. You could pump them for information or plant some type of suggestion or command. But it would be so short-lived. What can you do in such a short time? And there are drugs that are better for interrogation."

Steel tried to imagine a clan of vampires feasting on tainted blood reduced to a zombie state for a short time. Why was this useful to Wulf? It didn't make sense. He looked back at Miller. "I know this sounds strange, but if you were to ingest blood from an infected individual, would you become infected with the prion?"

"Yes. That's one way to pass on the prion. But it would only work for a few days."

"What do you know about Wulf?"

Miller shut the laptop. "I've heard about him through certain channels." She fell silent, and her eyes focused on the downturned picture. She looked back at Steel. "He was one of the main developers of biological and chemical weapons for Romania when it was under Communist rule. When the revolts took place, we assumed he was dead, just another victim of the executions. Then, a few years ago, Wulf Pharmaceuticals reappeared on the scene. The firm developed numerous vaccines and antibiotics to help in the aftermath of the collapse of the Soviet Union. Wulf seemed to have cleaned up his act and become a respectable man."

"And now he's shown up here in the United States with blood that's capable of reducing its victim to a zombie-like state," Steel said.

"For a short period of time." Miller leaned forward across her desk. "I don't know what else to tell you, Mr. Steel. But if I were you, I would be very careful."

Vampires, werewolves, and zombies, Steel thought. What did Wulf want with these monsters? He glanced once more at the picture frame.

"This prion, would it help your daughter?"

Miller looked up, and for a moment anger flashed across her face. "I said my daughter—"

"Dr Miller," Steel interrupted her. "My friend, Josh Knight, is in the hands of Wulf right now. I would do anything to find him. I think you would do anything to help your daughter. If this prion offers any hope, I'm glad that fate brought us together."

Miller sat back in her chair. "I'm sorry for being so abrupt, Mr. Steel. I just prefer to keep my private life out of the spotlight.

You're right. The prion may offer some insight into treatment. And I don't think it was fate or Dr. Lawrence that brought us together. I think it might have been a divine appointment."

Steel nodded. "Why is your brother interested?"

Miller frowned. "Anything that will raise his ratings interests him. The man is a charlatan."

Chapter 24

STEEL GOT A call from Kane that Elizabeth Washington had arrived from Shreveport and was waiting at the police station. Maybe she had found something useful from the card. Kane met Steel, Cephas, and Theo at the entrance to the police station. "Let's go to the conference room, Steel."

Steel nodded. "This is Theo King. And this is Dr. Cephas Lawrence."

"Nice to meet you. Dr. Washington is already here."

Kane led them down the hallway and into the conference room where Sergeant Raffle waited with Dr. Elizabeth Washington. Steel smiled as Liz stood up and grabbed him in a tight hug.

"Hey, hon. I'm so sorry to hear about Josh." Her amber eyes glittered with tears.

"We'll find him." Steel's voice almost broke.

"Yes, dear. We will." She patted his hand, and they sat down. Theo pushed past him and wedged himself into a chair. Cephas sat beside Liz, and she patted him on the shoulder. Kane eyed them with a dubious glance and remained standing at the end of the table.

"We now have dozens of missing person reports on people who attended the Bloodfest. And the phone is ringing off the hook with more every hour."

"Do you think Wulf is kidnapping these people?" Cephas asked.

"Possibly. More likely he's the Pied Piper leading them out of town. But to where?" Kane asked.

"Theo, hand me Claire's laptop," Steel said. Theo pulled the laptop from a backpack and handed it across the table. "I got a message from Josh." Steel turned on the laptop. "The message was sent today before dawn. It says 'Transylvania. Midnight. Friday. Alive?' My guess is the twins told him they killed me. I sent a message back, but I don't know when he'll be able to check his e-mail."

"Transylvania?" Theo said. "Ain't that Dracula territory?"

"Yeah. Romania. Why would they be going to Transylvania?" Raffle asked.

"In our last encounter with the thirteenth demon," Liz began, "Ketrick planned a ceremony at midnight on the summer solstice. Midnight Friday sounds suspiciously like Wulf has something else planned."

"Vampires. Demons. Transylvania! Why am I not surprised?" Kane threw up her hands and sat down. "Would someone tell me what this is all about?"

Liz smiled. "Honey, I got the goods from the files on that memory card. It's no codex, but there's enough information there to piece the story together. If it can be believed. You see, there were numerous scanned documents that appear to be very old. They're written in various ancient languages from some kind of early library called the Grimvox." She glanced at Cephas. "Have you ever heard of the Grimvox?"

Cephas rubbed his mustache. "I seem to have seen that name somewhere in obscure documents from the Middle Ages. I'd have to access my books, but they are in storage."

"Anyway, Kasey, my little computer expert, couldn't decrypt all the files. Some were keyed in a language I've never seen." Liz picked up her satchel and retrieved some folders. "Rudolph Wulf translated most of the documents and wrote a first-person narrative as if he were there for each historical event."

"Which, if he is indeed possessed by the twelfth demon, he

very well might have been," Cephas said. "Demons carry with them the memories of their past possessions."

"Thank you, dear." Liz patted his hand.

"Now, Wulf's story begins with Zamolxis. Zamolxis was considered by many to be a god. He journeyed from Greece northward to what we now know as Romania. Socrates wrote about him and claimed he was a healer who spellbound the people of early Romania with his incantations and potions. Legend has it he became a benevolent dictator and led the people into prosperity. One day he proclaimed that all humans were immortal, and he disappeared. He had built a secret underground throne room, and he lived there for three years before 'mysteriously' reappearing to his people, proving he was more than just a mortal."

Liz turned her laptop around and showed them the image of a mountain. "Mount Kogain is the location of Zamolxis's supposed sanctuary. Wulf, who calls himself Saitnoxis in the writings, claimed that Zamolxis's followers were trapped in the chamber, and only Zamolxis could leave. According to what I can glean from Wulf's writings, the day Zamolxis emerged from his hidden sanctuary, there was an alignment of planets and a lunar eclipse."

Raffle leaned forward over the table. "I heard something on the news last night about a lunar eclipse."

"When?" Steel asked.

"I think this Friday. And there was something about an alignment of planets too."

Liz perked up. "Wait a minute. Wulf mentions 'the Event' several times in his writings. He claims it happens about once every two thousand years."

"Every two thousand five hundred years," Cephas said as he rubbed his mustache.

Kane started tapping her fingers on the table. "Okay, guys,

let's get away from the pagan stuff. I want hard and fast answers. What does a planetary alignment and a lunar eclipse have to do with vampires?"

"Such a rare event would produce a change in the magnetic field of the earth through the gravitational pull of these planets," Cephas said. "But the effect would be minimal."

"But that may be all Wulf needs," Raffle pointed out.

"For what?" Kane's finger tapping grew more frantic.

Steel nodded slowly. "Liz, what about the symbol of the wolf that was on the leather pouch?"

"Ah, the Thracian wolf. A symbol of the Thracians, a race of fierce warriors who worshipped Zamolxis. They carried the symbol on a banner before them into battle. What's interesting is that these same warriors developed a ritual for communicating with their god. A group of warriors would stand together with their spears turned upward. Then the most righteous of young men would be chosen as a messenger. He would be given the message for Zamolxis, then he would be hurled into the air by the warriors to land on the spears. He would be impaled. If he died, he was considered worthy in life to carry the message. If he didn't die right away, he was considered unworthy, and another messenger was sent."

"It reminds me of Vlad the Impaler," Cephas said.

Liz's eyes twinkled. "You're absolutely right. Vlad the Impaler used similar 'impaling' as a manner of execution. But that was centuries later."

"Both in Romania though." Steel's mind was turning. "Any connection?"

Liz raised an eyebrow in thought. "Not that I'm aware of. But there didn't used to be a connection between Louisiana and the Incas. I'll look into it. You know who Vlad the Impaler inspired?"

Steel nodded. "Yes. The fictional character of Count Dracula."

Kane cleared her throat and leaned in to the table. "I've got to admit, I'm very uncomfortable with this whole idea. I once saw the crazed look in a killer's face in Florida—a young man who claimed he was a vampire and murdered thirteen people." She looked up from her hands, her eyes haunted by the past. "Those eyes contained pure, distilled evil."

Cephas pointed to the papers. "Lucifer gathered together the twelve most powerful of his demons and dispatched them to counteract each of Jesus's twelve disciples. A thirteenth demon, so vile and uncontrollable, was given the rest of the world, and he eventually settled in South America. But we see that the twelfth demon returned to his geopolitical area of influence during the Middle Ages. Who knows how long he fought against the early Christian church."

Liz's voice grew quiet. "What's interesting in Wulf's accounts is that Saitnoxis mentions the underground chamber at Mount Kogain on several occasions."

"The chamber where this Zamolxis hid," Cephas reminded them.

"Yes. Saitnoxis seems to indicate his cronies were buried in that chamber when Zamolxis left it."

"Maybe he sealed them in that chamber." Theo finally spoke up. "Sounds to me that's what they deserved if they were anything like this Noxis guy."

"It's possible." Liz paused at the end of the table. "But what's important is that Saitnoxis, the twelfth demon, wants something from that chamber."

"Where's this Mount Kogain?" Steel asked.

Liz returned to her laptop and brought up a new image. "There's no evidence of Zamolxis's palace, and no one is completely sure which peak is the original Kogain. As you can see, it is somewhere in these mountains in Romania."

Steel looked at the map. "Close to Transylvania."

"Exactly."

Steel looked up at Kane. "How can Wulf possibly get hundreds of vampires to Transylvania by midnight Friday?"

"Vamp Air?" Kane shrugged.

"Very funny," Steel said. He was interrupted by the door opening.

Agent Ross's mouth fell open as he walked in. "Oh, no. Not the God Squad again." Ross shook his head. "I'm not staying at this party. I just came to follow up a lead from a local hotel. You guys found a dead bellhop?" he asked Kane.

"You guys should hear this," Raffle said before he stepped outside and hollered to someone. Moments later a short man stepped in. "What did you find, Flynn?"

Flynn paged through a folder. "One of the older hotels downtown. Housekeeping found the body of one of their bellhops. Room had been trashed. Broken strings everywhere, and this." He held up an evidence bag containing a piece of hotel stationary with "Steel" written on it.

"Raven?" Steel asked.

Ross took the paper. "She likes strings. How did the bellhop die?"

"Throat ripped out. Looked like some kind of animal attack. Blood everywhere. Gave the crime scene guys the creeps."

Ross looked up at Steel. "Not Raven's style."

"No, but it sounds like those twins that tried to kill me. Why would they go after Raven?"

"Vivian's tying up loose ends," Kane said. "Or, in Raven's case, loose strings. She sent the twins after you, then sent them to kill Raven. After all, Raven botched two assassination attempts."

Ross took the folder. "Then it's my crime scene now."

Interlude
December 25, 1989
Romania

In the distance music drifted across the ravaged city for the first time in decades, carrying the songs of the Savior's birth. The regime that had destroyed most of the churches was over, and now the air rang with hope. But the songs were painful to my ears. How I hated their harmony, their glad tidings. This was not a time of good news. All I had worked so hard for was crumbling around me like the aging buildings in the courtyard below. The Alignment was coming in the new millennium, and my plans were not complete.

Snow fell from a leaden sky as I huddled on the icy balcony. Down below a bullet-pocked wall waited for more executions. It beckoned to me even as it had welcomed those who had gone before me. The soldiers of the new provisional government were moving house to house. I knew they had my name, and I would soon be facing my own execution. I stepped back into the office, hoping that the doctor had received my call and was coming. He knew what was at stake if he did not come; he still believed that I had his family as hostages.

The door opened, and the doctor stepped in. His eyes were wild, his face red from the cold. "Where are they? I don't care about your hidden memories or your failing mental faculties. I want my family!"

I pulled the rich, red robe around me and smiled. "There is no need to be so short, good doctor. You are not on the death list. The new provisional government is cleaning up the debris. They arrested Ceausescu and have just concluded his trial. He will be executed."

The doctor gasped for breath and paced back and forth. "I don't care. Ceausescu was doomed to failure."

"And do you not care about your family?" I asked.

The doctor stopped his pacing. "Of course I do."

I smiled and felt the feeble mind of my host recoil in shock at my plan. But he was too weak and too old to protest. He had served his purpose well. "I am an old man, doctor. You are so young and vital." I reached out and touched his cheek. He jerked away from my touch.

"Will you not tell me about my family?" he pleaded. "Colonel Rafash and his men will be here shortly to search the building."

"I do not fear Rafash." I paused and waited for the doctor to take a breath. This was going to be priceless. "I know about your pharmacy."

His face paled. "My pharmacy? I don't know what you are talking about."

"Of course you do. Secretly you have been working with Ceausescu's secret police to develop pharmaceuticals that affect the mind. You used some of them on me to help recover my memories. Don't deny it."

The doctor hurried across the room. "How do you know this?"

"I have seen things you cannot imagine. There were experiments in Auschwitz that no one has ever known about. If you were to learn of them, you could improve your formulas."

Something foreign and ghastly flickered across his face, and he blinked, putting the civilized façade back in play. "Why would I be interested in such things? You must tell me quickly where I can find my family."

I nodded. "Yes, there is the problem of your family. They tie you to your past. Your wife knows about the secret pharmacy, doesn't she?"

I raised an eyebrow and watched confusion fill his eyes. "But truth be known, you don't care for them. You see, good doctor, I know about your mistress. I know that you married your wife as a favor to one of the secret police, and you hate her. I know that your daughter is not yours but belongs to the man with whom your wife has been having an affair for the past seven years." I stepped toward him, and he fell back. "The only reason you care about your family is because they can implicate you. You don't want to rescue them. You want to destroy them."

The doctor shook his head. "This can't be happening. You are a fiend!"

I paused beside the mirror above my mantle, studying the wrinkled face and senile eyes of my host. He had been good for me. He had seen me through two world wars and now would be my salvation. I glanced back at the doctor. "You are the fiend, doctor. You reveled in my stories. You relished my memories. You wanted them. Now, you can have more than just the memories."

"What do you mean?"

"I can complete you. I can make sure your work is not discovered but continues." I thought of the precious ones beneath Mount Kogain. Yes. This time my plan would work.

"How?"

"You know how," I said. I took the pistol from my robe pocket. Out in the hallway I heard the sound of boots. Rafash would be hurrying our way, thinking that this time he would stop me. But once again the choice of one man would bring defeat. Muffled shouting echoed, and outside my window a fresh round of shots rung out from the firing squad. I handed the doctor the pistol.

"It is the same gun I used to kill your wife and daughter. Do not worry. It will not be painful. But you must be willing to accept me. You must want my memories. Do you?"

The doctor looked at the pistol, and his mouth fell open. "This is madness!"

I laughed and pointed to the door behind him. "Out there is madness. But I have survived thousands of years of your kind's madness, and with me, you will survive it also. Now, shoot me."

The doctor raised the pistol even as the door behind him rattled. His hand shook, and far down within the recesses of my host's mind, the old man whimpered and begged for release. But his suffering was only now beginning.

The shot rang out even as the door burst open. I swirled through empty air. I tasted the other dimensions. For a fleeting second I saw the heaven I was denied, and then the doctor's open mouth welcomed me, and I surged into him. Too late he realized the price of his decision. He saw the future his terrible past had brought to him.

Colonel Rafash looked at me, his dark hair wet with sweat and his hazel eyes gleaming with righteous fervor. I lifted my gun hand. "Stop! He was one of them." I pointed to the crumpled body of the old man.

A soldier raised his rifle at me. "Who are you?"

"I am a psychiatrist. I know all of his secrets. He was with Ceausescu. He killed my family, and I–I had to try and . . . stop him. I killed him." I fumbled with my words.

The soldier motioned to the dead body. "Search him. Is he on the list?"

Rafash glared at me and knew he had been defeated. He held up the photograph of the dead man. "Yes, he is on the list."

The soldier with the rifle clapped me on the shoulder. "You have done well. You have saved us precious bullets. What is your name?"

I handed Rafash the gun. "Doctor Rudolph Wulf."

[Chapter 25]

OURS LATER STEEL glanced at the clock on the police station conference room wall. They'd wasted too much time delving into Wulf's documents. It was almost two o'clock in the afternoon when his phone buzzed with an incoming message. After he listened to the message, he had tried to chase down Ross without success and finally managed to get a message to him to meet them as soon as he could. Lieutenant Kane came through the door with a mug of coffee.

"He just called and said he's on the way. They've been going over the hotel room with a fine-tooth comb. It's the first time he's gotten this close to her."

Steel sighed and turned to look at his friends sitting patiently at the table. "Doesn't he know we're on a tight schedule?"

Kane sat down. "He doesn't care about our problems, Jonathan. He's after Raven."

"Our problem just became his. Listen to this voice recording I just got from Josh from his iPhone." Steel opened Claire's laptop and pressed a button.

"I don't know if this will get to you, Jonathan. I'm walking up to first class to find out what Vivian and Wulf are up to. Dude, I'm just on the other side of the curtain. Armando is with them, and Spike and Fang are asleep."

The curtains rustled and the voices from first class became clear.

"Where is our final destination?" Vivian asked.

"Mount Kogain," Wulf said.

"Where's that?" Armando asked.

"We will fly into Because and take buses to the gorge. The cave entrance is not far from the dam," Wulf said.

"A dam?" Vivian asked.

"The temple is now under water, my dear. But there is a cave entrance near the base of the peak. We will find our way into the chamber. I already have men working on the preparations." Wulf said.

Their conversation became muffled. "What are you doing?" A female voice came over the speakers.

"I'm trying to find out where we're going. Are you going to kill them before we land?" Josh asked.

"No. Too complicated. Get back to your seat, or I'll tell them about your phone," the woman hissed.

There was a cacophony of sound and then Josh's voice. "Dude, Spike and Fang are coming. I'm going to e-mail this voice clip and hide the phone in the overhead compartment. I hope the battery lasts long enough so that when we land, it can get a signal and send the e-mail. Jonathan, I'm sorry I did this. Bro, I screwed up. But you gotta help. Hurry."

"Wait," Kane said. "The assassin is on the airplane?"

"My assassin?" Ross asked as he stepped into the room.

"Yes. That was Raven's voice on Josh's recording. They're on Wulf's airplane, and Raven is disguised as a flight attendant."

Ross smiled. "I think she's going after Vivian after what we saw at the hotel. Someone busted up that room trying to kill her."

"I'm convinced Vivian is behind the brothers' attempt on my life and Raven's. She's given up trying to kill Atchison." Steel said.

"Ross, Josh is on that plane. They're on the way to wherever it is Wulf is leading them. You've got to help us." Steel gave him the Cliff's notes version of what Liz found on the memory card.

"Steel, if they're headed for Romania, all I can do is deal with

Interpol and the Romanian government. I'm sorry. Now, if you'll excuse me, I have to coordinate a response to this and try and get my team to Romania." Before Steel could speak, Ross was up and out of the conference room. Steel slammed his fist on the tabletop.

"We've got to get to Romania!" he shouted.

"Steel, calm down," Kane said. "I'm as mad about this as you are. Armando is on the airplane, and I can't get my hands on him."

Steel drew in a deep breath. There had to be an answer. "We need to know exactly where they're headed."

Raffle played the recording again. "There's mention of a dam, a lake, and a gorge. Where can you find those things together in Romania? And this word, over and over."

He touched a button. Steel listened. "Because? What kind of word is that? Because!"

Cephas clapped his hands. "I've got it. I remember reading about several hydroelectric dams in Romania. If we can find a river that has cut a gorge that empties into a lake behind one of these dams…"

Liz reached for the laptop and began tapping away. "I remember something, old man. One of my students went on a hitchhiking trip through Eastern Europe and talked about a gorge with a river near a town, ah, here it is."

She turned the screen where everyone could see it. "Bicaz. Eastern Romania. A river cuts through a gorge and empties into Bicaz Lake behind a hydroelectric dam. And if you look at some of these photos from travelers, you'll notice something in the background."

Steel leaned toward the image of a verdant, green set of undulating mountains along a meandering river. And nestled on one of the highest peaks was a sharp, gray peak that pierced the sky. It was shaped like a fang. "Mount Kogain?"

Liz beamed. "That is where they're headed, Jonathan. It fits. Cephas, do you realize the significance of finding the actual site of Mount Kogain?"

Cephas nodded. "The historical and anthropological..."

"Wait a minute." Steel interrupted them. "We have to get there first."

Cephas paused and suddenly a smile crossed his face. "I think I know just who to talk to."

Steel tapped on the office door, and Renee Miller looked up from her desk. For a moment, irritation crossed her features, and then she relaxed. "Mr. Steel?"

"Your secretary isn't at her desk. I hope you don't mind."

Miller glanced at her watch. "Oh, it's after five. I didn't realize. What can I..." She stopped as Cephas stepped into view. She rocketed up from behind her desk. "You! What are you doing here?"

Cephas rubbed his moustache. "Now, Renee, we have to put the past behind us, and—"

"I don't have to do anything! The last time I saw you, my life fell apart at the seams, and you disappeared quicker than ice in a rain forest."

"Renee, you were not yourself. You had made some mistakes with your marriage to James and..." Cephas tried to speak.

"It's your fault that James was in that organization to begin with. You recommended him to the committee. You got him that job with the special ops. It's all your fault!" Miller's eyes were wet, and tears began to stream down her cheeks.

Steel walked over to the downturned picture and picked it up. He shoved it in front of Renee Miller's face. "Can the two of you shut up for a moment so we can talk about the people in our lives that matter most?"

Miller stepped back. "What are you talking about?"

"What would you do if your daughter were kidnapped?" Steel pressed the photograph toward her. "What would you do, Renee?"

"I would do anything to find her," Miller growled. She snatched the picture out of his hand. "Now, get out!"

"No!" Steel moved closer to her so she was hemmed up against the huge DNA molecule behind her desk. "Josh Knight has been kidnapped by Rudolph Wulf. I need to find him, and you are my only hope. I don't care what happened between you and Cephas in the past. It doesn't matter now. Look at your daughter. What would you do? Tell me."

Miller seemed to shrink. "I would do anything."

"I need to get to Bicaz, Romania, before Friday evening. You said you owned Miller Avionics so you could fly anywhere in the world at any time."

She wiped tears from her eyes and regarded him with a glare that cut to his core. "And I thought my ex-husband was ruthless." She eased around Steel and sat at her desk, taking a tissue from a box to wipe her face. "Okay, let me think. We do have connections in Eastern Europe." She brought up a schedule on her computer and tapped a few keys. Her hands were shaking. But as she studied the screen, she sniffed and sat up straighter in her chair. Her hands stopped trembling. She pointed to the screen. "We have several transports that move from Dallas to Eastern Europe delivering parts. I can probably get you there, Mr. Steel." Miller glared at him. "But there's one condition."

"What?"

"One day I may need you. Do you understand? If something were to happen to my daughter, you will help me." Miller held up the picture. "No questions asked."

"I promise. When do we leave?"

Steel sat in the truck outside Ingenetics watching the evening close in. A full moon was barely visible. and high in the sky three bright stars were almost one. "Cephas, what happened with you and Renee?"

Cephas clipped his seatbelt over his small chest. "My son, you don't need to know."

"Those were harsh words you spoke. I've never seen you like that."

Cephas's haggard face seemed more wrinkled than usual. "Renee and I have history. I have forgiven her, but she has yet to forgive me."

"That word keeps surfacing. Forgiveness."

Cephas reached out and touched his arm. "You must forgive yourself, Jonathan. And you must forgive Josh for running off."

Steel gripped the steering wheel. "Vivian orchestrated this, Cephas. She is to blame."

"What are you going to do to Vivian when you find her?"

Steel's mind raced with horrible images. He wanted to hurt her like she had hurt him. "I don't know."

"I guess she'll have to stand in line," Cephas stated coldly. "You've got it in for two other people, Wulf and Raven."

Steel blinked. What would he do to Raven if he found her? Maybe…and the past poured over him.

Amidst the explosions and gunshots the door to his cell opened. Steel looked up from the corner where he was trying his best to hide in case some stray bullet penetrated the cinder-block walls. A soldier stepped into the room wearing a uniform he had never seen. The

soldier motioned for Steel to stand up and then stood to the side. Mr. Kito entered the room. At least the man appeared to be Mr. Kito. He was slightly taller, and his hair was grayer. But the most striking difference was in his eyes. Both eyes were milky white.

"Mr. Steel?" he said.

"Who are you?"

"I am Mr. Kito." He bowed slightly. "Not the Mr. Kito you have come to know in the past few months. I am Mr. Kito's brother."

"What do you want?" Steel pressed the recovered pages of his Bible down into his coveralls to keep them from being seen by the guard.

"I am here to free you. The rightful government has retaken this prison camp. Most of the guards are dead. Unfortunately my brother has escaped." His sightless eyes drifted aimlessly.

"Are you blind?"

"As you would assume. But I can see far better than you can imagine. Would you please come with me?" He turned and stepped out into the hallway.

Steel hesitated but then followed. Three more of the new guards waited in the hallway, and Mr. Kito held out his arm. "If you would be so kind as to guide me, we will follow the guards to a special room."

Steel hooked his arm in the man's, and they made their way down the hallway. Other doors were opened into cells soaked with blood. Dead prisoners lay within.

"The dead prisoners were collaborators with the rebels, and I did not arrive in time to rein in the soldiers who arrived an hour ago. Fortunately they were told ahead of time not to kill certain people."

"Your brother ran this camp?" Steel followed the guards down another empty hallway. Lights were broken above, and glass littered the floor. He could still hear occasional gunfire outside.

"We are two sides of the same coin. He chose one path, and I chose another. I believe we have arrived." He stopped and pointed to a closed door to his right. "Guard, please give Mr. Steel the object."

Steel looked behind him, and a guard handed him the bat. Steel took it and studied the metal wire wound tightly around the heavy end. How many times had he felt the blows of the imbedded nails? How many times had Mazi struck him with the same bat? "Why are you giving me this?" he asked.

The door opened. Steel looked in. Mazi was crouched in the center of the room, his hands bound with duct tape. His face was swollen and bloody; one eye was swollen shut. He glanced toward Steel, and his gaze drifted to the bat.

"I give you ten minutes in the room with Mazi, Mr. Steel. You may do or say whatever you want." Kito's sightless eyes strayed toward Steel's face. His hand pushed gently on Steel's back, and Steel stepped into the room. The door shut behind him.

Mazi's good eye swiveled in panic. He tried to back away and fell against the far wall. Steel hefted the bat and let the heavy end smack into his left hand. His anger built with each blow until his face burned with fury. Mazi shook his head and lifted his bound hands.

"Don't kill me. Please," he said.

Steel stopped at the sound of Mazi's voice. He closed his eyes and reached into his coveralls with his left hand. His fingers strayed across the brittle pages. Moisture blurred his vision, and he gasped for breath.

"What should I do to you?" he asked.

Mazi froze and glared at him with the good eye. "What should you do to me? You should beat me. You should kill me. It is what I deserve. But I beg for mercy."

Steel blinked. "You have shown no one mercy."

"No, I haven't. So go ahead and kill me! Get it over with!" Mazi screamed, and his face streamed with tears.

"I want to bash your head in with this bat. I want to splatter your brain all over the wall." Steel lifted the bat above his head in both hands and then paused. "But I won't do that."

Mazi cringed and then glanced up with his good eye. "What?"

Steel lowered the bat and reached into his coveralls. He pulled out the pages of the Bible. "Do you know what these are?"

Mazi glanced at the wad of papers and licked his lips. "Paper?"

"You used it for toilet paper."

"Your Bible. Yes, I used it for toilet paper."

"Did you read it?"

"What?"

"Did you read it before you used it?" Steel screamed. "Did you look at the words on these pages before you wiped yourself with it? Huh? Just answer my question!"

Mazi shrank back, and his lips began to quiver. "Yes. I read the words. I hated them! I hated everything they told me!" He shook his head. "I ripped the pages from the book and threw them into the dung where they belonged." He started to sob. "Where I belonged."

Steel drew a deep breath and knelt before him. He reached out with the wad of papers. "I found these in the latrine. They saved my life. Now they can save yours."

Steel placed the bat on the floor. He tore at the duct tape with his right hand and unwound it from Mazi's hands. Mazi nervously glanced down at his freed hands. "What are you doing?"

Steel tossed the duct tape aside and offered the pages. "You don't have much time left. You need these now more than I do. Make peace with God."

Mazi wiped at his nose and looked at the stained paper as if it was a poisonous snake. "There is no mercy left for me, man of steel. I am beyond your God's forgiveness."

Steel placed the papers in the man's grasp. "You are never beyond forgiveness, Mazi. I could have bashed your brains out, and I must confess I wanted to. But I have felt the power of forgiveness, and it is far more painful than a blow from this bat. I cannot do anything but show you mercy."

Steel picked up the bat and turned toward the door. He was aware that at any minute, Mazi could jump him from behind and break his neck with one twist. But he moved slowly to the door without hesitation and rapped against it with the bat. When he looked back, Mazi was sobbing with the pages pressed against his face.

The door opened, and Mr. Kito stood in the hallway alone. "Have you made your peace, Mr. Steel?"

"Yes, I have." He handed the bat to Kito. "I won't be needing this."

Kito frowned as if greatly disappointed and took the bat. He motioned to one of the guards, and the man stepped into the room with Mazi and closed the door.

Steel watched Kito's snow white eyes. "What did you expect me to do?"

"Make a choice, my friend. The choice you made unfortunately means you are not the person I was hoping you would be." He turned his lifeless eyes on Steel. "You may go."

Steel nodded and turned to walk down the hallway. He was almost to the outer door when he heard the guard's gun fire three times. Mazi was at rest.

Steel gasped as the present returned. He looked over at Cephas.

"Another flashback?" Cephas whispered.

"Yes." Steel said hoarsely. He had forgiven Mazi. Could he find it in his heart to forgive Raven? And what about Vivian? He didn't want to forgive her. He wanted to kill her.

[Chapter 26]

ELCOME TO ROMANIA," Wulf said. Vivian smiled and breathed in the clear air as she walked down the airplane stairs to join him at the limousine. The door to the limo opened, and the man that stepped out was hardly recognizable.

"Bile?"

"Jerome is my real name," he said. His hair was thicker and had a lustrous sheen. His eyes were shockingly red, and his fake fangs had been replaced by two real fangs on his upper teeth. He wore a long, black coat much like Armando's and a dark purple turtleneck. "I am Master Wulf's personal assistant."

"Nice makeover. But I'm still going to call you Bile." Vivian slid into the backseat of the limousine. Wulf sat quietly beside her as they drove up the mountain road. "Did you waste a demon on Bile?"

"He showed true loyalty to me, Vivian, when he identified Jonathan Steel at the Bloodfest. Which is more than you did."

"You were right next to the man and didn't recognize him." Vivian pulled out a makeup mirror and adjusted her lipstick.

"I sensed he was with the Other. That was more than your puny demons could do."

"If I had my third demon back, I would have recognized him," Vivian said.

"I will give you back your demon. But first there is something you can do for me."

"What do you want me to do?"

"There is an object that is very powerful. Robert Ketrick had it hidden somewhere. I want it."

"He had hundreds of artifacts, and the FBI confiscated them all."

"That is your problem. If you want your demon back, then you will find it. A wooden chest with a metal cover. The ark of the demon rose. Once we finish here, you will return to America and find the ark. With it I will have control over the members of the Council."

"Will you give me a seat on the Council?"

Wulf laughed and shook his head. "You, on the Council? Vivian, you are a triviality, a nuisance. Members of the Council have earned their status. They show loyalty to the master, not to their own personal needs. My plan stretches back thousands of years, a plan approved by the master, a plan that will glorify the master's reign over humanity."

Vivian looked away. With Jonathan Steel out of the picture, her hope of defeating Wulf was dwindling. But this ark? It might give her an advantage. "And I will still be your second. Agreed?"

"Of course," Wulf said as the limousine pulled up to an ancient, dilapidated hotel nestled against the foot of the mountains. Vivian watched Armando push Joshua Knight toward the limousine. Spike and Fang followed.

"We have arrived, Master." Bile opened the door.

"Wait with the car." Wulf got out, his dark cloak ruffling in the mountain air. Vivian followed. Armando bowed before Wulf while keeping a tight grip on Josh's arm. "We are here, Master."

"Good." Wulf studied the hotel. "This is the closest establishment to the site?"

"Yes."

"Any trouble from the pilots or the flight attendants?"

"None. They remained with the airplane, but I left a lookout behind. It seems the authorities showed up at the hangar. They may be on our trail." Armando glanced at Vivian with his burgundy eyes.

"And did you leave any evidence behind?"

"No. There was nothing to lead them here unless someone tipped them off."

"The crew of the airplane?" Wulf asked.

"They never left the airplane before our departure."

"You should have killed them," Wulf said casually. "Send the twins to take care of it."

Armando nodded. "Yes, sir."

"That will be harder than you think." Josh spoke up. Vivian glanced at him.

"What do you mean?"

Josh glared at her. "One of the flight attendants is an assassin."

Vivian felt the two remaining demons constrict in panic within her. Her skin cooled, and she leaned back against the car. "An assassin?"

"Yeah. She's the same woman that tried to kill Mr. Atchison at the mall the other day. Jonathan called her Raven. She was on the airplane."

Wulf reached out and grabbed Josh's chin, jerking it harshly in his direction. "The same assassin that tried to kill Atchison at my luncheon?"

Vivian watched Josh's muscles strain as he tried to pull away from Wulf's grasp. "I don't know what you're talking about."

"Why would an assassin be trying to kill the lawyer?" Wulf glared at Vivian.

"He was in my way. I didn't know she was going to try and kill him with you around. Besides," Vivian threw an acid gaze on the twins, "she's supposed to be dead."

Spike looked at Fang then back at Vivian. "We watched her fall, love. She had to be dead."

"Bloody dead!" Fang growled.

"At least you didn't botch the job with Jonathan Steel." She turned her gaze back to Josh in triumph. Josh didn't flinch.

He grinned. "Jonathan is still alive."

"What? How do you know?"

Josh's mouth fell open, and then he glanced away. "I just do. He can't be dead."

Vivian gasped for breath, trying to gain control. "Rudolph, it's obvious these idiots are incompetent. I sent them to do a job, and they failed."

"You little…" Spike took a step forward, his fist clenched.

Armando placed a restraining hand on the huge man's chest. "You sent them to do *your* work, Vivian, not Master Wulf's. And you sent Raven for Wulf."

Vivian felt the tentacles close around her and sensed the tide turning against her. "That's nonsense. I sent Raven after Atchison to tie up loose ends. It was her mistake to try to kill him with Wulf around."

"You were trying to get rid of me," Wulf interrupted her. "And now our little friend has confirmed it."

Armando beamed in her direction. Vivian felt something wrap itself around her arms. She tried to move, but invisible bindings kept her immobile. She looked back at Armando.

"A little trick your old demon taught me."

"What?" she barked.

"Wulf gave me your demon. I now have two within me. And he knows all your tricks."

Vivian struggled against the invisible bindings as Wulf pulled the blade from his cane and held the poisoned tip inches from her face. "You never should have betrayed me, Vivian." His hand disappeared into her chest, and she felt his grip tighten on one of the remaining demons. He pulled it from her, ripping her soul asunder. Wulf held the writhing ball of energy aloft and then offered it to Armando. Armando sucked it into his mouth like vapor. "Now you will never have the power to teleport, Vivian. You are my prisoner." He turned to Spike. "Find the assassin and kill her."

Chapter 27

I T'S OFFICIAL. WE'RE lost in Romania." Theo said.

Steel pounded the hood of the rental van and rubbed his tired eyes. They had spent hours in one of Renee Miller's transports and had landed in the city of Belapo, only to get lost somewhere along the winding, ancient roads of Romania.

"Calm down, Steel," Raffle said. He spread out a map on the hood. "We should have sprung for the GPS."

Steel drew in a deep breath and glanced at his watch. Time was running out. He walked into the edge of the woods next to the road. The road wove its way like a black snake through the forest of fir trees and leafy annuals. Huge gray and black rock towered above him, ominous in their severity. He breathed in the fresh air and the scent of resin and tried to calm down. They had been driving for almost an hour along the bumpy road, with cobblestone walls as old as America holding back the rock and the soil from the incline to the forest.

Raffle and Theo continued leaning over the map. Raffle had accompanied them as a member of the Dallas PD with Theo as his "prisoner" since Theo had no formal identification. Steel had a suspicion about Raffle. He recognized the voice from his flashback. There was more to the man than met the eye.

A tour bus passed on the road, and Steel stood up and quickly made his way through the swaying trees to the van. "Tour bus. I bet that's how Wulf got them here. We need to look for tour buses parked along the base of the mountains. That's where the entrance to the cave would be."

Raffle nodded. "Cephas told us the cave was probably under

the water of Lacul Bicaz." Raffle tapped the map. "That means there may be another entrance above the waterline along the shore here. We're almost there."

They loaded back in the van and soon crossed a bridge over a finger of the giant lake. The water was a deep azure in stark contrast to the harsh, gray rock that towered above. On the other side of the bridge a restaurant and gift shop sat against the shoreline, and a half dozen tour buses were pulled into parking spaces across the road. Raffle parked the van at the far end of the buses. A stream ran along the base of the road and poured over a precipice at the end of the bridge in a powerful waterfall. Tourists crowded an overlook, snapping photographs.

Theo climbed out of the van. "Chief, I'll go have a look in the gift shop. Wulf don't know me." He lumbered across the road.

Raffle pointed to the buses. "Shall we?"

There were four buses angled against the steep mountainside that towered above them. Steel glanced in the open door of the first bus. Looked like an ordinary tourist bus. Not a vampire in sight. The same was true for the second and third bus.

Steel stepped into the lengthening shadow beside the fourth bus and leaned against the grimy exterior. Above him the three planets had become one brightly burning star. The full moon hovered in the center of the sky. He was tired and growing increasingly discouraged. It was getting late. Raffle stepped around the end of the bus. In the shadows his eyes gleamed, and for a moment Steel was back in the cell looking through the tiny hole in the wall at his neighbor.

"You were with me in Africa, weren't you?"

Raffle smiled. "God was watching over you, Steel. I made sure you got His message."

"And Josh?"

Raffle's frowned. "He hasn't asked for the right kind of help. He's still pretty mad at God."

"Because he lost his mother?" Steel glanced at the man.

"No, he's mad at himself for that. He's mad at God because of you."

"Me?" Steel leaned away from the bus. "Why?"

Raffle stepped toward him and placed a hand on his shoulder. "He wants God to make him like you."

Steel felt his face burn. "I don't want him to be like me. I don't want anybody to be like me. I don't even remember who I'm supposed to be."

"You showed mercy to Mazi."

"Yes, I did."

"Then prove you're worthy of Josh's respect. Show mercy again, when it is time."

Steel studied the man's face. He didn't have time to think about what Raffle meant. He had to find Josh. He pushed past Raffle and stepped inside the bus.

It was empty, but there was the unmistakable odor of blood and leather: vampire funk. Steel heard someone move inside the bus restroom far in the back. He slowly made his way down the aisle. Could Josh have hidden in the restroom?

The door burst open, and a woman in long black pants, a white blouse, and a black vest stepped out. A flight attendant? She pulled off a blonde wig and tossed a pair of sunglasses in the seat even as her eyes met Steel's.

"Raven?"

The bus lurched sideways and threw them both into a seat. Something huge came through the side window, showering them with broken glass as the bus settled back on the ground. Fang landed in the aisle, his hair long and his snout that of a wolf.

"There you are, love!" He reached over and grabbed Raven by

the arm. Raven swiped at him with her knife, and he slapped it out of her hand. His yellow eyes glittered with evil as he noticed Steel. "You're supposed to be dead!" He grabbed Steel by the arm with his other hand.

"Now, let me show you a new trick Master Wulf showed me." Fang closed his eyes, and they were somewhere else. Steel felt himself slipping through other dimensions, his mind skittering along the surface of the universe like a stone on calm water. Out of the chaos they rematerialized on a rocky shelf.

"This time you'll both actually die." Steel looked out over the lake at the road far below. They were near the pinnacle of a fang-shaped mountain that had to be Mount Kogain. Fang had tele-ported just as Wulf had done at the gathering. But suddenly Fang's grip weakened. Steel watched the man's eyes roll back in his head and his snout disappear back into a normal human face. They fell backward, away from the mountain edge and into a huge chasm.

Raven kicked and screamed, and Steel tore at Fang's hand as they plummeted into darkness. Suddenly the air crackled and Spike appeared, falling with them. As the darkness swallowed them, Spike grabbed Fang in a bear hug, and the two disap-peared, leaving Steel and Raven falling into blackness.

In a flash of light, he saw a huge cavern with a platform and the red banner of the wolf dragon hung on a wall. And then they were falling again.

Raven had stopped screaming, and Steel tried to think of what to do. Suddenly a strong arm encircled his chest, and he was pulled tight with Raven tucked in beside him. In the dark-ness he saw nothing, but he heard the unmistakable sound of wings unfurled, catching the air, and their descent slowed.

Fluorescent light glimmered off distant cave walls, and for a second he saw the figure of Raffle, huge white wings beating at the air as they fell headlong into water.

Steel struggled to the surface of the cold underwater river and fought for air. The current grabbed him and pulled him along. He bounced against rough rock and reached up to grab the edge of a sharp ledge, hauling himself out of the water. A faint green glow surrounded him, and he looked up into the face of Raven, a glow stick in her hand.

"You working with those twins?"

Steel managed to sit up and slid away from Raven. "No. They're trying to kill me."

Raven glared at him. Sergeant Raffle appeared behind her dressed in his regular clothes. No hint of wings.

"How did you do that?" Raven asked. "Some kind of parachute?"

"No, just wings," Raffle said.

"Yeah, right. You're the cop from the mall."

"Speaking of the mall, why didn't you kill me?" Steel asked.

Raven looked away, and the pale green light silhouetted her face. "You know why."

"Actually, I don't. I have amnesia."

Raven kept her face averted. "So, it's true. He used the phrase on you."

"Who?"

"The Captain."

Steel clenched his fists. "What do you know about my father?"

"I know he didn't approve of our...relationship. And then I was ordered to kill you. And I thought I had." Raven pushed past him toward an open tunnel in the nearby wall of the cavern. "These tunnels lead up to the cavern. We need to go."

Raven held the glow stick up and disappeared into the tunnel. Steel hurried after her. "Wait! What do you know about my past?"

"Forget about the past." Raven's face dipped into darkness. "What happened to the guy trying to kill us?"

"Teleportation," Steel said. "Wulf teleported at the Bloodfest. I guess Fang wasn't ready yet."

"The human body was never designed to move through other dimensions. It takes years of practice to be good at it. Fang is probably dead," Raffle said. "But I made sure the two of you suffered no permanent damage."

"Thanks." Steel hurried ahead and grabbed Raven by the arm and spun her around. "I need to know."

Raven jerked out of his grasp, and her hand came up. She paused. Her hand was empty. "I lost my knife. You're in luck, Steel." She looked at him and leaned closer. "We were close, Steel. We were very close. How could you forget that? How?"

She was inches away, and he didn't move. He was entranced by her eyes, her lips, her fragrance. She touched his cheek with a cold hand, and he shuddered. Her eyes were close now, and it was if he were gazing into her very soul. "This close," she said, and she brushed his lips with hers.

She was sitting at the table in the corner, just as he had suspected. Raven would make sure she could see anyone who entered the restaurant. Steel adjusted his tie and drew a deep breath. He had to make this work, or he would be dead within the hour.

She saw him and visibly tensed. She was nervous. Good! Raven rarely got nervous. Steel paused at the end of the table and motioned to the empty booth. "May I?"

Raven motioned to the empty seat. "Please."

He slid into the opposite seat and placed his hands on the table. "Where should we start?"

"How about I just kill you now?" Raven whispered.

"People are watching."

"You know I can kill you in a dozen different ways. I can kill you and get up and walk away from this booth, and the waiter would think you were still reading the menu ten minutes from now."

"Do you feel that?" Steel asked.

Raven blanched. She must have felt the metal tip against her stomach. "What is it?"

"A retractable blade. One thrust and you die."

"Not before I fire the pistol hidden in my purse. It has a silencer."

Steel withdrew the blade. "Then shall we call a truce for tonight?"

Raven studied him and nodded. "Very well. But if I see you tomorrow, I'll have to kill you."

"You didn't want to kill me six months ago."

Raven flushed. "Don't remind me. I was foolish."

"We both were fools to think we could hide this from him," Steel said.

"We were doomed from the start."

"There is no place for love in our lives," Steel said.

"I realized that long before you did." Raven laughed and dabbed at her eyes with the napkin. "It's over, and all that is left for us is the day I finally kill you."

Steel felt his heart constrict with anger and disappointment. "If not my father, then who wants me dead?"

"Now, you know it isn't nice to kiss and tell." Raven picked up the menu. "What's good?"

The waiter came and took their order. Once he was gone, Steel placed his hands in front of him. "Do you ever grow tired of the killing?"

Raven reached for her purse and placed it on the table. She took out a mirror and lipstick and studied her face. Steel saw the glint of the pistol in the purse.

"My private life isn't up for discussion."

"Raven—"

"Don't call me that in public." She dropped the mirror back into the purse.

"Victoria," Steel continued. "I don't want to kill you. And I don't want to die. I only want one thing, to find the Captain. You work for him, and you can help me with that."

Raven laughed. "What makes you think I know where he is?"

"Because he hired you to find me." Steel leaned back as their meal arrived.

Raven toyed with her steak knife. It caught the candlelight and reflected it onto her face. "You have no idea who hired me to find you. Things have changed in the past few months."

She started cutting her prime rib, and its juices gushed onto the plate. Steel ignored his plate and reached out to put a restraining hand on hers. "Don't you think we should say grace?"

Raven jerked her hand away from his. "You want to pray?"

Steel watched her panic-filled eyes. "I know about your past, Victoria. I know about Lucas. I know about your stepfather."

Raven's knife clattered onto the plate, and she reached for her purse. Steel snatched it away before she could get the gun. She glared at him.

"What gives you the right to pry into my life?"

"You talk in your sleep." Steel reached into his pocket and pulled out the plastic bag. He placed it on the table in front of her. "You haven't been able to find me because I was in a prison camp in Africa. My father put me there. I escaped, and I know he's looking for me. Who better to find me than you?"

Tears trickled down her cheeks. Steel reached over and touched her face. She jerked away.

"Victoria, not long ago all I wanted to do was to kill my jailer. But God brought me back to my senses. I know where you started, Victoria. I know you can stop this and get your life right."

Raven shook her head. "You're insane!"

"Maybe I am. But in my moment of deepest despair, when I was ready to give in to the chaos and the lies of Satan, I found this." He tapped the piece of paper in the bag. "I want you to have it. If I can stop you—if I can help you—you'll understand these people do not have to die."

Raven picked up the piece of paper. "Where did this come from?"

"It was a gift from God. Read it. Consider my words. Turn your back on the world you now live in. From this day forward I want to help people, not kill them, Victoria. And finding the Captain is the first step in that process. If you won't help me, then let me help you. Turn around. Head back to the world you abandoned when your stepfather died. Find forgiveness before it is too late."

Raven stared at the piece of paper as Steel slid out of the booth. "I'll see you around." He walked out of the restaurant, afraid that at any minute he would feel the bullet pierce his skull. But he did not die that night.

Steel opened his eyes as Raven pulled away. He studied her dark hair clinging to her face. Her eyes danced with fire. Had he once loved this woman? "Why didn't you kill me at the mall?"

Raven blinked and looked away. "I couldn't."

"Because you still care?"

Raven ignored him and hurried down the tunnel. Steel rushed after her. The memories of the past had changed everything. "You just said you wished you could forget your past. What happened to you? Why do you do it, Raven? Why do you kill?"

Raven stopped so abruptly he plowed into her, and she stumbled. He grabbed her arm to keep her from falling, but she jerked out of his grasp. She turned, and her eyes were alive with anger. "It was *him*. Okay? Every time I was killing *him*. *My* Captain. That monster that took my life from me; took my God from me; took my lamb." She stepped closer, and Steel backed up. "Every bullet, every knife stroke, I was killing him over and over and over. And they deserved it, Steel. Every one of them deserved it. They took life from someone, left them empty and broken on the side of the road, left them without love, and moved on. I was the hand of vengeance. I was the one that brought justice for those victims."

"You played God," Steel whispered.

"Don't mention that name."

"Raven, you were just teleported through space by a demon and rescued by an angel! I don't have to mention God's name!"

"Just shut up already!" Raven screamed. "I have to think."

"About your next victim?"

Raven's face was pale in the reflected light. "I've got to clean up after someone."

"Vivian?"

Raven laughed. "Don't tell me she doesn't deserve punishment. I know what she did to that kid of yours."

Steel tensed. "Josh? You've seen Josh?"

"Yeah, he was on the airplane. He tried to get me to help him, but by then we were airborne."

Steel sat down on a rock. He held his head in his hands and watched water drip onto the cave floor. "I can't let him die, Raven. I made a promise."

"What kind of promise?"

"I promised his mother..." Steel stood up and looked Raven in the eyes. "He has no one, Victoria. Just an old uncle too ancient to be his father. He's alone. Like you were. Will you help me?"

"I'm not in this to rescue your strays."

"Yes, you are. You're here to rescue yourself. Tell me, have these killings brought you any peace at all? You still see your stepfather's eyes, don't you? You still feel his breath on you. He's still there, Raven. He's still there in every blow you deliver, in every act of hatred and death. He's still there. You're not killing his memory. You're feeding it."

"Stop it!"

"Maybe it's time to try something different. Maybe..." Steel paused and shook his head. He couldn't believe he was saying this. "Maybe it's time to forgive and move on. Let the angry spirit of your father die."

"You asked God to forgive you, and that's why Lucas couldn't touch you." Raffle appeared behind her. Steel had forgotten about him.

Raven's face paled with shock. "How did you know?"

Raffle's eyes glowed in the dark. "Who do you think made Lucas's skin boil? Who do you think has watched over you all these years? You should have listened to Max."

Steel didn't know what was going on. Who was Max? He looked back at Raven. "You met Lucas?"

Raven's eyes clouded with memories of the past. "He wanted me to join him, but when I touched him, he disappeared."

"He told you to kill your stepfather, didn't he?"

Raven shook her head. "He got tangled up in the strings and was choking, and all I had to do was cut the strings. One snip, and he would live. But I just stood there and watched him die." She glared at Steel. "You know what it is like to want your father to die, don't you?"

Steel stepped back like he had been kicked. "Yes," he whispered. "But I fight the hatred."

Raven stepped closer to him. "And when you do find him, what will you do? Huh? What will you do? I tell what you'll do. You'll kill him."

"If I do, I'll feel no better than I do right now. I would become you."

"And what am I supposed to do, Steel?"

"Ask for forgiveness. God has sent an angel to protect you, Victoria. What does that tell you?" Steel reached out and touched her arm. "There was a time when you asked God to forgive you."

Raven jerked out of his grasp. "I've killed people!"

"Raven, no wrong is unforgivable." He thought about the line that Cephas had drawn on the notebook paper.

"And you think there's a place in heaven for me right next to all my victims?"

"Yes." Steel felt his face heat up. He couldn't believe he was saying this. "It's tough. You think you can't be forgiven because it is so hard for you to forgive."

Raven's eyes hardened with anger. "Stop preaching to me, Steel. I'm here to kill Vivian, not forgive her."

Steel grew quiet, his thoughts going back to the church basement. "Vivian was a part of Claire's death too. I've never thought about forgiving her."

Raven smiled. "See, it's not that easy."

"Raven, it's not supposed to be easy. Imagine wiping the slate clean. Imagine truly putting all of that behind you and not ever being reminded of it again. It's like having amnesia. God forgives, and it is as if it never happened. Whatever I did in the past is gone for me. I can't remember it. And it can be gone for you too."

Raven studied him for a moment, lost in thought. "Listen, count yourself lucky that you can't remember your past. Don't go looking for it. Follow your own advice." Raven's face softened in the dim light. "If I can help with Josh tonight, I will. I promise. I don't have any beef with him. But Vivian comes first." She turned and headed deeper into the mountain. Steel turned to say something to Raffle, but he was gone.

[Chapter 28]

OSH FELT ARMANDO'S iron grip tighten as they stepped from the mouth of the tunnel into the huge cavern. The open space was gigantic, dwarfing the puny humans who dared to challenge its silence and secrets. From far above a beam of pale moonlight fell upon the far wall. The milky light filled the cavern with an unearthly glow. Far in the highest reaches of Mount Kogain bats dipped and whirled in the moonlight on their way out of the secret darkness.

Vivian, still secured by the invisible demonic bonds, was pulled along after Armando. Josh wished he could enjoy her misery, but his mind was furiously trying to work out an escape plan. Ahead of him Rudolph Wulf, accompanied by Ila, led the entourage. He wore a huge red robe with the emblem of the wolf dragon on the back. The satiny red fabric rippled and moved as he walked, catching the snatches of moonlight. The wolf dragon seemed to come to life, bright eyes glaring at Josh, teeth dripping with hungry saliva.

A huge rent in the earth gaped across the far edge of the cavern, and mounted across the chasm sat a triangular-shaped platform.

"Mr. Knight, you would appreciate the irony of the chasm you see before you. It opened up at the urgings of a strong earthquake and swallowed a dozen Romanian archeologists who had come to see the hidden chamber of Zamolxis," Wulf said. "The cavern was soon closed because rumor had it the chasm was in actuality a bottomless pit leading to hell." He laughed and looked back over Josh's shoulder at the swelling tide of vampire clans filing into the cavern. "Of course, there is no hell or heaven. There is no god. My followers don't believe in those things." Wulf leaned forward so only Josh could hear. "And yet they do. And there, my friend, is my quandary. How do you convince loyal followers to invite in a demon when they don't believe? Ah, that is where my precious blood comes in and where you will play a vital part. In a short time, with the planets now aligned, the moon will be eclipsed, and so will your life."

Wulf turned his gaze toward the platform. "Behold your destiny, Josh Knight." In the center of the platform a tripod stretched toward the ceiling of the cavern. Dangling from the apex of the tripod was a cage in the shape of a human torso. The cage hung above another elevated platform bearing three ten-feet-tall spears, all thrust toward the ceiling.

Below the elevated platform a system of clear tubes led from the base of each spear to a crystal cask surrounded by dozens of shot glasses on a table covered with a white tablecloth and a spray of black roses.

"Your table awaits you, my young friend," Wulf said. "And soon you will feed my sheep."

They crossed the walkway over the chasm, leaving Wulf's followers on the floor of the cavern. Armando led Vivian over to a leg of the tripod and secured her with real ropes. Josh turned to look for a way to escape and ran into Ila standing at the foot of the stairs leading up to the cage. "Ila, help me. I came to save you. We need to leave now."

Ila pulled aside the collar of her shirt, and Josh gasped. The mark of the wolf dragon adorned her collarbone. "Too late."

Armando pushed Josh up the winding stairway leading to the platform bearing the spears. Ila was now in the hands of Wulf's demons. Josh had failed, utterly, miserably, totally. He didn't even resist as Armando shoved him onto the upper platform.

Armando retrieved a remote control from the platform and began lowering the cage.

"Your final resting place, Josh."

The cage thudded to a stop beside him. Wulf appeared mysteriously from the air beside the cage and opened it like the lid of a box. Josh backed away toward the edge of the platform and felt two strong arms grip his. The vampire called Bile grabbed him by the arms and shoved him toward the box.

"Far above me, Josh, the moon and the planets are aligned." He pointed upward, and Josh saw the full moon moving into place through a huge gap in the top of the mountain. Already the edge of the moon that was visible was turning red. "Soon the eclipse will take place, and the alignment will be complete. An event unlike anything that has happened in over two thousand years will fill this cavern with power. Place him in the cage," Wulf directed.

Bile ripped the black T-shirt off Josh's chest and crushed his arms tightly by his sides. The lid of the cage snapped into place.

"That is good, Jerome. You may wait over there," Wulf said. Bile bowed before his master and scuttled to the side, out of Josh's sight.

Wulf reached through a slit in the cage and grabbed Josh's jaw in a tight grip. The other hand held a tiny vial of blood. "Drink, my young friend, of a new blood that will change the world." He flicked the stopper out of the vial and shoved it between Josh's lips. Josh tried to spit, but he felt the skin on his face grow warm, felt his neck swell as if blood could no longer make its way to his heart. His eyes throbbed with every heartbeat, and he gasped for breath. As he did, the blood gushed into the back of his throat and the pressure ended. He swallowed involuntarily, choking on the thick liquid.

The cage swiveled horizontally, his body now facing down,

and swung over the spears. He tried to struggle, but he couldn't move within the confines of the cage. Fire blossomed in his mid-section. A sudden fever seized him, and he began to shake with a rigor so violent the cage rattled. His vision clouded, and his mind grew muddled. Sweat popped out on his forehead, and he tried to focus on the spears pointed at his body. He blinked away tears, trying to clear his confused mind.

"Please, dear God, I need some help. Do not let me betray You. I want You to control my thoughts. Don't let me become one of Armando's zombies," Josh whispered.

With his eyes closed, Josh found himself once again in the stone chamber of his deepest imagination, just as he had been on that night long ago in the basement of the church in Lakeside. It was here he had faced the controlling thirteenth demon and defeated him. Torches burned brightly, and from the ceiling a butterfly appeared. It landed deftly on the floor and suddenly enlarged into the figure of Sergeant Raffle.

"Raffle?" Josh stood up from the muddy floor.

"I have been given permission to help you, Josh. You asked for help, and you will have it. You will remain in control with my help, but you must think carefully of how to use this for your advantage."

"Are you an angel?"

"Raphael. I helped your mother, Josh. And I was with you on the mountainside. Now, what is your plan?"

Raven placed a hand on Jonathan's chest as they stepped into the light coming through the end of the tunnel. "We're here," she whispered.

"Let me see."

"No, we can be seen from up here. Just a minute." Raven

flattened herself on the floor of the tunnel and left just enough room for him to squeeze up beside her. Below them a huge crack in the floor of a cavern led down into darkness. A platform straddled the chasm, and he felt a wave of panic pass over him as he saw Josh dangling in a cage over three huge metal spears.

"What are they doing?" Raven whispered.

Jonathan studied the spears and the tubes leading to the tables below. He watched Wulf toss a glass vial into the chasm and turn to face a room filled with hundreds of his vampire followers.

"That was one of the vials of his blood." Steel thought quickly. The prions. The effect they had. Momentary great power and what else? What had Renee said? A flattening of will. Bile had said vampires didn't believe in God or Satan. They couldn't accept a demon they did not believe in. But if they drank the blood…

"They're going to drink Josh's blood. Wulf infected it, making them feel powerful and yet susceptible to demonic possession. I've got to save Josh."

He started forward and felt Raven's hand grip his shoulder. "Wait. You can't just barge down there. Wulf has hundreds at his command. What are you going to do, fight them all?"

"If I have to."

Raven glanced down at the ledge just below the mouth of the tunnel. It led to the left just beneath a huge banner hanging on the wall. From behind the banner a face appeared. Raffle motioned to them.

"How did he get over there?" Raven asked. Steel didn't give her an answer. "Well, never mind. It looks like it's dark enough along this ledge to get to that banner. Then we'll need a diversion to get down to the platform."

They crawled out onto the ledge. Dark shadows cast upward

from the lights below provided them ample cover to reach the bottom of the huge banner, and they slid behind it into total darkness. Steel leaned down and looked through the gap at the bottom of the banner. There, tied securely to one of the legs of the platform, slumped Vivian.

"Looks like Vivian has become a victim," Steel said.

He felt Raven press against his shoulder as she leaned forward. "At least she's a sitting duck for me."

Josh fought the confusion growing over his mind. Would his plan work? If not, it would at least delay Wulf long enough for…what? If the angel was here to help, maybe Jonathan was here too. The very least he could do was to buy Jonathan some time.

"Followers of vampire magick." Wulf stood on the platform in front of the spears. His crimson robe billowed around him, and he held the wolf cane in his outstretched arms as it if were a scepter. "Welcome to your Awakening."

A chorus of cheers moved across the sea of upturned faces, and Wulf gestured them to silence. "Tonight, at the dawning of a new age of man, you will receive the mark of the wolf dragon."

Shouted affirmations and catcalls echoed from the crowd. "Behold the sacrifice." Wulf turned and gestured toward Josh. "Through his veins courses the new blood that will give you power beyond human imagining. At the appointed time you will come forth and receive my new cup and enter this new life. For behind this banner of your allegiance lies the source of your magick."

The lights extinguished in one quick gesture of Wulf's hand. The crowd below began to murmur. "Behold the blood of the wolf dragon." Wulf gestured above as the moon reached its full eclipse. Blood-red light filled the cavern, shining down the opening from the peak of Mount Kogain, falling fully on the huge banner behind the platform. The crowd began to whisper and murmur in awe.

Wulf turned and motioned with his cane, and the banner released at the top, rippling downward to collapse on the ledge below. A huge stone door, twenty feet across, was set into the rock face of the cavern. A series of dull metal rods crossed the top, bottom, and sides securing the ancient stone door. Around the periphery of the door the symbol of the wolf dragon glowed a dull red in the ray of crimson moonlight.

Wulf gestured with his hands, and the center of the doorway grew translucent. Behind that clouded surface *things* moved. Faces pressed up against the glass. Deformed eyes, snarling fangs, huge tongues all swirled in an orgy of anger. The demonic creatures were every obscene configuration of nightmarish creatures man had ever imagined. They writhed and pressed against the translucent window, yearning to be free.

Wulf turned back to his followers. "Centuries ago an army of vampires served me. Then a force beyond my reckoning trapped them behind this gate. Tonight the planets have aligned, and the moon has been eclipsed. Soon I will open the portal for these ancient souls to give you their magick as they fade from existence."

The crowd moved and swayed as voices arose in praise of Wulf. "I will make with you a new covenant on this new blood. I will be your master, and together we will change this world and bring the mundanes to their knees."

A wave of shouted affirmation ran across the crowd, and they began to press forward toward the walkway. Wulf looked up at Josh. "I think they're thirsty!"

[Chapter 29]

STEEL STRUGGLED OUT from beneath the heavy folds of the collapsed banner. He glanced upward at the rock face and recoiled in revulsion. Demons swarmed behind the stone door, trapped in the underground chamber of Zamolxis, waiting to be loosed upon the world. The red beam of moonlight cast a circle on the stone cavern wall below the door, slowly creeping upward, and would soon shine fully on the stone door. When that happened, Wulf's power would complete the process.

"I don't understand," Raven said.

"The vampire believes there is no god, no heaven, no hell, and therefore no demons." Steel pulled the fabric off of her. "Wulf trapped hundreds of demons in a chamber in Romania thousands of years ago. With his blood he can convince those people down there to invite the demons in. They'll invite in the 'vampire magick,' and Wulf will then lead an army of demonically controlled humans." He turned to Raffle. "You were there?"

"I sealed the chamber myself. I did not imagine Saitnoxis would wait two thousand five hundred years to free them. But we are ancient creatures with long memories. And we're very patient," Raffle said.

"I saw Wulf and Vivian as demons in her office. I didn't want to believe it," Raven said.

Steel took her by the shoulders and looked into her eyes. "Believe it, Raven. You still belong to God."

Raven shoved his hands away. "No. It's not possible." She inched away from him, her face clouded over with confusion.

"You locked God away in your heart just as these demons were locked away," Steel said.

"You are correct, Jonathan," Raffle whispered behind him. "She holds the key. Everything hangs on the choice she will make this night."

Steel turned and gazed into his hazel eyes. "What is your real name?"

"Claire knew me as Ralph. Some have called me Raphael."

Steel gasped at the mention of Claire's name. Raffle grabbed his arm. "Jonathan, when the time comes, God will allow me to act, but only if Raven makes the proper choices."

"Master Wulf, I want to speak to your vampire spirit," Josh shouted. "We want to see your ancient soul tonight. Let me speak to your spirit directly."

Wulf waved his hands and floated into the air, pausing at Josh's level. His cloak billowed behind him as they hung in the crimson beam of moonlight. "Silly child. You are far too young in the Spirit and far too young in your soul to fool me."

"I am weak. I can renounce God," Josh said quickly. "You can use me as your new host…"

Wulf shook his head. "Joshua Knight rode his white steed to the rescue of Ila. Such a hero could never embrace the macabre as I have. You would have to cover your newly acquired salvation with layer after layer of guilt." Wulf drifted closer, hovering just below Josh's face. "Only the blood of the retched souls you had slain or the pain of those you had betrayed could cover up your soul. Your light may be only a glimmer, but it still shines out for the Other, and once you belong to Him, you cannot be taken away." The cage began to descend toward the spears.

Raven gasped as she watched Wulf hover in the air before the boy. What had Wulf said? Once you belonged to God, you always belonged to God. Even when you turned your back on Him?

Jonathan pushed past her toward the stairs leading down to the platform. As she grabbed his elbow, he turned those intense, violent eyes on her. She touched the amulet beneath the fabric of her shirt. He was the same man she had once loved, and yet, he was different. He had changed. She felt a string snap inside of her mind, freeing her struggling conscience, filling her with a desire she had not felt in years. She would help Josh.

"Let me go after Vivian and draw Wulf's attention. Once he leaves the platform, go for Josh." She lurched past him and ran down the stone stairs and across the walkway. As she neared the platform, Vivian raised her face.

"You are a persistent witch, aren't you?" Vivian whispered. "You're here with Steel, aren't you?" Something passed across Vivian's features, and she glanced over her shoulder. "It's a tough choice, isn't it? Kill Vivian or save the boy. Did you make Steel a promise?"

"Shut up."

"Go ahead and kill me. But if you do, the boy dies. What will it be, Raven?" Vivian smiled. "Your choice."

Raven closed her eyes and tried to clear her mind. Her memory cabinet burst open and the strings tumbled out, snaring her, lifting her into the air and pulling her up over the vampires waiting for Wulf's salvation. Wulf still floated above the platform in the ray of bloody moonlight, but a bright light descended around her. Raffle hovered before her, resplendent in white clothing and gleaming wings. From behind him strings and threads appeared, writhing and interlocking.

"They cannot see, Victoria." He gestured to the motionless crowd. "The adversary is the father of lies, and you have lived that lie for years. It is time to embrace the truth."

"Why didn't He stop my stepfather?"

"Such questions are always asked. I am but a messenger. I do not claim to know the will of God. But your suffering, your pain, has brought you here to this place. For tonight you have a choice to make. If you make the right choice, those below you will see the truth about Wulf and perhaps get a glimmer of eternity. If you make the right choice, Josh will live, and the man known as Jonathan Steel will fulfill his destiny. All of this is in your hands." He gestured, and the strings moved through the air, intertwining, coalescing, and forming a fabric alive with color and movement.

"My choice?" she whispered. "I want peace. I want forgiveness for all the pain I have caused."

The strings formed into a huge tapestry that hung between her and the stone door, behind which a hundred demons writhed in eternal anger and fury. A face formed from the strings. It was her stepfather, cruel and angry. And for the first time she felt something other than anger. She felt pity. For she understood now how hatred and anger could have twisted him to be the monster he became. It had made her into a monster, and the only way to undo that was to let him go. Tears ran down her cheeks, and she closed her eyes.

"Let me go to Wulf," she whispered. She opened her eyes and found herself standing on the platform with Wulf hovering above her. Behind him the circle of reddened moonlight was moving across the face of the stone door. The very wall was beginning to vibrate under the pull of the combined planets in a supernatural display of force. Stones began to dislodge around the edge of the door and fall into the chasm. She had to hurry.

"Wulf! I want to speak to your demon," she shouted up to him.

Wulf glanced down at her and smiled. "Raven? I seem to be very popular tonight. First the boy tries to fool me, and now you." He flicked a finger in her direction, and she was pulled up into the air to hover before him. "If I let my demon come forth, you could send him to hell."

Raven held up her hands. "Not me. I have blood on my hands. I have killed."

"How many?"

"Twenty-seven."

Wulf drew closer, and his eyes bored into hers. She felt his hypnotic power and fought to keep control. "I saw you in the office, my dear. I touched your mind in the restaurant. You are truly tainted with evil."

"Then take me as your next host. The man is old. I am young and strong," she whispered.

Wulf smiled, now only inches from her face. "Show me your guilt. Show me your pain. Let me see them. One by one."

Raven gasped and nodded. She opened a panel on her memory cabinet, and the most recent face emerged, bound in dark twine. The twine dripped putrid decay, and the dead eyes stared at her. The twine broke and fell away, and she felt the string constrict around her heart as she allowed the guilt to wash over her.

One by one the faces emerged from hiding. Tighter and tighter the strings of guilt bound her heart until she could hardly breathe. Wulf pushed his mind into hers, reveling in the dead faces, lapping up the putrid puddles of guilt. He was ecstatic.

"Yes, I feel their deaths. I smell their blood."

"Then throw off Wulf, Saitnoxis, and take me," she said with trembling lips.

Wulf waved a hand, and a wall of mist hid them from the crowd. He closed his eyes, and his skin began to stretch. His mouth elongated into the snout of a wolf. His hands became clawed appendages. He threw off the red cloak, and his clothing burst as a huge, scaled tail tore through the air. Giant leathery wings unfurled. He opened yellow eyes and regarded Raven with naked lust. Wulf's old body fell into the folds of the red cloak. He hovered closer to Raven and wrapped his wings around her body, hiding her from the world. The red moonlight played upon his features, casting him in bloody light. "Now, my child, I will come into you. Together we will wreak such havoc as this world has not seen. Let me see him, the first one, the stepfather."

Steel vaulted up the spiral staircase toward the upper platform just as Raven ran toward the twelfth demon. A hand grabbed his ankle, and he fell forward onto the metal stairway, striking his upper lip. Blood gushed into his mouth. He looked back at Armando. Suddenly a cool mist shrouded the platform, tainted crimson by the bloody moonlight.

"Not so fast, man of steel." Steel sat up, blood streaming from his cut lip, and kicked Armando in the face. Armando dodged the kick with ease, and his free hand slapped down on something on the platform. He held up the remote control.

"Looking for this?" He grinned as he tossed the control over his shoulder, into the chasm below. He released Steel's ankle and slid out of sight into the mist.

"Jonathan, help!" Josh shouted.

Steel struggled to his feet. He could barely see the cage through the cloying mist, and Saitnoxis, the wolf dragon, hovered in the air, throwing shadows across the platform. Steel briefly glanced at Raven, hanging in front of Saitnoxis as if suspended by strings.

Steel turned back to Josh's descending figure. If he couldn't stop the cage, he'd have to try something else. He grabbed one of the nearest spears and pulled hard to dislodge it. The spear was made of stainless steel and bolted to the platform. He tried to climb up the spear to the top, stretching out his hand to try and push the descending cage away, but the surface was slick with an oily substance, sliding him back down to the platform. The cage emerged from the mist, and Steel stared into the boy's pleading eyes. There was nothing he could do to stop this. Josh was going to die.

Vivian felt her old energy returning at the sight of Steel grappling with Armando. She might just pull out of this smelling like a rose. As Armando ran down the stairs, she called to him.

"Armando."

"What?"

"I want to speak to my two demons."

Armando's face twisted. "I don't have time."

"We are facing defeat if we stay on the side of Wulf. Listen to my plan. That's all I'm asking. I don't want to talk to Armando. Put him away somewhere." Vivian put as much authority into her voice as she could.

Controlling factions warred across Armando's face, and then it twisted into a familiar form. "Yes, my lovely one."

Vivian breathed a sigh of relief. "Can you control Armando's original demon?"

"Yes. It is weak. And your other demon is in Ila now," Armando rasped.

"If we invite the other demon, the two of you can rejoin within me—we can have our unholy trinity restored plus one more."

"Lovely plan. If Wulf fails," Armando nodded.

"Then you've got nothing to lose. When the time comes, follow my lead."

At Wulf's request Raven began sliding down the strings of guilt and torture until she was once again standing in the living room over the dying face of her stepfather. She looked into his eyes and felt the hate that had consumed her all these years melt away. Above her the tapestry changed to reveal the face of her father, then shifted again as the strings rewove into the image of a crown of thorns. She gasped and shouted.

"Father, I forgive you."

Deep within her the memory cabinet fell apart, and a tiny, flickering flame filled the darkness of her mind. The flame caught one of the strings, and it raced along its length to another and then another until all the strings of her past were burning bright with forgiveness. Warmth filled her soul, and for the first time in months, she smiled.

Saitnoxis pulled her to him with his wings. "What did you say?"

"I said, 'You can go to back to where you came from,'" Raven hissed.

Suddenly Saitnoxis's wings burst into flame. The skin on his face bubbled with bloody, steaming pustules. His mouth opened in a horrid scream, and he flew backward into the red moonlight. His wings dispersed the mist, and the vampires screamed in horror at the sight of the twelfth demon. Raven dropped to the platform. A beam of light so bright, so utterly illuminating poured from above, driving the red moonlight away, filling the chamber. Raffle appeared above her, wings unfurled, the light emanating from behind him.

"Good choice, my child. I'll take it from here." His hazel eyes beamed with power.

Raphael soared down to hover above Saitnoxis's smoking wings. "First, I will allow your minions freedom to greet their long-lost master. They've been waiting for you. And I don't think they're very happy." With simply a gesture from Raphael, the great stone gate shattered, and the metal bars fell into the chasm. The symbol of the wolf dragon glowed red hot. Saitnoxis was sucked upward by a powerful vacuum into the new opening. Hands, talons, tentacles, and other unspeakable appendages wrapped themselves around his struggling, pestilent torso from within the other chamber. Saitnoxis screamed, and his voice echoed with eternal pain throughout the chamber.

Shouts came from behind her, and Raven spun. FBI agents in armored gear streamed into the cavern. The vampires panicked, some running headlong into the chasm. Others were trampled by the surging wave of humanity. Raven recognized Agent Franklin Ross in the lead, and for a moment his gaze locked on her. He was here for her. It was time to stop running.

Then Ross's gaze was drawn upward, and it seemed he, of all the people in the confusion below, saw what she saw. Raphael hovered in front of the gaping maw of the demon cavern. He reached out and touched the glowing red symbol of the wolf dragon. It grew white hot, constricting toward the center of the opening, closing like an iris. Behind the glowing rock, the hungry demons tore away at Saintnoxis's body until they disappeared beneath the melting symbol. Raphael fanned the heated rock with his wings, and the stone cooled, merging imperceptibly into the surrounding wall. The demons were sealed away forever, and Raphael disappeared.

[Chapter 30]

SOMETHING WARM DRIPPED on Steel's cheek, and he looked up to see the first spear pierce Josh's chest. Josh cast a long look at Steel.

"I'm so sorry for running away. I just wanted to help Ila."

"I'm sorry I hit you," Steel said. In his mind he saw the hovering form of Mazi. Mercy. "God, please show Josh some mercy. We need a miracle."

Steel heard the screams of Wulf's followers. A huge figure burst through the crowd, tumbling and fighting. Theo's eyes roved around the cavern until he saw Steel. He hurried across the cavern floor, tossing aside vampires and shoving through FBI agents until he reached the rock platform. He rushed up the stairs and knelt before Steel.

"Chief, sorry I'm late. I ran into one of those twins."

Steel pointed up at the descending cage. "I can't stop the cage from dropping."

Theo's dark features stiffened with panic, and he stepped up to the spear piercing Josh's chest. Wrapping his huge arms around it, he pulled with all his might. The metal groaned before it snapped away from the platform with a sharp ping. Theo hurled the spear away and jumped up to catch Josh's cage with one hand. Placing his feet against the other spears, he pushed it outward and swung the cage away from the spears. Once Josh was over the open platform, Theo jerked downward on the bottom of the cage, and it opened. Theo fell back from the open cage and caught Josh's tumbling body with his own as they crashed onto the metal platform.

Raven watched the angel disappear above her, then felt the platform shake as Theophilus King saved Josh from certain death. She stumbled over a body and looked at the body of Rudolph Wulf. He was shrugging into his red robe as he stood up from the platform. His eyes were glazed, slowly taking in the scene around him. He glanced out at the approaching FBI agents and then back at Raven.

"What is happening? Where am I? Where is my master?"

Bile helped the man stand up. "Don't worry, Master. I'm here. I can help you, Master. I can find you a new demon. We must use the girl to stop them." He pointed at Ila.

Wulf reached into the folds of his robe and pulled out a pistol. "Get the girl."

Ila looked just as confused as Wulf. She clutched the spiral stairs as if she were sliding off a tilting ship. Bile grabbed her by the arm and shoved her toward Wulf. Wulf grabbed her around the neck and pressed the pistol against the girl's head.

"Back off! Or my master will kill the girl. Back! Now!" Bile screamed. Beneath them Ross held up his hand and motioned the agents back.

"Everyone back off." Ross shouted. Steel stood halfway down the stairs, and he vaulted over the railing, landing behind Wulf. He pulled Ila from his grasp. Steel shoved Bile aside and ran toward Josh, pushing Ila ahead of him.

Wulf blinked in confusion and looked down at the pistol. He slowly raised the gun and pointed it at Steel. Time seemed to slow as Raven recognized the gun she had given to King the night he was to have died along with Steel. She felt the weight of the amulet at her neck and gasped. Now she was certain. She did not want Steel to die.

She felt the strings of her past binding her still, holding her back, keeping her safe from harm. Survival, she reminded herself. It was all about taking care of herself. But for the first time in her life she couldn't stand and let another person die. Time lurched forward, and she ran across the platform. Steel's gaze met hers, and he knew what she was about to do.

"No!" he screamed, but it was too late. Raven shoved him aside, throwing herself between Steel and the gun. Wulf pulled the trigger, and a bullet plowed through her rib cage. White-hot pain lanced across her chest as the bullet burrowed into her lungs. She whirled and started toward Wulf. He pulled the trigger again, and another bullet tore through her chest, splintering bone and shredding muscle. Is this what her victims felt in the microseconds before their death? Were the final moments of their lives filled with the sharp, eviscerating pain she felt? She paused, blood spurting from the wound in her chest, her vision swimming with the pain. And still she moved toward Wulf.

Wulf tightened his grip on his cloak and aimed the pistol at her head. He pulled the trigger for the last time as Raven extended her arms, jumping up into the air to shield the others as much as she could.

The air exploded in hot shrapnel. Bits of metal flayed her face and arms, tearing into her abdomen, her legs, her chest. The concussion grabbed her and threw her across the platform toward the front edge. She landed hard, sliding across the slick metal on her own blood until she came to rest just inches from the chasm.

In the place of Wulf's body misted a haze of atomized bone, flesh, and brain. His entire upper torso was missing. The residual flesh and bone toppled backward and fell into the pit, dragging the red robe after it. For a second it fluttered in the breeze like the crimson banner of the wolf dragon.

Raven's pain was incredible, the pain of every bullet she had ever fired, every wound she had ever inflicted. Steel's face appeared, and she felt her strength quickly fading.

"Raven?"

"It's okay." She coughed blood in a fine spray. "You were right."

Steel gently picked up her head and placed it in his lap. Blood pooled and ran down her side as he teased her hair out of the lacerations on her face.

"Hold on, and I'll get help."

Raven coughed, and a bloody bubble burst from her lip. "We're in the middle of nowhere." Raven studied his bright turquoise eyes, damp with tears. The cold was spreading, and her hand went into her blouse. She grabbed the amulet with all her might and jerked until the blue twine broke. "Take this." She pressed it into his hand. "It's the key. Call Max. Tell him you redeemed me. He'll want to know." She coughed, and blood sprayed on Steel's face. "Promise me. Pay them all back. Make it right. Promise," she begged.

"I promise, Victoria." Steel's hand closed on the amulet.

Raven felt her hand fall, losing strength, and it snagged against Steel's torn shirt. She pulled the shirt away. "I thought I killed you…" She swallowed blood. "How did you live?" Her vision blurred, and she refocused on his chest. With her remaining strength she pulled herself upright and leaned forward to study Steel's chest. There was no wound.

Even as the life began to fade from her, the realization dawned. She laughed, blood bubbling on her lips. "You're not…" For a second she thought she heard Jonathan's voice. Was he asking her a question? It didn't matter anymore, for she was once again in a pink dress with the warm spring air on her face. She looked down at the cake shaped like a lamb. A shadow fell across it.

"I am here." His voice was kind and gentle. A hand reached out for hers, its perfection marred only by a red wound. She looked up into the face of her Maker.

As Raven died, she tumbled away from Steel toward the dark shadows of the pit. He tried to grab her bloody hand, but she slipped from his grasp and disappeared down the chasm. He stood up and teetered on the edge of the precipice. He never heard her hit the bottom. A hand grabbed him by the arm and pulled him back from the edge before he followed after her.

Ross pulled off his helmet. "Careful, Steel. Don't want to follow your girlfriend."

Steel jerked his arm out of Ross's grasp and tucked the amulet in his pocket. "You don't get it, Ross." He shoved his way past Ross and crossed the platform. Josh sat by Ila, a small trickle of blood drying on his bare chest.

"I ought to beat the living daylights out of you."

Josh stood up and blinked. "Dude, you did."

Steel studied the bruise on the boy's cheek and the tears forming in his eyes. He reached toward the boy and paused. "Don't you ever run off from me again, you understand?"

"I won't, bro. I promise," Josh said, and he took Steel's hand and shook it.

Steel nodded and blinked away tears. "Your lip's bleeding."

"You can have this. I don't want it anymore." He dropped the gold lip bead into Ila's hand.

Ila looked up from her hand. "Where am I?"

"You're safe," Steel said. It seemed Ila's demon had fled the scene. He looked at Josh. "From now on you leave the rescuing to me. Got it?"

Josh nodded and walked across the platform to where Theo sat. "Thanks, Theophilus."

Theo rumbled, "I was just doing what the Chief asks me to do."

Ross walked past Jonathan and stopped to study Vivian's struggling figure. "Well, looky what the cat dragged in."

Vivian threw a caustic look back at Ross and Steel. "Would you kindly untie me? I'm as much a victim here as he is."

Ross raised an eyebrow. "I don't think so. You hired that assassin to kill Atchison. And Wulf. And Steel."

"No, that was my doing," Armando said behind them. Steel turned. Armando stood in the shadows, his face twisted in hate and despair. "I did it all. I even killed Gloria Sanchez and her mother. Her mother wanted Gloria to drop out of my clan. So I killed her. Then Gloria changed her mind, so I had to make it look like a suicide."

Ross's mouth fell open, and he looked skeptically at Vivian. "How did you do that?"

"Demonic deal of the century," Steel said as he stepped up to Vivian.

Vivian wore an innocent look. "Wulf Pharmaceuticals and Ketrick Enterprises are now one. But Armando was planning to kill me and make Wulf the sole owner."

Steel stepped closer. "So this is your new plan?"

Vivian's eyes flared. "You don't have any proof I did anything wrong, Jonathan Steel. But I will say one thing. Thank you for doing away with the twelfth demon. I'll call you when I go after number eleven." Steel felt his anger boil within as she smiled and giggled beneath her breath.

[Chapter 31]

JUDGE BOLTON LOOKED out over the courtroom filled with spectators until his eyes came to rest on Steel. He nodded and motioned to the bailiff.

"The court will now consider Joshua Knight," the bailiff said.

Steel stood up and motioned for Josh to approach the bench. Josh came forward. Since they had returned, Josh had gotten rid of the black hair dye and the earrings. The bruise on his cheek had turned to an ugly yellowish-green, but the swelling had gone down. Charles Atchison met them before the bench.

"Your Honor, Ruth Branson got in touch with me from London and has prepared the paperwork you see before you. She wanted me to tell you that these documents testify to Jonathan Steel's rescue of Joshua Knight and his—"

"All right, already. I got it. I read the documents." Bolton turned his piercing eyes on Steel. "You kept your promise, I see."

"Yes, sir."

Bolton nodded. "And you, Mr. Knight. I see you've been in and out of considerable trouble lately."

"Yes, sir. But I did it to help my girlfriend, Ila."

"And how is Ila?"

"She is doing pretty good. Back with her mom."

Bolton looked around the courtroom. "Dr. Lawrence, where are you?"

Dr. Lawrence got up from a chair and joined Jonathan and Josh. "Right here."

Bolton cleared his throat. "So, what are we to do with all

of this? According to the electronic will submitted by Josh's mother—"

"Will?" Steel interrupted him.

"Yes, Mr. Steel. She e-mailed it to me right before she"—Atchison glanced at Josh—"passed away."

Steel thought back to the e-mail that had sent right after he turned Claire's laptop on for the first time after she died. Claire had known she wasn't going to live.

Bolton tapped his gavel. "May I finish?"

Steel nodded. Bolton adjusted his reading glasses.

"Claire Knight asked for Cephas Lawrence to be made primary guardian of Joshua Knight and for you, Jonathan Steel, to be secondary guardian in the event health issues prevent Dr. Lawrence from fulfilling his role."

Steel blanched. "Me? Guardian?"

Cephas chuckled. "Only if I kick the bucket."

Steel swallowed. This was moving too fast. He looked at Josh. "What do you think?"

Josh shrugged. "Dude, I don't have much choice. I guess it's okay with me. If not, I'll just run away again."

Steel tensed, and Josh shook his head. "Bro, I'm joking. Yeah, it's fine. You're growing on me."

Bolton glared at them. "I'm not totally happy with this arrangement. Since Mr. Knight's house has burned down, where will he live?"

Cephas lifted a crooked finger. "Well, I have just acquired a large piece of property in Shreveport. It will give me ample room for my artifacts. It's not here in Dallas, but—"

"Good!" Bolton nodded. "I don't want Josh in this city right now. I want him away from these vampire friends of his. But I need to be able to check on him on a monthly basis. And where do you live, Mr. Steel?"

"With me," Cephas said before Steel could answer. "There's plenty of room in my new house, and I will need Mr. Steel's help in cataloging and interpreting my artifacts, in light of the events surrounding the thirteenth and the twelfth demons."

"But I have a beach house," Steel said.

"Cool!" Josh said. "We can go cruise some hot chicks."

Steel opened his mouth to speak and then closed it in frustration. He had totally lost control of this situation.

"I need to know that you will cooperate with this arrangement, Mr. Steel. Mr. Knight will be eighteen in a little over a year, and until then he is a minor. I would prefer that both you and Dr. Lawrence oversee his safety. Do you agree?" Bolton stared at him over his reading glasses.

"Uh, yes."

"Josh, will that be a problem with you?"

"No, sir. I'd just as soon put all this behind me."

"Mr. Atchison?"

"I can handle the sale of what's left of Mrs. Knight's property and see that the proceeds go into the trust fund set up in his mother's will."

"To be overseen by Ruth Branson, not you!" Bolton said. "Now, on to another matter. Theophilus King." Bolton sat back in his chair. "I understand he was instrumental in saving Joshua Knight from these vampires of yours."

"Yes, sir," Steel said. "He, uh, couldn't be here today."

Bolton snickered. "Wise decision on his part. However, it will take more than one dramatic rescue to convince me of his new path. Since you have pulled him from the fiery abyss, so to speak, and returned him to the pathway of righteousness, I would think he would benefit from your guidance."

"Guidance?"

"He did help you out on this latest ordeal with your little demons?" Bolton leaned forward.

"Yes, sir."

"He has expertise in religions matters, and he was once on the LAPD before he became a preacher, right?" Bolton continued.

"Yes, but—"

"Well, Mr. Steel, there are two officers waiting to arrest Mr. King and bring him to face charges of drug peddling. Now, I don't like what Mr. King used to be. But I truly believe he has reformed. So if you would agree to apprentice him as your associate for the next year, I will waive the charges against him."

Steel stood speechless before the bench. Cephas shrugged. "There will be plenty of room for the four of us in my new house."

Bolton nodded. "Now, I think the issue with Vivian Ketrick has been settled, so you won't be needing to stay around and testify."

Steel stepped closer to the bench. "Sir, she shouldn't be trusted. She has influence over Armando—"

"Ah, yes. Armando. The fellow who signed a full confession. I understand that he's now trying to claim the insanity defense." Bolton raised an eyebrow. "Says he was demon possessed when he made the confession, and now the demons are gone. But he will be indicted for the murder of Mrs. Sanchez and her daughter. As to the other business, Special Agent Ross has assured me he is satisfied with the fact that this Raven character is dead."

Steel sighed and felt the cold amulet in his pocket. "Very well, Your Honor."

Bolton leaned forward. "Mr. Steel, you and Dr. Lawrence take Josh and go make a home for him. Put all this demon nonsense behind you."

Steel looked back at Josh. "I'll certainly try."

Once out of the courtroom Steel motioned Josh on down the hall. "See if you can find Theo and tell him it's okay for him to come out of hiding. Go on out to the truck, and I'll be there in a minute."

"Jonathan…I don't remember much about what happened in the cavern."

"It's blurry, isn't it?"

He nodded. "Just like in the basement of the church."

"Your mother's precious dimensions. She told us our minds would have problems retaining what we saw."

"Dude, I prefer the blur." Josh turned and followed Cephas down the hall.

Steel pulled the amulet out of his pocket and studied the number etched on the back. He put the number into his cell phone and listened.

"Is she dead?" The voice was filtered and distorted.

"Yes. She said to tell you"—Steel paused and suppressed the wave of sudden sorrow—"she was redeemed."

"Good. I will need the key to—"

"She told me to pay them all back."

Silence answered, and for a second Steel thought the connection had been broken. "That is more than I could have asked for." He could hear the tremble in the man's voice even through the filter. "I will contact you in the near future. Thank you."

The line went dead, and Steel ducked into the men's restroom. He leaned against a stall, wiping the tears from his eyes with a tissue. He pulled off his tie and shoved it into his coat pocket before shrugging off his coat and tossing it on the sink. He looked at himself in the mirror. Slowly he pulled his shirttails from his pants and lifted the shirt away from his chest. He examined the skin on his left side, trying to see what Raven had been looking at. No scars. Nothing.

He dropped the shirt and reached up and ran a finger along his scalp. Two years before he had awakened with a huge cut at the hairline. No scar. He pulled up the shirtsleeve on the arm where Raven had sliced his skin with the knife. The red line was gone. No wound. No scar.

Steel studied his reflection. Now that he thought about it, he had always healed quickly. And, apparently, completely. Why?

He felt the amulet in his pocket and took it out. He fumbled with a tiny latch, and the pendant swung open like a clamshell. Inside it a tiny key was taped to one side. On the other was a folded slip of paper. He took it out and unfolded it. It was the piece of paper he had given Raven.

> Who shall separate us from the love of Christ? Shall tribulation, or distress, or persecution, or famine, or nakedness, or peril, or sword? As it is written: "For Your sake we are killed all day long; we are accounted as sheep for the slaughter." Yet in all these things we are more than conquerors through Him who loved us. For I am persuaded that neither death nor life, nor angels nor principalities nor powers, nor things present nor things to come, nor height nor depth, nor any other created thing, shall be able to separate us from the love of God which is in Christ Jesus our Lord.

Tears clouded his vision, and he sighed. It was the Bible verse he had found in the latrine. His life had come full circle. His hope and faith were vindicated.

"So, you have no idea where this house is?" Josh glanced at the map. Sunlight danced across his lap as Steel drove the RV along Lakeshore Drive.

"The Realtor said it was a steal," Cephas shouted from behind him. "She said it was right on the lake in a secured neighborhood and had over twelve thousand square feet."

"Cool! On the lake. Did you hear that, Theo?" He glanced over his shoulder at the huge man crammed into a seat.

"Sure did, Josh. But it's been a long time since I been swimming."

"Bro, I'll teach you." Josh was all smiles.

Steel pulled up to a stop sign and glanced to his right at the bait shop sitting along a bayou that emptied into the lake. He had been here before, searching for the thirteenth demon. He began to get a sinking feeling in the pit of his stomach. Without saying a word, he pulled across the street into Pineshore Hills subdivision. A security guard stopped them at the gate.

"I'm with Dr. Cephas Lawrence. We're moving in."

The guard glanced down at his clipboard and peered into the backseat, where Cephas waved. "Sure are. Have a nice day." He opened the metal gate, and Steel checked the road sign before going on.

"Tell me the address again."

Cephas rattled it off. Steel's heart sank even more as he rounded a curve and saw the address on the mailbox. He pulled up the long driveway that wound around the right side of the house to the yard facing the lake, where he stopped the RV at the side of the huge castle.

Josh's mouth fell open. Steel hung his head and moaned. Theo

King leaned forward and smiled. He clapped Cephas on the back. "Papaw, you did good. Man, oh man, what a house!"

Steel looked at Josh. "It's Ketrick's house."

[Epilogue]

S HE FLOATED IN chilling waters as a net of gray threads closed around her and pulled her into the light. She felt more threads pierce her chest, her abdomen, her face. Her skin tightened and scarred as the bones in her face reshaped. And still she floated on a sea of confusion. The man with the scar in his wrist had smiled at her and told her it wasn't over yet. In fact, it was just beginning.

What did he mean? Where was she?

Images of a man with turquoise eyes flashed in and out of the dark shadows of her memory. And then her vision cleared. The doctor in the white coat nodded to a nurse.

"Our Jane Doe is awake," he said in Romanian. And she understood it. How did she understand a foreign language? From her darkness the strings began to emerge, weaving a new tapestry, showing her the life she could only barely remember.

"I will get her uncle." The nurse said. She paused to lean over her. "He's been waiting for weeks for you to wake up. But he refuses to tell us your name. Such secrets!"

The nurse reappeared and ushered a man up to the bedside. He was short and wore a wide-brimmed Panama hat. He clenched a meerschaum pipe in his teeth. His bright, blue eyes glittered from the shadows beneath the hat brim. "Hello, honey."

The woman's eyes widened. "No!"

He leaned forward. "Beware the wicked numinosity."

The woman felt the strings break, felt the growing light fade back into darkness, saw the fires and the tall tower with a huge clock face, heard thunder roll across a green field where huge stone slabs towered, felt herself dwindling fast, hands clawing at the man with the turquoise eyes sitting alone in a restaurant; the man with the knife and the blood of a lamb faded away until she was empty. She relaxed and blinked.

"Where am I?"

The Captain tucked his pipe into a shirt pocket. "You're safe."

She looked up at him and then around here. "Who are you? Who am I?"

"Don't worry. The Captain is here to make all things right."

[Selected Bibliography]

Florescu, **Radu R.** and **Raymond T. McNally.** *Dracula, Prince of Many Faces: His Life and Times.* N.p.: Back Bay Books, 1989.

Gromacki, Robert Glenn. *Salvation Is Forever.* N.p.: Moody Press, 1973.

Lewis, C. S. *The Screwtape Letters.* San Francisco: Harper San Francisco, 1982.

Lightner, Robert P. *Sin, the Savior, and Salvation.* N.p.: Kregel Acadamic and Professional, 1996.

Melton, J. Gordon. *The Vampire Book: The Encyclopedia of the Undead.* Canton, MI: Visible Ink Press, 1999.

Ramsland, Katherine. *Piercing the Darkness: Undercover With Vampires in America Today.* New York: Harper Paperbacks, 1999.

Ross, Hugh. *Beyond the Cosmos.* Revised and updated. Colorado Springs, CO: NavPress, 1999.

RZIM. Steel's flashback is based on a true story from Ravi Zacharias International Ministries. www.rzim.org.

COMING IN FALL 2013—

THE ELEVENTH DEMON, THE ARK
OF THE DEMON ROSE

BOOK THREE IN THE CHRONICLES
OF JONATHAN STEEL

[Prologue]

November 1963
Dallas, Texas
Grimvox reference USNA-FCaskey111563

HALL I KILL the human?"

I lifted my weary head to look at the demon. He was oddly dressed in a brown Nehru jacket, and his features were dark beneath a shock of black hair. His eyes were disturbing, totally white and devoid of pupils.

"We need him." The pale man standing next to the demon turned his red eyes in my direction. His face was ageless and marred only by a star-shaped scar on his cheek. He wore a long black overcoat, black pants, and no shirt. His bare chest glowed in the darkness, and he moved across the debris-strewn floor to crouch before me. "He is subdued. He will cause us no harm."

"Then why do we keep him alive?" The demon crossed his arms over his chest. "I must meet with the Council in an hour and give them a progress report."

The pale man nodded and licked his large teeth with a very red tongue. "He is our only connection with the girl."

I gasped and tried to look away. The girl's mother had been my downfall.

"Don't look away from me, Father. Unlike most of your kind, the touch of your flesh does not harm me." He pressed his cool fingertips against my cheek and pushed my face around so that all I could see were his hideous red eyes. "For you see, Father, you are a failure. You think you serve your master, but your love for another has pulled you away from that commitment. The girl's mother must be extraordinary."

I jerked away from his touch and felt the cold, harsh burn of guilt. I struggled against the ropes holding me to the chair. "If you harm her, I will kill you."

The demon laughed, and his voice echoed up into the empty rafters of the warehouse. "You cannot kill Lucas, human. Now, Lucas, where is the girl? I need her."

I glanced at the demon. "Please don't harm her."

"*Please don't harm her.*" He mocked me and shook his head. "I have plans for her, human. Why would I want to harm her? Lucas, take me to the girl, and then we will no longer need this human."

Lucas reached out and grabbed my collar and tore it from my neck. His cold, long-fingered hands grasped the top of my shirt and tore it from my body. I shivered in the cold air. "You will live if you swear allegiance to the eleventh demon. When you do, this mark"—he brushed his chest, and the hideous tattoo of a beast of combined forms struggled to life on his pale skin—"will be yours. It will live right here." His fingers caressed my chest, and he touched my left shoulder.

I recognized the tattoo: a beast with the head of a lion, the head of a goat coming out of the thing's back, and a snake for a tail. It was the ancient symbol for the chimera. If I swore allegiance, she would be safe. I closed my eyes and saw Molly standing at the church altar with the girl's hand in hers. God forgive me! "What will you do with the girl?"

The eleventh demon raised an eyebrow. "The plans of the Council are deep and long and often flawed. I have plans of my own that defy the Council, but that is none of your concern.

Now, Lucas, let us go. My patience with you is growing thin. I know you are a toady for the Council."

"Toady?" Lucas's crimson eyes glowed with anger. He straightened, and a wicked smile crossed his lips. "I do not serve the Council of Darkness, Chimera. I serve the master, and you defy the master."

"Do not speak to me that way. You may be the right hand of the master, but I am far superior to you."

"I need this human to insure the girl lives long enough to fulfill the Council's plans, not yours. When the deed is done, I will leave this human to you for your pleasure. But until then I keep the girl safe. I will make sure your plans succeed. That is the master's instruction."

"The master trusts me, Lucas. Take me to the girl. Now!" His voice grew in volume, and for a second I saw the beast that possessed the human rear its ugly head like a specter surrounding the man.

Lucas smiled, and his impossibly white teeth gleamed in the darkness. "I have a message from the master." Lucas held out his hand. A swirl of red smoke billowed from his palm like a small tornado. A pleasing and handsome face appeared from the smoke and addressed the demon. "I want your talisman."

The eleventh demon stepped back. "No!"

Lucas closed his palm, and the face disappeared. "I am the right hand of the master, Chimera. He is gathering the talismans of the Council for his own purposes. If you want the girl to fulfill your plans, you will give me the talisman. It is the leverage the master desires. Or do I summon the master to speak to you in person?"

The eleventh demon grew pale and blinked his empty eyes furiously. "I will not allow this human to see my talisman."

Lucas glanced at me. "He does not want you to see his

talisman, Father." Then Lucas smiled and rubbed his hands together. "I will make sure the good Father does not remember the talisman. There is no memory in death."

Chimera nodded and reached into his pocket. Something long and golden flashed in his palm. I tried to focus on it, but it seemed blurred…indistinct…otherworldly. "What is that?"

Chimera came toward me, and the odor of fire and soot engulfed me. He knelt before me, and the golden talisman flickered in the periphery of my vision. His right hand was on my forehead, hot and sweaty, and I tried to pull away. Lucas moved behind me and took my head in his cold hands.

"I will let you keep one eye so that you may see the fate that awaits those who follow in my footsteps. For the eleventh demon demands total commitment, Father! Will you renounce your allegiance and find love with the mother of this girl? If so, you will be mine, and your death will be avoided."

I was paralyzed with fear, paralyzed by their inhuman power as the thin, gold needle appeared at the edge of my vision, plunged toward my right eye, and then there was pain far greater than the fires of hell!

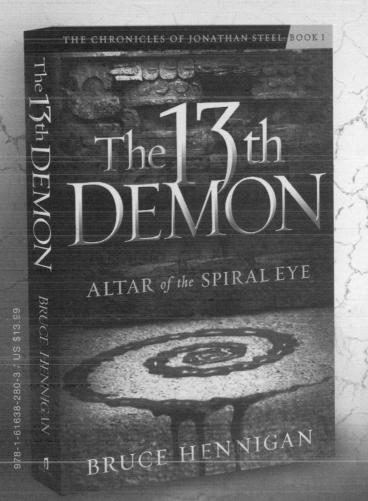